PENGUIN BOOKS

TEMPORARY SHELTER

Mary Gordon says of her work: 'What I want to accomplish is to tell stories about real people, to tell the truth about human beings in human situations, the way in which people live their lives.' The enthusiastic critical and popular reception which has greeted all her novels testifies that she has more than succeeded in this ambition. In the words of *The New York Times Review of Books* she is 'a gifted novelist, a writer whose stylistic attainments are on a level with her intelligence and insight'. Mary Gordon's three previous novels are *Final Payments* ('One of the best novels of any kind I have read in recent years' – *The Times*), *The Company of Women* ('Generous-hearted, shrewd, sad – and very funny too' – Marina Warner, *Sunday Times* Books of the Year) and *Men and Angels* ('A brilliant study of the insatiable demands of the unlovable' – *Standard*).

Mary Gordon lives in upstate New York with her husband, Arthur Cash, the biographer of Laurence Sterne, and their two children, Anna and David.

Mary Gordon

TEMPORARY SHELTER

SHORT STORIES

PENGUIN BOOKS

PENGUIN BOOKS

Published by the Penguin Group
27 Wrights Lane, London w8 5TZ, England
Viking Penguin Inc., 40 West 23rd Street, New York, New York 10010, USA
Penguin Books Australia Ltd, Ringwood, Victoria, Australia
Penguin Books Canada Ltd, 2801 John Street, Markham, Ontario, Canada L3R 1B4
Penguin Books (NZ) Ltd, 182–190 Wairau Road, Auckland 10, New Zealand

Penguin Books Ltd, Registered Offices: Harmondsworth, Middlesex, England

First published by Bloomsbury Publishing Ltd 1987
Published in Penguin Books 1988

Printed and bound in Great Britain by
Cox & Wyman Ltd, Reading

TO JAN ZLOTNICK SCHMIDT

CONTENTS

TEMPORARY
SHELTER

TEMPORARY SHELTER

*H*e hated the way his mother piled the laundry. The way she held the clothes, as if it didn't matter. And he knew what she would say if he said anything, though he would never say it. But if he said, "Don't hold the clothes like that, it's ugly, how you hold them. See the arms of Dr. Meyers' shirt, they hang as if he had no arms, as if he'd lost them. And Maria's dress, you let it bunch like that, as if you never knew her." If he said a thing like that, which he would never do, she'd laugh and store it up to tell her friends. She'd say, "My son is crazy in love. With both of them. Even the stinking laundry he's in love with." And she would hit him on the side of the head, meaning to be kind, to joke, but she would do it wrong, the blow would be too hard. His ears would ring, and he would hate her.

Then he would hate himself, because she worked so hard, for him; he knew it was for him. Why did she make him feel so dreadful? He was thirteen, he was old enough to understand it all, where they had come from, who they were, and why she did things. She wanted things for him. A good life, better than what she had. Better than Milwaukee, which they'd left for the shame of her being a woman that a man had left. It wasn't to be left by a man that she'd come to this country, that her parents brought her on the ship, just ten years old, in 1929, when they should have stayed home, if they'd had sense, that year that turned out to be so terrible for the Americans. For a few months, it was like a heaven, with her cousins in Chicago. Everybody saying: Don't worry, everyone needs shoes. Her father was a cobbler. But then the crash, and no one needed shoes, there were no jobs, her mother went out to do strangers' laundry, and her father sat home, his head in his hands before the picture of the Black Madonna and tried to imagine some way they could go back home.

"And I was never beautiful," his mother said, and he believed that that was something he would have to make up to her. Someday when he was a man. Yes, he would have to make it up to her, and yet she said it proudly, as if it meant that everything she'd got she had got straight. And he would have to make it up to her because his father who'd lived off her money and sat home on his behind had left them both without a word. When he, Joseph, was six months old. And he would have to make it up to her that she had come to work for Dr. Meyers, really a Jew—once you were one you always were one—though he said he was a Catholic, and the priests knelt at his feet because he was so educated. And he would have to make it up to her because he loved the Meyers, Doctor and Maria. When he was with them, happiness fell on the three of them like a white net of cloud and set them off apart from all the others. Yes, someday he would have to make it up to her because he loved the Meyers in the lightness of his heart, while in his heart there was so often mockery and shame for his mother.

He couldn't remember a time when he hadn't lived with the Meyers in White Plains. His mother got the job when he was two, answering an ad that Dr. Meyers had put in the *Irish Echo*. No Irish had applied, so Dr. Meyers hired Joseph's mother, Helen Kaszperkowski, because, he had explained with dignity, it was important to him that the person who would be caring for his daughter shared the Faith. Joseph was sure he must have said "The Faith" in the way he always said it when he talked about the Poles to Joseph and his mother. "I believe they are, at present, martyrs to the Faith." He would speak of Cardinal Mindszenty, imprisoned in his room, heroically defying Communism. But the way Dr. Meyers said, "The Faith" made Joseph feel sorry for him. It was a clue, if anyone was looking for clues, that he had not been born a Catholic, and all those things that one breathed in at Catholic birth he'd had to learn, as if he had been learning a new language.

But of course no one would have to search for clues, the doctor never tried to hide that he was a Jew, or had been born a Jew, as he would say. He would tell the story of his conversion calmly, unfurling it like a bolt of cloth, evenly, allowing it to shine, allowing the onlooker to observe, without his saying anything, the pattern in the fabric. He had converted in the 1920's, when he had been studying art, in Italy, in a city called Siena. Joseph had looked up Siena in Dr. Meyers' atlas. He had been pleased when Dr. Meyers came into the library and found him there, rubbing his finger in a circle round the area that was Siena, touching the dark spot that marked it, as if he were a blind child. He was seven then, and Dr. Meyers took him on his lap. How comfortably he fit there, on Dr. Meyers' lean, dry lap, a lap of safety.

Not like his mother's lap, which he had to share with her stomach. Holding Joseph on his lap and not afraid to kiss a little boy the way all of Joseph's uncles were, Dr. Meyers showed him the pictures in the book of Cimabue and Simone Martini and explained to him the silence and the holiness, the grandeur and the secrecy. He used the pictures for his business now, his business in liturgical greeting cards, holy pictures, stationery. The business that had bought him this house and all these things. And Joseph understood why he had left his family (his family said he could never see them again) and all he had been born to. For the quiet sad-faced mothers and their dark commanding baby sons.

He understood it all; so did Maria. They had loved it all, the silence and the grandeur, since they had been small, before they went to school when Dr. Meyers took them with him to Daily Mass, the only children there, kneeling together, looking, very still as every other person rose and went up to Communion. They made up lives for all the people, and they talked about them even when they no longer went to Daily Mass; when they were older, in the parish school, they talked about those people. The woman who was always pregnant (they said expecting, thinking it more polite) and the crippled woman, and the Irish man who wore a cap, and the old, the very old Italian lady dressed entirely in black who sat at the very back of the church and said the Rosary out loud, in Italian, during the whole mass, even during the silence of the Consecration. But the person they thought of most and considered most theirs was the very small woman who was extremely clean. They imagined her in her small house alone (they were sure she lived alone), brushing her hat, her black felt hat with the feather band around it, brushing her purple coat with its velvet collar and buttons of winking glass, polishing her old lady's shoes till they looked beautiful. Then putting on her hat without looking in the mirror because if she did she would have to see the horror that was her face. For on the side of her nose grew a shiny hard-skinned fruit, larger than a walnut, but a purple color. Joseph and Maria talked about it, never once mentioning it to Dr. Meyers. They thought that the woman must be a saint, because, despite the terrible cross God had given her, her face was as sweet as an angel's.

Joseph thought that Maria, too, must be a saint because she never lost her patience with his mother, although she lost patience with everything else. His mother was terrible to Maria; every day of her life she was terrible. If he didn't know how good a woman his mother was, and how much she loved the Meyers and how grateful she was to them, he would think she hated Maria. That was how she acted. It was mainly because Maria was sloppy, she really was, his mother was right, much as he loved her, much as he thought Maria was a saint, he knew his mother was right. She left the caps off of pens so that the pockets of her skirts turned black; she threw her clothes around the room, she dropped her towels on the floor, she scrunched up papers into a ball and threw them into the wastebasket, and missed, and didn't bend to put them properly into the bin; she made her bed with lumps, sometimes the lumps were just the blankets or the sheets, sometimes they were her socks or underwear or books she'd fallen asleep reading. As if she didn't understand you made a bed for the look of it, not just so that if someone (Joseph's mother) asked if you had made your bed you would be free to answer yes.

He wondered what Maria thought about his mother. They never spoke about her. No, once they had spoken about her, and it would have been much better if they'd never had the conversation. Once his mother had said such awful things, called Maria a pig, a slut, a hussy, a disgrace, and she'd just stood there, going white. Although she always had high coloring, this day she had gone dead white and made her body stiff and clenched her fists beside her body as if she wanted, really very badly wanted, to hit Joseph's mother and all her life was put into her fists, keeping them clenched so they would not. She had excused herself and left the room, walking slowly as though she had to show them, Joseph and his mother, that she didn't need to run. And Joseph for once had shouted at his mother, "Why are you so horrible to her?" And his mother had shouted, opened her lips, showed her strong yellow teeth; her tongue spat out the words, "How dare you take her part against me. The filthy, filthy pig. They're all alike. Fine ladies, with someone like me to clean up their shit. And you too, don't forget it. You're not one of them, you're *my* flesh and blood, whether you like it or you don't. They'll leave you in the end, don't you forget it. In the end I'll be the only thing you have."

She couldn't be right, the Meyers would not leave him. So he left his mother sobbing in the kitchen and went upstairs to where he knew Maria would be sitting, still and white as if she had shed blood. He knocked on her door and then walked in. He saw her sitting as he knew she would be, and he sat down beside her on her bed.

"I'm sorry she's so mean. You should do something. You should tell your father."

"No," she said. "If I say something, he might say something to her, and she might want to leave, or he might make her leave, and you'd leave too."

He should not have come into her room; he wished he hadn't heard it. And wished later that he hadn't heard, been made to hear, the conversation at the table, Dr. Meyers talking to them both, Maria and his mother, calmly, saying that he understood both sides and that they must be patient with each other. Our Lord had loved both sisters, Martha and her sister Mary, there was room for all beneath the sight of God.

What he said made nothing better. His mother said she just did it for the girl's own good, these things were important in a woman's life, she, Helen Kaszperkowski knew that. And then Maria said she would try to be better at these things. And Dr. Meyers lifted up his knife and fork and said, "Good, good." And Joseph knew he had no home, there was no place that was his really, as Maria's place was with her father. He was here or he was there, but it was possible, although he felt himself much happier beside the Meyers, that his mother had been right and it was beside her that he must find his place, must live.

———

But what was it, that happiness he felt beside the Meyers if it was not where he belonged? He thought about the things the three of them did together. The train into the city and the dressing up, the destination always one of those high, grey-stoned buildings with the ceiling beautiful enough to live on, carved or vaulted, and the always insufficient lights. The joy those buildings gave him, the dry impersonal air, the rich, hard-won minerals: the marble and the gold, where no wet breath—of doubt, of argument or of remorse—could settle or leave trace. And how the voice of Dr. Meyers came into its own; the thick dental consonants, the vowels overlong and arched, belonged there. Everybody else's speech offended in those rooms, seemed cut off, rushed, ungiving and unloved. But Dr. Meyers' voice as he described a painting or a pillar wrapped around whatever he called beautiful and made it comfortable and no longer strange. It belonged then, to Joseph and Maria; Dr. Meyers had surrounded it with their shared history and let its image float in slowly, like a large ship making its way to harbor, safely to its place inside their lives.

And then there were the treats, the lunches at the automat, the brown pots of baked beans or macaroni, the desserts at Rumpelmayers and the silly games, the game they played with cream puffs. "It is important," Dr.

Meyers would say in Rumpelmayers, in the room that looked just like a doll's house, pink and white and ribboned like a doll, "it is important," he would say, making his face look pretend-serious "to know exactly how to eat a cream puff. When I was in Paris, very great ladies would say to me, *"C'est de la plus grande importance savoir manger une creampuff comme il faut."* He would keep on his pretend-serious face and cut into one cream puff deliberately, carving up pieces with the right mix of pastry and cream, then popping them into his mouth like Charlie Chaplin. "But, my children," he would say, "it takes a lot of practice. You must eat many cream puffs before you can truly say you know how to eat them *comme il faut.*"

Then he would order one cream puff for each of them and say, "That's good, you're getting the idea, but I don't think it's quite yet *comme il faut.*" So, with a pretend-serious face he would order another for them, and then another, then when he could see them stuffed with richness and with pleasure at the joke he would say, "Ah, I think you're getting there. You are learning the fine art of eating cream puffs *comme il faut.*"

Then they would go to the afternoon movies, the Three Stooges, Laurel and Hardy, movie after funny movie, and Dr. Meyers laughed the hardest, laughed till he coughed and they hit him on the back, then laughed at how hard they were hitting him. And then they would walk outside. Outside, where, while they had pleased themselves in warmth and darkness, the sky had grown somber. And quickly, sharply, they left behind the silly men who fought and shouted just to make them laugh. They'd wend their way through the commuters to St. Patrick's for the five thirty, the workers' Mass. And pray, amidst the people coming from their offices in suits, the women, some in hats, some taking kerchiefs from their handbags, all of them kneeling underneath the high dark ceiling where the birettas of dead cardinals hung rotting; always they chose a pew beside the statue of Pope Pius, waxy white, as if he were already dead. Then, blurred by the sacraments and silenced, they walked to Grand Central, boarded the train, too hot or too cold, always, and looked out the windows, pressed their cheeks against the glass and played "I Spy."

And at home Joseph's mother waited, served them dinner when they arrived, served them in anger for she knew they had left her out. Once they invited her to come with them to the Metropolitan Museum. Dr. Meyers showed her the Ming vases and her only comment was "I'd hate to have to dust all those," and Dr. Meyers laughed and said it was extraordinary how one never thought of all the maintenance these treasures took, and then his mother smiled, as if she had said the right thing. But he could see Maria look away, pretending not to be there for his sake, and his heart burned up with shame, and he was glad that Dr. Meyers never asked his mother to come along again, and he knew it was one more thing he would have to make up to her when he was grown up and a man.

What was Maria thinking when she pretended not to look and not to be there? Sometimes he couldn't keep the thought away, the thought that those two hated each other. It must not be true. His mother said she was doing things for Maria's own good, and Maria never said a thing about his mother. But could they both be lying to him? No, not lying, but the sin, as Father Riordan called it, of concealing truth. A venial sin, but did they live it? It was more likely that his mother lived in sin, in venial sin of course. God forbid that she would live in mortal sin. But was her unkindness venial sin? And the way she found wrong everything about Maria? Why did she hate Maria's hair?

As far as he could see and understand there could be nothing in Maria's thick black hair to hate. His mother acted as if Maria's hair were there to balk, to anguish, to torment her. "Nobody thinks of me," she would say after she had begun, "and that disgusting hair. Nobody thinks of what it means for me, that hair all over the place. In the shower, in those brushes. Think of it, she never cleans them out. I tell her and I tell her, and she leaves it in there, that disgusting hair until I don't know what use it is to her, a brush in that condition, and I clean it out myself. Because he likes things right, likes her to have things right, although he don't mind if somebody else does it for her. To tell the truth, that's the way he likes it best, some fat Polack cleaning up after the princess."

How could she stay with them, the Meyers, hating them so? She did it for him, so he could grow up here, in this house, with these "advantages." The large house with its high walls full of pictures. Scenes of European streets and buildings. Drawings by people hundreds of years dead. Velasquez. Goya. The house with its green lawn and dark enshadowed garden and its vivid shocks: the day lilies, orange-yellow; purple lupins; columbines with veins like blood. And the things that Dr. Meyers taught that she knew she could not teach her son: poetry and how to use a fork, the names of emperors and which tie went with which suit, and all the lessons. All the lessons that Maria got, Joseph got too: piano, French, and in the summer, tennis. "The teacher comes for one, he comes for two," said Dr. Meyers shrugging. "Still he has to come." He said it as if it were a joke, the statement final and yet supplicating, and the lifted shoulders. Joseph knew, though no one had told him, that Dr. Meyers learned this kind of sentence, how to say it, from his grandfather the rabbi. Joseph heard the words like that, the tone of them when he and Maria sneaked into the synagogue for Yom Kippur.

It was something Maria had wanted badly. She was not like him. When something rose up before her eyes as if it were a figure on a road she was approaching, she would run to it the way she always ran, headlong and holding nothing back, the way she ran in games, and in the garden on a summer night, just for the pleasure. How beautiful she looked then after running, her hair falling out of her barrette, the sweat that beaded in the cleft above her lip like seed pearls, her white cheeks flushed as if a wing had touched them, a wing dipped in roses. Or in blood. No one could beat her when she ran; it was one reason why the other children in the neighborhood didn't want to play with her. She had to win, and she held nothing back. It didn't bother Joseph; he was glad to let her win. He understood her rages when she lost; the things she said were horrible; sometimes she hit him hard, wanting to hurt. He knew just what she felt. She felt that it was meant for her to win, so when she lost it was as if some plan had been spoiled or some promise broken. And then she was so sorry afterwards, she came to him with such important gifts, wonderful gifts, thought up in heaven. Sometimes they were too good; what she had done was not so bad that she should give them. Like the time she went into her savings to buy him a fountain pen just like her father's, from the jewelry store in town. Because when he had beaten her in tennis she'd hit him on the back so hard he'd fallen over, and his teeth had bitten through his lip. "It's too much," he said, though she knew how he loved it: the black shiny bottom and the silver top. "Real silver," she said, "here, look at the mark." And then they both got scared. "Don't use it where anyone can see it. Not your mother and not anyone at school. The nuns will ask you where you got it. Keep it someplace secret." And he had, for he was good at that, was best at keeping secrets. No one had ever found the pen. Or found the thing she had no right to give him: the gold necklace with the Jewish star that was her mother's mother's.

Maria's mother had been Jewish too, but renounced it to marry Dr. Meyers. She'd died soon after Maria was born, puerperal fever, it was called; Joseph imagined she had turned completely purple. He and Maria often looked at her pictures. It was the only thing he envied that she had: pictures of the absent parent. He had no pictures of his father; his mother talked with happiness about the day she burnt them up. "I held a match to them and—pfft—goodbye." One day Maria said, "Maybe one of my mother's sisters had a baby in Milwaukee on the day that you were born. Then the hospital had a mixup, you know you hear of these things all the time. And that baby was you, and the baby that your mother had is living now with my aunt." She spat on the floor. "It serves them right." She'd never seen her aunt, her mother's favorite sister, who had told Maria's mother that she had no sister, her sister was dead.

Joseph had been frightened when she'd made that story up, frightened that she really believed it. Frightened too, because he wanted to believe it. And knew what that meant: he wished his mother not his mother. And he wanted to run downstairs, run down to his mother, ask was there something he could do to help her, sit beside her, tell her about school, remind her Dr. Meyers said he had the seeing eye, the clever hand, that Dr. Meyers said he was training him to take over the business one day, so the Lord would be honored with things of beauty. See, Mother, Joseph wanted to say, I have the seeing eye, the clever hand. You will never have to worry about money. I will take care of you, and everything you suffer now I will make up to you when I become a man.

But he did not do that; he sat instead beside Maria, looking at the photographs, thinking about the dark, sad-faced woman who had never held her child, who left her brothers and her sisters and her parents to marry Dr. Meyers. His people, too, had refused to speak to him, but he could bear it, Dr. Meyers could, you could see it in his eyes that could go cold. Maria's, too, could do that. She didn't have her mother's eyes, light brown as if they had once been Maria's blazing color, but she had wept so for her family that they had faded.

It was after Maria had given Joseph her grandmother's necklace that she got the idea: they must go into the synagogue. He could imagine how she'd thought it up, alone, at night in bed, her eyes wide open in the dark, awake and lying on her back in the first cold of autumn. It must have been then she decided that she would ask Moe Brown. Moe Brown who owned the candy store and loved her. He always gave her an extra soda free, and he gave one to Joseph too. She'd told Moe both her parents had been born Jewish. "But they gave it up," she said, as if it was a car they had got tired of. It frightened Joseph to hear her say it like that, so lightly, when it was the most important thing Dr. Meyers had ever done, had won for himself the salvation of his soul, the fellowship of Christ, a place in heaven.

But she had been right to talk about it that light way. It made Moe feel that he could talk about it, it was not so terrible. "The way I figure, honey," Moe said, "is live and let live. But personally I don't get it. Once a Jew always a Jew. Ask the late Mr. Hitler."

"Oh, if the Germans won the war, my father and I would have been sent to concentration camps. We would have died together," Maria said, her eyes getting tearful. Which was the kind of thing that made Moe love her. And made Joseph feel if that had happened, he would go with them, Maria and her father, and would die with them, suffer their same fate. But what would happen to his mother?

Moe had no idea that when Maria asked him all those things about the temple and the services she was planning to sneak in. Joseph had no idea himself, and when she told him, he was shocked. Didn't she know that Catholics were forbidden to attend the services of other faiths? And they would be sure to be found out. Moe said that there were people in the back collecting tickets.

"Listen, dodo," she said, "we'll wait till it's started. Way started. Then we'll sneak up to that balcony Moe said there was. With the people that have no tickets. Everyone'll be paying attention to the service. It's a very sad day. The day of atonement."

"But we won't know what to wear or what to do. I don't have one of those little hats."

"A yarmulke," she said, casually, as if she'd used the word every day of her life. "It's a reform temple. You don't need one."

"It's a terrible idea," he said, stamping his foot and feeling close to tears, because he knew he couldn't stop her.

"All right, don't go. I'll go myself. It's not your heritage anyway."

He couldn't let her go. To let her go meant he was not a part of her, her life, her past, her family. And then suppose she got in trouble. He could not leave her alone.

The plan worked perfectly. They waited ten minutes after the last person had gone into the temple. Carefully, they opened up the heavy door and saw the staircase to the balcony, just as Moe had described it. No one saw them climb the stairs or sit in the last seat in the back. How happy she seemed then, her face filmed with the lightest sweat, the down above her lips just moistened, her eyes shining with the look he knew so well: her look of triumph. They watched below. The man who sang, whom Moe had called the cantor, had the most beautiful voice Joseph had ever heard. The cantor's voice made him forget Maria. He rode the music, let it carry him. The sadness and the loneliness, the darkness and the hope. The winding music, thick and secret. Like the secrets of his heart. The secrets he had had to keep from everyone, that he would have to keep forever. When he felt Maria pulling at his arm, he realized that for the first time in his life when he was with her he had forgotten she was there.

"Let's go," she whispered silently.

"Why?" he mouthed at her. He didn't want to go.

"I hate this. I'm leaving."

He knew he must leave with her. It was the reason he was here, to be with her, and to protect her if danger came. He couldn't leave her now, and she had broken it, the ladder of the music. He had lost his footing; now he must drop down.

When they got outside, she ran away from him. He ran after, knowing he couldn't catch her, waiting for her to be out of breath. When he caught up to her, he saw that she was crying.

"I hated it. It was so dark and ugly. It was disgusting. Let's not talk about it ever again. Let's just forget we ever did it."

"Okay," he said. He let her run home by herself.

But he did not forget it, the dark secret music, like the secrets of his heart. The music that traveled to a God who listened, distant and invisible, and heard the sins of men and their atonement in the darkness and in darkness would forgive or not forgive. But would give back to men the music they sent up, a thick braid of justice and kept promises and somber hope.

He knew she didn't like it because it was nothing like the music that she loved, the nun's high voices that had changed her life, that made her know that she would never marry but would join them, singing in the convent, lifting up to God those voices which except for these times, were silent the whole day. That day in the convent she was far away from him, and knew it, and looked down at him from the lit mountain on whose top she stood, and kept him from the women's voices, rising by themselves into the air, so weightless, neither hopeful nor unhopeful, neither sorrowing nor free from sorrow, only rising, rising without effort above everything that made up life. You never saw the faces of the women who made these sounds that rose up, hovered high above their heads and disappeared. You saw only the light that struck the floor, shot through the blue glass and the red glass of the windows, slowed down, thickened, landing finally as oblong jewels on the wooden floor. He saw Maria rise up on the breaths of the faceless nuns, rise up and leave him, leave the body that ran and knocked down, that lay on the grass. The body she loved that did always what she told it, that could dance and climb or run behind him and put cool hands over his eyes and say "Guess who?" as if it could be someone different. But in the chapel she rose up and wanted to leave the body life that she had loved. Leave him and all their life together. The men singing in the temple did not want to rise up and leave. And that was why he liked them better. And why she did not.

They heard the nuns' music the day Sister Lucy was professed. Sister Lucy who had been Louise La Marr and who had worked for Dr. Meyers. For five years she had been his secretary. "She was, of course, much more than a secretary. I deferred to her in so many questions of taste," Dr. Meyers had said. Neither Joseph nor Maria remembered her very well; they had been seven when she entered Carmel, and she'd not made much of an impression. "God, when I think she was right there, right in my father's office, and I didn't talk to her. I didn't pay attention to her. But that's the way it is with saints, from what I've read," Maria said.

Maria had begun reading all the books she could get about cloistered nuns. She would come to Joseph, holding in her hands the story of a Mexican woman, who had seen the Virgin Mary, a French woman a hundred years dead, a Spanish woman whose father had been a count, and say, "Listen to this. Do you think it sounds like me?" Of course it would sound nothing like her, but he saw how much she wanted it and he'd say, "I think so. Yes. The part when she was young, our age, sounds like you."

Then she would slap the book against the outside of her thigh, the front, the back, twisting her wrist. Then she would lie down on his bed or on the floor and put her hands behind her head and look up dreamily toward the ceiling. "I know they'll let me write to you in Carmel," she would say, "so don't worry. We'll always be best friends. Even though we'll never see each other again. Except through the grille. The last time we'll see each other without the grille will be the day of my profession." Then she would rise away from him, rise up into that world that was the breath of all those women, whose faces were never seen by men.

It was the end of everything, he understood now, her idea to join the convent. It was the first thing of hers he couldn't be a part of, the first thing that she kept back. He'd always known that there were things she hadn't told him before, things she thought about his mother, for example. But he had understood that. Always before, when they were together something pushed forward, pushed against him. She was always running toward him, running away from something else, something she didn't like, or was afraid of, or was bored by, or despised. And then, whatever she ran from became theirs: they opened it, like a surprise lunch, devoured it, took it in. Nothing was wasted; nothing could not be used. With her the hurts, the slights, the mockery of boys who found his life ridiculous, his mother's mistakes and tricks and hatreds, his sense that he was in the eyes of God unworthy, and in the eyes of man a million times inferior to the Meyers, all meant nothing when he was with Maria. Over all that she threw the rich cloak of her fantasy and all her body life.

Now she was taking back the cloak. Bit by bit she pulled it, leaving naked the poor flesh of all his doubts and failures and his fears. She began spending hours with Sister Berchmans, who had terrified them both. But now Maria said that Sister Berchmans was her spiritual adviser and a saint. Maria said that Sister had confided to her that she knew she frightened the children, but it was because she felt she must be distant to avoid establishing particular affections for her students, which would get in the way of her life with God. Maria said she wouldn't be surprised if Sister Berchmans entered Carmel, although it was nothing the nun had said, it was an idea that Maria had picked up "from certain hints which I'm not free to tell you."

For the first time, he disliked Maria, when she made her lips small and her eyes downcast and spoke of Sister Berchmans and the letters Sister Lucy had sent her "which I don't feel free to show." To punish her, he became friends with Ronald Smalley who collected rocks and vied with Joseph for the eighth grade mathematics prize. When he came home one day, holding a crystal of rose quartz, she mooned around him asking what he did at Ronald's house. "Nothing," he said, to taunt her.

"You're disgusting," she said, stamping her foot. "You don't even care that I had a completely disgusting time here all alone on this rotten Sunday while you were off with your stupid friend and his disgusting rocks."

But to please her he gave up Ronald. And she was pleased, and he was pleased to know that he had pleased her. For she had no friends; she could not keep a friend. When she tried to make a friend, the friendship ended sharply, and with grief. For no one but he understood her, he felt, and for the gift of her was willing to put up with her tempers and her scenes. For he knew that to keep them together she kept silent about his mother, kept silent so he would not be sent away. So she was his. His and her father's. And now Sister Berchmans', who must keep herself for God.

But he suspected it was Sister Berchmans at the back of everything. Her white face looking out at him from her white coif. What did she see when she looked at him? And what had she told Dr. Meyers? Or did she never dare to speak to Dr. Meyers; had she spoken only in confession to Father Cunningham, who did the nun's bidding like a boy?

Joseph knew it was her fault. Because Maria told her things, and she had got things wrong. He knew the nun had spoken in confession, and then Father Cunningham had come to Dr. Myers, and now everything was gone. He looked up at his mother, now, holding the Meyers' laundry.

"Look, it's not the end of the world. For me, it's a good thing. Listen, Butch, for both of us. A house to call our own. With my name on the deed. No one else's, only mine. And yours, someday, if you don't leave your mother in the lurch."

They were sending him away, though they were keeping on his mother. Every day his mother could come back here to their home, the white house with the green shutters, the green-striped awning in the summer and the screened-in porch that in the winter turned into a house of glass. But how could he come back? He would have no part in the house now. What had been his room would become—what? What did they need a new room for, what could they do with his when they already had so many? The library and Dr. Meyers' study, Maria's room, the playroom (now their toys were gone and workmen years ago set up a Ping-Pong table there), his mother's laundry room, her sitting room (though never once in all the years had she had a guest). Would the Meyers move from the house themselves? Would they buy some place smaller, thinking to themselves, "Now Joseph and his mother are not here the house is wrong for us?" No, they would never leave the library with its bookshelves specially made, the deep shadowy garden with its day lilies and columbines, the willow that grew roots into the plumbing that Maria made her father promise never to cut down. No, they would never leave the house. It was their home.

But he had thought it was his home. What would he be allowed to take from this house with him? They had come, his mother often told him (he could not remember coming here) with nothing. And where had all the things he had lived with come from? The dresser and the beds, the Fra Angelico Madonna, the picture of the squirrel by Dürer and the horse by Stubbs, the paperweight that dropped white snow on the standing boy? He asked his mother which of all these things were theirs.

"You've got a head on your shoulders, I'll tell you that," she said. "It's good stuff, the stuff in your room. I've got an eye for things like that, and I can tell you. Ask him, when he takes you on this little trip to tell you with the priest. Ask him if you can take the stuff in your room. But don't tell him that I told you first."

Dr. Meyers had arranged for Joseph and himself to go on a weekend retreat with the Passionists in Springfield, Massachusetts. He had told Joseph's mother he would tell Joseph about his decision, his decision that they would have to leave the house. But he had asked Joseph's mother to keep quiet, to let him tell Joseph himself. But she had not kept quiet. She had told him: they are sending you away.

"I guess they want to get rid of you before the two of you get any bright ideas. Of course, she'd be the one to think it up, but you'd be the one to get the blame."

His mother was right: Maria was the one with bright ideas, ideas that rose up, silver in a dark sky, shimmered and then flew.

"It's like he just noticed what you've got between your legs. Like he just figured out she don't have the same thing between hers. Or maybe he needed the priest to tell him."

Put the clothes down, Mother, he wanted to say. You have no right to touch them. You are filthy, with your red hair that you dye one Sunday night a month, with your fat body and your ugly clothes, your red hands and your yellow teeth. And with your filthy heart. The thing he had between his legs, his shame, that did things he could not help, that left the evidence of all he wished he could not be, the body life that he, because he was her son, was doomed to. And his mother knew, she found the evidence, the sheets, showing the thing he could not help, there in the morning. It all happened while he slept, and not his fault, even the priest said not his fault. But still it happened, all because he was her son. And now they knew, and they were sending him away. Because they did not want him in the house now with Maria. But Maria had nothing to do with all that. She hovered above it, like a nun, a saint. He prayed that they would never tell her, she would never know the things they knew about him. Perhaps if he left and said nothing they would not tell.

"I guess you're okay to be her playmate, but God forbid anything else. And for a husband, let's face it, he's got something better in mind than some dumb Polack whose mother washed his shitty underwear for ten years straight."

Why wouldn't she stop talking? He wanted something terrible to happen. She wouldn't be quiet till he said something to make her.

"Maria doesn't want to get married," he said, quietly so she would not know how he hated her and how he dreaded living with her by themselves in some house that belonged to her alone. "She's going to be a nun."

Joseph's mother snorted. Her lips lifted and she showed her yellow teeth. He thought of Maria's mother in the photograph, her sad face frowning, looked at his mother, snorting, throwing laundry into the machine and wondered how it was that he could be her son.

"Wise up, buddy. There's no convent in the world that would take that one."

He was almost as tall as his mother. She could say anything about him, terrible things, he wouldn't answer back. But she could not say things about Maria.

"Sister Berchmans said they'd take her when she finished school."

"The nun tell you that?"

"No, but I know it's true."

"Yeah, and you can buy the Brooklyn Bridge for fifteen bucks. Listen, nobody tells you this, or tells them it, because they're too polite. But they don't take Jews in the convent. And she'll always be a Jew."

"You made that up. Who told you that?" he said. Now he was shouting at his mother. Now he clenched his fists. It was the first time in his life that he had clenched his fists at her. And it just made her laugh.

"Just look at them, those nuns. Just look at all their faces. Ever see a face like hers? Just think about it. She'll find out and get her heart broken to boot, but it'll be too late. All his money won't be able to buy her way in. Cause they don't let them in."

She poked her finger at his chest. *They. Don't. Let. Them. In.* Each word the blow she wanted it to be. Could she be right? They wouldn't be so terrible. Was it the word of God? The God who sent unbaptized babies down to limbo? Who would separate a mother and a child because no water had been poured. He mustn't think about it. It was the sacrament of baptism he thought of. The indelible, fixed sign.

Was there a sign on them because their blood was Jewish? No, it couldn't be. He would find out from Dr. Meyers. He would ask him a clever way. This weekend at the monastery, when they were alone.

———

He packed his suitcase for himself. Pajamas, underwear, a shirt, his slippers. Then he packed an extra pair of pajamas. In case it happened. That thing in the night.

Maria was angry when they left. She dreaded being home for a whole weekend with Joseph's mother. But where could she go? She had no friends. She couldn't go to Sister Berchmans. For a moment Joseph was glad, then he hated the thought of her alone with his mother. He was glad when Dr. Meyers left her money for the movies and suggested she go to the library. She brightened at the thought of that. Then she would go to Moe's she said, "And get a double black-and-white and think of you two fasting."

Her father pretended to slap her, then kissed her on both cheeks.

"What will become of you? I ask myself. I suppose you will have to live with your father forever."

Maria smiled her pious smile and looked at Joseph, as if they two knew the truth. But Joseph looked away. Over Maria's shoulder he could see his mother.

=====

They drove four hours to the monastery, speaking easily of things, of school and politics, of Dr. Meyers' days in Europe, of his promise one day to show Joseph Chartres.

"One day you may decide that you would like to go away to school. Remember, you have only to ask. I know what it's like to be a young boy. You can always come to me, you know, with any problem."

No I cannot, he thought, you are sending me away. The home you call yours I called mine. And now I have no home.

"Thank you," he said, and looked out the window where the rain was turning the grey pavement black.

A lay brother named Brother Gerald showed them to their room. Two iron beds and on the green walls nothing but a crucifix.

"Well, no distractions. That can certainly be said. Better a bare room than an excrescent display of Hallmark piety," said Dr. Meyers, flipping the gold clips of his suitcase. He hung up his shirts and put his shaving kit out on the bed. "And now to supper, whatever that will be. Certainly not as good as what your mother cooks."

Why had his mother told him? Every second now, he had to wait for Dr. Meyers' words. Each bite of food might bring those words closer, every step around the grounds. Each time Dr. Meyers laid a hand on Joseph's shoulder, he was sure it was the time. But Saturday went by, the early Mass, the Rosary, Confessions, Vespers, dinner time. And when it was his turn to speak to the retreat master, Joseph sat dumbly, listening to Father Mulvahy talk about bad companions and the dangers of the flesh. He knew what dangers of the flesh were. They could make you lose your home. He thought about the garden, deep in shadow. He thought about Maria and his mother's words. Perhaps he should ask Father Mulvahy if she'd told the truth. But he did not know how.

"Joseph, I have something difficult to tell you," Dr. Meyers said, Sunday after Mass, when Joseph thought the time was wrong. Fresh from Communion, polished by the glow of silence, of the Sacrament, they walked to the refectory alone.

"In some ways, Joseph, you are like my son. I've always loved you as a son. And because I love you as a son, I fear for the salvation of your soul. I pray for it, I pray for it every morning, as I do for my own daughter's."

Dr. Meyers kept his hand on Joseph's shoulder. Their feet made ugly sounds in the wet grass. He thought of Maria, of the gift of her ideas and words. He thought of the gold star, the secret gift nobody knew she gave him. Was his living in the house a danger to their souls? It could not be. Dr. Meyers must have got it wrong.

"Your nature, Joseph, is not passionate, like my Maria's. Nevertheless, you are a young man now. And to put difficulties in a young man's path is a cruelty I hope I would not be guilty of."

You are guilty of the cruelty of sending me away. Of separating me from everything I love. Of sending me to live alone, in ugliness and hatred with the mother whom I cannot love.

Joseph nodded soberly when Dr. Meyers said, "I thought it best," and ended with the news of his gift to Joseph and his mother of the house.

"But you must never be a stranger, Joseph. You are like our family. Our home is yours."

But you have sent me from your home, my home. I have no home. There is no place for me.

"Thank you, sir," he said.

"You're a good boy, Joseph," said Dr. Meyers squeezing his shoulders. "For you I have no fears. But what will happen to Maria?"

He felt his spine light up, as if a match had been struck at the base. A hot wire went up into his skull, and then back down his spine.

"I think she'll become a nun," said Joseph, looking daringly at Dr. Meyers.

Sadly, Dr. Meyers shook his head. "Think of how she is. There is no convent that would have her."

Joseph felt his throat go hot like melting glass. It could not be that what his mother said was right. It could not be that they knew the same thing, his mother and Dr. Meyers, knew this thing he and Maria did not know.

Why did they know and never tell their children? They were cruel the both of them. The cruelty he thought was just his mother's, Dr. Meyers shared. He might have thought that he kept silent out of kindness, but it was not kindness. It was fear.

But Joseph knew what he would do. He would get Dr. Meyers to send him away to school. He would not see Maria. He would write to her. And his letters would make her think of him in the right way. Make her think of him so she would love him, want to live with him, the body life, and not the life that rose up past the body, not the life of Sister Berchmans and the white-faced nuns. He would make her feel that only with him could her life be happy. He would make her want to marry him before they went to college. He would do that so that she would never know that they would never let her have it. He would marry her before she could find out that because of her blood they would keep back from her her heart's desire.

"I would like to go away to school," he said to Dr. Meyers.

"Of course, Joseph," Dr. Meyers said. "We can arrange anything you want."

THE IMAGINATION
OF DISASTER

am aware of my own inadequacies, of course, but if this happens, no one will be adequate: to be adequate requires a prior act of the imagination, and this is impossible. We are armed; they are armed; someone will take the terrible, the unimaginable, vengeful step. And so we think in images of all that we have known to be the worst. We think of cold, of heat, of heaviness. But that is not it; that does not begin to be it. A mother thinks: how will I carry my children, what will I feed them? But this is not it, this is not it. There will be no place to carry them, food itself will be dangerous. We cannot prepare ourselves; we have known nothing of the kind.

But some days I think: I should prepare, I should do only what is difficult. I think: I will teach myself to use a gun. I hide behind the curtain, and when the mailman comes I try to imagine his right temple in the gunsight as he goes down the sidewalk. How sure one must be to pull the trigger, even to kill for one's own children, for their food, their water, perhaps even poison. The imagination is of no use.

The imagination is of no use. When I run two miles a day, I make myself run faster, farther, make myself feel nauseated, make myself go on despite my burning ribs. In case this one day will be a helpful memory, a useful sensation. Of endurance and of pain. My daughter comes and asks my help in making clay animals. On days like this, I want to say: no, no clay animals, we'll dig, we'll practise digging, once your father was a soldier, he will teach you to use a gun. But of course I cannot do this; I cannot pervert her life so that she will be ready for the disaster. There is no readiness; there is no death in life.

———

My baby son is crying. Will it be harder for males or females? Will they capture boy children to wander in roving gangs? Will my son, asleep now in his crib, wander the abashed landscape, killing other boys for garbage? Will my daughter root among the grain stalks, glistening with danger, for the one kernel of safe nourishment? Ought I to train them for capitulation? I croon to him; I rock him, watch the gold sun strike a maple, turn it golder. My daughter comes into the room, still in her long nightgown. Half an hour ago, I left her to dress herself. She hasn't succeeded; she's used the time to play with my lipstick. It is all over her face, her hands, her arms. Inside her belly is another tiny belly, empty. Will she have the chance to fill herself with a child, as I have filled myself with her and with her brother? On days like this I worry: if she can't dress herself in half an hour, if she cannot obey me in an instant, like the crack of a whip, will she perish? She can charm anyone. Will there be a place for charm after the disaster? What will be its face?

When the babysitter comes, I get into my car. She can make my daughter obey in an instant; she can put my son to sleep without rocking him, or feeding him, or patting him in his crib. On days like this I think I should leave them to her and never come back, for I will probably not survive and with her they will have a greater chance of surviving.

To calm myself I read poetry. When it comes, will the words of "To His Coy Mistress" comfort me, distract me as I wait to hear the news of the death of everything? I want to memorize long poems in case we must spend months in hiding underground. I will memorize "Lycidas," although I don't like Milton. I will memorize it because of what Virginia Woolf said: "Milton is a comfort because he is nothing like our life." At that moment, when we are waiting for the news of utter death, what we will need is something that is nothing like our life.

━━━━━

I come home, and begin making dinner. I have purposely bought a tough cut of meat; I will simmer it for hours. As if that were an experience that would be helpful; as if that were the nature of it: afterwards only tough cuts of meat. I pretend I am cooking on a paraffin stove in a basement. But I cannot restrain myself from using herbs; my own weakness makes me weep. When it comes, there will be no herbs, or spices, no beautiful vegetables like the vegetables that sit on my table in a wooden bowl: an eggplant, yellow squash, tomatoes, a red pepper and some leeks. The solid innocence of my vegetables! When it comes, there will be no innocence. When it comes, there will be no safety. Even the roots hidden deep in the earth of forests will be the food of danger. There will be nothing whose history will be dear. I could weep for my furniture. The earth will be abashed; the furniture will stand out, balked and shameful in the ruin of everything that was our lives.

We have invited friends to dinner. My friend and I talk about our children. I think of her after the disaster; I try to imagine how she will look. I see her standing with a knife; her legs are knotted and blue veins stick out of them like bruised grapes. She is wearing a filthy shirt; her front teeth are missing; her thick black hair is falling out. I will have to kill her to keep her from entering our shelter. If she enters it she will kill us with her knife or the broken glass in her pocket. Kill us for the food we hide which may, even as we take it in, be killing us. Kill us for the life of her own children.

We are sitting on the floor. I want to turn to my friend and say: I do not want to have to kill you. But they have not had my imagination of disaster, and there can be no death in the midst of life. We talk about the autumn; this year we'll walk more in the country, we agree. We kiss our friends good night. Good night, good night, we say, we love you. Good night, I think, I pray I do not have to kill you for my children's food.

=====

My husband puts on red pajamas. I do not speak of my imagination of disaster. He takes my nightgown off and I see us embracing in the full-length mirror. We are, for now, human, beautiful. We go to bed. He swims above me, digging in. I climb and meet him, strike and fall away. Because we have done this, two more of us breathe in the next room, bathed and perfect as arithmetic.

I think: Perhaps I should kill us all now and save us from the degradation of disaster. Perhaps I should kill us while we are whole and dignified and full of our sane beauty. I do not want to be one of the survivors; I am willing to die with my civilization. I have said to my husband: Let us put aside some pills, so that when the disaster strikes we may lie down together, holding each other's hands and die before the whole earth is abashed. But no, he says, I will not let you do that, we must fight. Someone will survive, he says, why not us? Why not our children?

Because the earth will be abashed, I tell him. Because our furniture will stand out shamed among the glistening poisoned objects. Because we cannot imagine it; because imagination is inadequate; because for this disaster, there is no imagination.

But because of this I may be wrong. We live with death, the stone in the belly, the terror on the road alone. People have lived with it always. But we live knowing not only that we will die, that we may suffer, but that all that we hold dear will finish; that there will be no more familiar. That the death we fear we cannot even imagine, it will not be the distinguished thing, it will not be the face of dream, or even nightmare. For we cannot dream the poisoned earth abashed, empty of all we know.

DELIA

People talked about how difficult it was to say which of the O'Reilley girls was the best-looking. Kathleen had the green eyes. She came over by herself at seventeen. She worked as a seamstress and married Ed Derency. The money that she earned, even with all the babies—one a year until she was thirty-five—was enough to bring over the three other girls. Bridget had black hair and a wicked tongue. She married a man who was only five feet tall. She had no children for seven years; then she had a red-haired boy. Some believed he was the child of the policeman. Nettie was small; her feet and her ankles were as perfect as a doll's. She married Mr. O'Toole, who sang in the choir and drank to excess. She had only daughters. Some thought Delia the most beautiful, but then she was the youngest. She married a Protestant and moved away.

In defense of her sister, Kathleen pointed out that John Taylor looked like an Irishman.

"He has the eyes," Kathleen said to Nettie and to Bridget. "I never saw a Protestant with eyes like that."

"Part of the trouble with Delia all along is you babied her, Kathleen," Bridget said. "You made her believe she could do no wrong. What about the children? Is it Protestant nephews and nieces you want?"

"He signed the form to have them baptized," said Nettie.

"And what does that mean to a Protestant?" Bridget said. "They'll sign anything."

"He's good to the children. My children are mad for him," said Kathleen.

"Your children are mad entirely. Hot-blooded," said Bridget. "It's you have fallen for the blue eyes yourself. You're no better than your sister."

"He's kind to my Nora," said Kathleen.

Then even Bridget had to be quiet. Nora was Kathleen's child born with one leg shorter than the other.

"There was never any trouble like that in our family," Bridget had said when she first saw Nora. "It's what comes of marrying outsiders."

John Taylor would sit Nora on his lap. He told her stories about the West.

"Did you see cowboys?" she would ask him, taking his watch out of the leather case he kept it in. The leather case smelled like soap; it looked like a doll's pocketbook. When Nora said that it looked like a doll's pocketbook, John Taylor let her keep it for her doll.

"Cowboys are not gentlemen," said John Taylor.

"Is Mr. du Pont a gentleman?" asked Nora.

"A perfect gentleman. A perfect employer."

John Taylor was the chauffeur for Mr. du Pont. He lived in Delaware. He told Nora about the extraordinary gardens on the estate of Mr. du Pont.

"He began a poor boy," said John Taylor.

"Go on about the gardens. Go on about the silver horse on the hood of the car."

Delia came over and put her hands on top of her husband's. Her hands were cool-looking and blue-white, the color of milk in a bowl. She was expecting her first baby.

"Some day you must come and visit us in Delaware, when the baby's born," she said to Nora. She looked at her husband. Nora knew that the way they looked at each other had something to do with the baby. When her mother was going to have a baby, she got shorter; she grew lower to the ground. But Delia seemed to get taller; she seemed lighter and higher, as though she were filled, not with a solid child like one of Nora's brothers or sisters, but with air. With bluish air.

Delia and John Taylor would let her walk with them. She would walk between them and hold both their hands. Their hands were very different. Delia's was narrow and slightly damp; John Taylor's was dry and broad. It reminded Nora of his shoes, which always looked as if he were wearing them for the first time. They knew how to walk with her. Most people walked too slowly. She wanted to tell them they did not have to walk so slowly for her. But she did not want to hurt their feelings. John Taylor and Delia knew just how to walk, she thought.

After only two weeks, they went back to Delaware.

"She's too thin entirely," said Bridget.

"She's beautiful," said Nora. Her mother clapped her hand over Nora's mouth for contradicting her aunt.

———

Delia never wrote. Nora sent her a present on her birthday, near Christmas. She had made her a rose sachet: blue satin in the shape of a heart, filled with petals she had saved in a jar since the summer. She had worked with her mother to do the things her mother had told her would keep the smell.

Delia sent Nora a postcard. "Thank you for your lovely gift. I keep it in the drawer with my linen."

Linen. Nora's mother read the card to her when the aunts were to tea at their house.

"Fancy saying 'linen' to a child," said Bridget. "In a postcard."

"She has lovely underthings," said Nettie.

"Go upstairs. See to your little brother, Nora," said her mother.

"When they came back to New York, he gave her twenty-five dollars, just to buy underthings. Hand-hemmed, all of them. Silk ribbons. Ivory-colored," said Nettie.

"Hand-done by some greenhorn who got nothing for it," said Bridget. Now Nora knew what Delia meant by linen. She had thought before it was tablecloths she meant, and that seemed queer. Why would she put her good sachet in with the tablecloths? Now she imagined Delia's underclothes, white as angels, smelling of roses. Did John Taylor see her in her underclothing? Yes. No. He was her husband. What did people's husbands see?

She was glad the aunts had talked about it. Now she could see the underclothes more clearly. Ivory ribbons, Nettie had said. Delia's stomach swelled in front of her, but not as much as Nora's mother's. And Nora's mother was going to have a baby in May, which meant Delia would have hers first. March, they had said. But Delia's stomach was light/hard, like a balloon. Nora's mother's was heavy/hard, like a turnip. Why was that, Nora wondered. Perhaps it was because her mother had had five babies, and this was Delia's first.

When her mother wrote to Delia, Nora dictated a note to her too. She asked when John Taylor's birthday was. She thought it was in the summer. She would make him a pillow filled with pine needles if it was in the summer. In July, the family went to the country for a week, and her mother would give her an envelope so she could fill it with pine needles for her Christmas gifts.

March came and went and no one heard anything of Delia's baby. Nora's mother wrote, Nettie wrote, even Bridget wrote, but no one heard anything.

"She's cut herself off," said Bridget. "She hasn't had the baby baptized, and she's afraid to face us."

"First babies are always late," said Kathleen. "I was four weeks overdue with Nora."

"Perhaps something's happened to the baby. Perhaps it's ill and she doesn't want to worry us," said Nettie.

"Nothing like that used to happen in our family," said Bridget, sniffing. "Or anyone we knew in the old country."

"What about Tom Hogan? He had three daft children. And Mrs. Kelly had a blind boy," said Nettie.

"If you'd say a prayer for your sister instead of finding fault with her, you might do some good with your tongue, Bridget O'Reilley, for once in your life," said Kathleen.

"If she'd of listened to me, she wouldn't be needing so many prayers," said Bridget.

"God forgive you, we all need prayers," said Kathleen, crossing herself.

"What's the weather in Delaware?" said Nettie.

"Damp," said Bridget. "Rainy."

"They live right on the estate," said Kathleen. "They eat the same food as Mr. du Pont himself."

"Yes, only not at the same table," said Bridget. "Downstairs is where the servants eat. I'd rather eat plain food at my own table than rich food at a servant's board."

"Will we not write to her, then?" said Nettie, to Kathleen mainly.

"Not if she's not written first. There must be some reason," said Kathleen.

"It's her made the first move away," said Bridget.

"If something was wrong, we'd hear. You always hear the bad. She must be all wrapped up. Probably the du Ponts have made a pet of her," said Kathleen.

Nora remembered that John Taylor had said that on Mrs. du Pont's birthday there was a cake in the shape of a swan. And ices with real strawberries in them, although it was the middle of November. And the ladies wore feathers and looked like peacocks, Delia had said. "They're beautiful, the ladies," John Taylor had said. "You should know, tucking the lap robes under them," Delia had said, standing on one foot like a bird. "God knows where you'd of been if I hadn't come along to rescue you in good time." "You've saved me from ruin," John Taylor had said, twirling an imaginary moustache.

Nora remembered how they had laughed together. John and Delia were the only ones she knew who laughed like that and were married.

"Do you think we'll never see Delia and John again?" said Nora to her mother.

"Never say never, it's bad luck," her mother said. She put her hand to her back. The baby made her back ache, she said. Soon, she told Nora, she would have to go to bed for the baby.

"And then you must mind your Aunt Bridget and keep your tongue in your head."

"Yes, ma'am," said Nora. But her mother knew she always minded; she never answered back. Only that once, about Delia, had she answered back.

———

When Nora's mother went to bed to have the baby, the younger children went to Nettie's, but Nora stayed home. "Keep your father company," her mother had said. "At least if he sees you it'll keep him from feeling in a house full of strangers entirely."

But even with her there, Nora's father walked in the house shyly, silently, as if he was afraid of disturbing something. He took her every evening, since it was warm, to the corner for an ice cream. She saw him so rarely that they had little to say to one another. She knew him in his tempers and in his fatigue. He would walk her home with a gallantry that puzzled her, and he went to sleep while it was still light. He woke in the morning before her, and he went away before she rose.

Bridget made Nora stay outside all day when her mother went into labor. She sat on the front steps, afraid to leave the area of the house, afraid to miss the first cry or the news of an emergency. Children would come past her, but she hushed them until they grew tired of trying to entice her away. She looked at her hands; she looked down at her white shoes, one of which was bigger than the other, her mother had said, because God had something special in mind for her. What could He have in mind? Did God change His mind? Did He realize He had been mistaken? She counted the small pink pebbles in the concrete banister.

She could hear her mother crying out. Everyone on the block could, she thought, with the windows open. She swept the sand on the middle step with the outside of her hand.

Then in front of her were a man's brown shoes. First she was frightened, but a second later, she recognized them. She did not have to look up at the face. They were John Taylor's shoes; they were the most beautiful shoes she had ever seen.

"Hello, Nora," he said, as if she should not be surprised to see him.

"Hello," she said, trying not to sound surprised, since she knew he did not want her to.

"Is your mother in?"

"She's upstairs in bed."

"Not sick, I hope."

"No. She's having another baby."

John Taylor sucked breath, as if he had changed his mind about something. The air around him was brilliant as glass. He looked around him, wanting to get away.

"How is Delia?" said Nora, thinking that was what her mother would have said.

"She died," said John, looking over his shoulder.

"And the baby? Is it a boy or a girl?"

"Dead. Born dead."

"Do you still drive a car for that man?" she said, trying to understand what he had told her. Born dead. It did not sound possible. And Delia dead. She heard her mother's voice from the window.

"I'm on holiday," said John, reaching into his pocket.

She was trying to think of a way to make him stay. If she could think of the right thing, he would take her for a walk, he would tell her about the cars and the gardens.

"How've you been, then?" she said.

"Fine," said John Taylor.

But he did not say it as he would have to an adult, she knew. He did not say it as if he were going to stay.

"Nora," he said, bending down to her. "Can we have a little secret? Can I give you a little present?"

"Yes," she said. He was going away. She could not keep him. She wanted something from him. She would keep his secret; he would give her a gift.

He reached into his pocket and took out a silver dollar. He put it in her hand and he closed her hand around it.

"Don't tell anyone I was here. Or what I said. About Delia, or about the baby."

It was very queer. He had come to tell them, and now she must not tell anyone, she thought. Perhaps he had come this way only to tell her. That was it: he had come from Delaware to tell her a secret, to give her a gift.

"I won't say anything," she said. She looked into his eyes; she had never looked into the eyes of an adult before. She felt an itching on the soles of her feet from the excitement of it.

"I'll count on you, then," he said, and walked quickly down the street, looking over his shoulder.

She went into the house. Upstairs, she could hear Bridget's voice, and her mother's voice in pain, but not yet the voice of the baby. She lifted her skirt. She put the silver dollar behind the elastic of her drawers. First it was cold against her stomach, but then it became warm from the heat of her body.

THE ONLY SON OF
THE DOCTOR

*L*ouisa was surprised that she was with a man like Henry, after all she had been through. She liked to tell him that he was the best America could come up with. She told all her friends about his father, who had built half the houses in the town where Henry lived, who had gone broke twice but had died solvent; about the picture of his eighteenth-century ancestor, dumb as a sheep but still a speculator; about his mother, who had founded the town library. And she told them—it was one of her best stories now —that when she had agreed to go to bed with him, he had said to her, "Bless your heart."

It was to expose him that she had wanted to meet him in the first place. There had been a small piece about him in the *Times*, and she had not believed that he could be what he seemed, a country doctor who ran a nursing home that would not use artificial means to keep the old alive. The story said he was in some danger of being closed down; the home was almost bankrupt.

If things looked simple, Louisa's genius was to prove that they were not. She wrote to the doctor about his home, hoping to unmask him and his project. The *Times* had been almost idolatrous; they described reverentially his devotion to the aged. They described the street where he lived as if they had dreamed of it over the Thanksgiving dinners of their childhood. Louisa drove the hundred and twenty miles from New York hoping to see behind the golden oaks a genuine monstrosity, hungering to discover, in the cellar of the large farmhouse the doctor had converted, white skeletons behind the staircase, whiter than the Congregational church that edified the center of the village. At the very least, she hoped to find the doctor foolish, to catch him in some lapse of gesture or language so that she could show the world he was not what he seemed.

When he opened the door to her, she saw that his face was not what she had expected. The eyes were not simple: blue, of course they were blue, but they were flecked with some light color, gold or yellow, warning her of judgment, of a severeness at the heart of all that trust. And she knew he was a man who was used to getting whatever woman he wanted. She could tell that by the way he closed the door behind her, by the way he led her into the living room.

"Tell me about yourself," she said, pressing the button of her tape recorder. "Tell me how you came to such work."

His voice was so perfectly beautiful that she felt she had suddenly stepped into a forest where the leaves were visible in moonlight. He said he was devoted to stopping the trend of prolonging agony. That was what had made her love him first: those words "the trend of prolonging agony." It made change sound so possible; there was such belief implicit in that construction: that life was imperfect but ordinary, and not beyond our reach.

He had thought he would be an actor, he said, after college. He said his dream was to play light comedy; he had wanted to be Cary Grant. But she could see his gift was not for comedy. His gift was for breaking news. She knew, sitting in his living room, that his was the voice she would have preferred above all others to speak the news of her own death. He said he had decided to take up this work, after years of practice as an internist in Boston, because he had seen how impossible it had been for his mother to die well. So he had come back to his home town, where his father had

built half the houses, where his mother had founded the library, to start
an old-age home.

He asked Louisa for her help in keeping the home alive, for it was, as
the *Times* had suggested, in danger of bankruptcy. The piece she wrote
about him and his work brought floods of contributions. She talked her
friends into helping him with a fund-raising campaign. His own efforts had
been small, and local, and hopelessly inefficient. He wrote all the fund-
raising letters himself, at a huge black manual typewriter. He was always
writing letters, always meeting with the board of directors. The board was
made up of townspeople: the lawyer, the minister, the principal of the high
school. When she came up from the city to speak to the board, to advise
them on the first steps of their fund-raising campaign, her differentness
from them made her feel like a criminal. Later she would be able to sit
with them at the doctor's table and joke or help them peel potatoes. But
that first meeting of the board made her think of the city mouse-country
mouse tales she had read as a child. Sitting around her at the doctor's table,
all those people made her feel edgy and smart-alecky and full of excessive
cleverness suspiciously come by. She felt as if she were smoking three
cigarettes at once. They turned to her with such trust; they were so
impressed by her skills; they were so sure that she could help them. Their
trust made them seem very young, and it annoyed her to be made to feel
the oldest among them when in fact she was the youngest by fifteen years.
The night of that first meeting of the board, she went to bed with the
doctor because he seemed the only other adult in town.

By the time the campaign was over and the committee had raised its
money, she had got into the habit of spending her weekends with him.
They never said that she would do this; she simply called on Thursdays
to say what train she would be taking Friday. And he would say: "This is
what I've arranged for us. We'll have the Chamberlains on Saturday;
Sunday we'll take a picnic lunch to the river."

It was partly his voice that made her love doing these things. His voice
made everything simpler; it could reclaim for her pleasures she had be-

lieved lost to her forever. Her first husband had told her she was a disaster with tools. The doctor (his name was Henry; she did not like his name; she did not like to use it, although she admitted it suited him) taught her simple carpentry. He made it possible for her to ask questions that were radically necessary and at the same time idiotic: "When you say joist, what exactly do you mean? How does a level work?" He made it possible for her to work with things whose names she understood.

She had learned, particularly in the years since her divorce, when people had invited her for weekends out of kindness, that it was impossible for a person living in the country to take a city guest for a walk without reproach, implied or stated. She could see it in the eyes of whatever friend she walked with, the unshakable belief in the superiority of country life. People in the country, she thought, believed it beyond question that their lives had been purified. They had the righteousness of zealots: born again, free at last.

This had kept her out of the country. The skills she prized and possessed were skills learned in the city: conversation, discrimination. She remembered a story she had read as a child about a princess who had to go into hiding on a farm. How she suffered at the hands of the milkmaid, who set up tests that the princess was bound to fail: the making of cheeses, jumping from hayloft to haycart, imitating the call of birds. The milkmaid took pleasure in convincing the princess of the worthlessness of the princess's accomplishments. And she did convince her, until a courtier arrived. The milkmaid was tongue-tied; she fell all over her feet in the presence of such a gentleman, while the princess poured water from a ewer and told jokes. Louisa saw herself as the princess in the tale, but the courtier had never come to acknowledge her. Always she was stuck in the part of the story that had the princess spraining an ankle on the haycart, unable to imitate the cry of the cuckoo! On the whole, she had found it to be to her advantage to decline invitations to any place where she would be obliged to wear flat shoes.

But she loved simply walking in the country with Henry. He had a way of walking that made her want to take month-long journeys on foot with him. He did not spend time trying to get her to notice things—bark, or leaves, or seasonal changes. He would walk and talk to her about his mother's father, about his days in the theater, about his work with the aged. He would ask her advice about the wording of one of his letters. Always, when they were walking, he would soon want to go home and begin writing a letter. So that for the first time in her life it was she who begged to stay outside longer, she who did not want to go indoors.

And his house was the most perfect house she had ever known. It had been his family's for generations. The living room had thirteen windows; he kept in a glass-and-wood cabinet his great-grandmother's wedding china. But his study was her favorite room. He had a huge desk that he had built himself, and on the desk was a boy's dream of technology: an electric pencil sharpener, a machine that dispensed stamps as if they were flat tongues, boxes for filing that seemed to her magic in their intricacies. He had divided his desk by causes; it was sectioned off with cardboard signs he had made: nuclear power, child abuse, migrant workers. He never mixed his correspondences. But the neatness of his desk was boyish—not an executive neatness, but the kind of neatness that wins merit badges, worried over, somewhat furtive, somewhat tentative, more than a little ill at ease.

And he had pictures of ships on the wall of his study. Ships! How she loved him for that! It was impossible that any other man she had ever known well—her father, her husband, any of her lovers—would have had pictures of ships. All the men in her life had doted on the foreign, which was why they were interested in her. Why, then, was Henry interested? Sometimes she was afraid that he would realize he had made a mistake in her, that he would wake up and find her less kind, less generous, less natural, than the women he was accustomed to loving. She was afraid that he had misunderstood her face because he liked it best after sex or early in the morning. He liked her best without makeup, and he didn't notice her clothes. Other men had loved her best when she was dressed for the theater or parties. Henry preferred her naked, with her hair pulled back. This disturbed her; it made her feel she was competing in the wrong event.

She could never win against girls who dashed down to breakfast after taking time only to splash cold water on their eyes. She had some chance against women who invented their own beauty. But he would dress her in his shirts; he would kiss her before she had washed her face. Now she did not wear makeup when she was with him—he had asked her not to so simply. How could she refuse such a desire, spoken in the voice she loved? But she was afraid that she could lose his love, in some way she could not predict, if he loved her for herself the first thing in the morning.

And it troubled her that she could not predict in Henry the faults that would cause her one day not to love him. Would she one day grow tired of his evenness; would she long for storms, recriminations? She felt she had to ask him about his wife; they had gone on for months saying nothing about her. What kind of woman would leave such a house, such furniture? Henry said only that she was living in New Mexico, she had a private income, they wrote twice a month. He said nothing that would allow her to look into herself for the wife's faults, to see in Henry the wife's objections. In time she grew grateful for his reticence. She was, for the first time, safe in love. He did not look, for example, at other women in restaurants. He did not see them. Perhaps it was because she and Henry spent so much of their lives away from each other. It made her gentler, that lack of access. It made him, she thought, less curious.

———

She asked him once if he had ever thought of asking her to come and live with him. He looked at her strangely; she could tell that the had not thought of it. That look surprised her, and it embarrassed her deeply. And then she began to feel that look as an extreme form of neglect. They had been together for six months; they had been in love. And he had not thought of living with her. He said (one of those truths he thought there was no reason not to tell), "I just don't think of you as making much impression on a house. I don't think of you as caring about it."

"Of course I do. I like having a beautiful place to live."

"Yes, but I mean you don't become attached to a house itself. You become attached to the things in it."

There was no way she could prove him wrong. She would have to do something so extreme that everything in her life would have to change utterly. She would have to build herself a house in the woods and live in it for years to prove to him that she cared about houses. And she was ready to do it; she awoke next to him at four in the morning and she thought that that was just what she would do. She would quit her job; she would stop seeing him. She would build herself a house to prove to him that she cared about houses. In the morning she laughed to think of herself writing a letter of resignation, buying lumber, but she was frightened that because of him she had entertained, even for a moment, such a fantastic renunciation. She saw that loving someone so calm, so moderate, that being loved so plainly and truthfully, could lead to extremes of devotion, of escape.

He accused her of being unable to resist the habit of separating sheep from goats. It was a loving accusation. He told her that her habit of sheep and goats had lifted from him a burden; he did not have to look so clearly at people when he was with her. She made a list of the phrases he used to defend the people she criticized: "good sort," "means well," "quite competent at his job," "very kind underneath it all." He put the list on the corkboard above his desk. He said he kissed it every morning that she was not there. He touched it for good luck, he said, before writing a letter.

———

One Thursday in August when she called he said, "My son is with me." She had made his son one of the goats. Partly it was an accident of their ages; his son was nearly her age and she resented him for it. But it was a class resentment as well, and a historical one. Henry's son—with, she thought, using a phrase her mother might have used, all the advantages —had gone the way of the children of the affluent sixties. He had dropped out. Dropped out. It was such a boring phrase, she had always thought, such a boring concept. Dropped out. And yet she resented his hitchhiking through Denmark while she was working as a waitress or in the library to support her scholarship, resented him for not carrying on his father's line, for not having an office by this time, with pictures of ships. And she did not comprehend how he could resist all this. All this: she meant the house with all the windows, the attic full of old letters, the grandmother who was named for her great-aunt, killed during the Revolution. Before Louisa met him, she decided the boy was thickheaded. She could not be sympathetic to this boy who had left his father. When his father was the man she loved.

On the train up, she tried to remember what Henry had told her about his son. There had been the same reluctance to talk about his child as there had been to talk about his wife, and she had been as grateful. He had said something about the boy's hitchhiking through Denmark. And there was something about a fight. She remembered now that there was some reason for her wanting to forget it. She had not liked Henry's part in it.

The family had been vacationing in Europe and Henry's son had refused to return home. He was fifteen at the time, and he wanted to spend the year in Scandinavia, hitchhiking around, earning money at odd jobs. Why Scandinavia? she had asked, searching for some detail that would make the boy sympathetic. It simply took his fancy, Henry had said. He had, of course, insisted that his son come home and finish high school. His son had refused. Finally, after a week of silence, the boy had said, "Well, there's only one thing to do. We'll have to go outside and fight."

"What did you do?" Louisa had asked, with that combination of thrill and boredom she felt when she watched Westerns.

"I let him go."

Of course. What had she wanted him to do? Arrange some display of paternal weapons? He would not be the man she loved if he had forced his son to succumb to his authority. But why was she so disappointed? How would her own father have acted toward her brother? Her brother, a lawyer now with three children, would never have had the confidence for such defiance. He would have known, too, physical anger at his father's hand. Such knowledge would have prevented risk. Louisa resented Henry's son for knowing, at fifteen, that he could survive without the sanction of his parents. She wanted to tell that boy what a luxury it was—that defiance, that chosen poverty. She wanted to tell him that with less money and position, he could never have been so daring. She wanted to tell him he was spoiled. By the time the train pulled into the station, she was terribly angry. She realized that she had ridden for miles with her hands clenched into fists.

She was exceptionally loving in her embrace of Henry. He told her, with some excitement, that Eliot had spent the last few days painting his barn. He said, with a gratitude that touched and frightened her, that his barn was now the most beautiful in the county. He told her what good stories Eliot had to tell, about Alaska, about South America. She closed her eyes. Nothing interested her less than stories about men in bars, and fights, and roads and spectacular views, and feats of idiot courage. She knew she would have nothing to say to his son. Would this make Henry stop loving her? By the time they were in front of the house, she knew she was wrong to have come.

He was sitting at the kitchen table with his legs spread out, at least halfway, she thought, into the room. Henry had to step over his son's legs to get to the table. She followed behind Henry, stepping over his son's black boots. She hated those boots; there was something illegal-looking about them. They were old; the leather was cracked so that it looked not like leather but like the top of a burned cake. It was an insult to Henry, she thought, to wear boots like that in his house.

"Eliot, I'd like you to meet Louisa Altiere. Louisa, my son, Eliot Cosgrove."

"Hey," said Eliot, not looking up.

Louisa walked over and extended her hand.

"I'm very glad to meet you," she said.

He did not take her hand. She went on extending it. With some aggressiveness she thrust her hand almost under his nose. He finally shook her hand. She wanted to tell him that she had got better handshakes from most of the dogs she knew.

"Why are you glad to meet me?" he said, looking up at her for the first time.

"What?"

"I mean, people say they're glad to meet somebody. But how do you know? You're probably really a little ticked off that I'm here. I mean, you don't get to spend that much time with Henry. And here I am cutting into it."

"On the contrary, I feel that knowing you will enable me to know your father better."

"Watch out, Eliot," said Henry. "Watch out when she says things like 'on the contrary.' "

The two men laughed. She felt betrayed, and excluded from the circle of male laughter. Henry had put his feet up on the table.

"I'll go and unpack," she said, feeling like a Boston schoolteacher in Dodge City. She wondered if Henry had told his son what she was like in bed.

———

She looked at the barn through the window of Henry's bedroom. She used to like looking at it; now it bulked large; she resented its blocking her view of the mountains. She kept walking around the bedroom, picking things up, putting them down, putting her dresses on different hangers, anything so that she would not have to go downstairs to the two men. My lover, she was thinking, and his son.

Henry had a drink waiting for her when she did go down. He stood up when she walked into the room. How much smaller he was than his son. It did not have to do entirely with Eliot's being born after the war and having more access to vitamins. She had loved Henry for being so finely made that his simplest gestures seemed eloquent. Once she had wept to see him taking the ice cubes out of the tray. She remembered his telling her that when Eliot was a child they called him "Brob," for "Brobdingna-gian."

While Henry talked to her about his work on the Child Abuse Commit-tee and the letters he had received from a prominent U.S. senator, Eliot sat at the table, whittling. It distracted Louisa so much that she was not exactly able to understand the point of Henry's letter. She stared at Eliot until he put down his knife.

"I thought whittling was something that dropped from a culture when people became literate," she said.

"What makes you think I'm literate?" said Eliot, throwing the pop top of his beer can over her head into the garbage.

"I assume you were taught to read."

"That doesn't mean I'm still into it."

Henry put his head back and laughed, a louder laugh than she had ever heard from him.

———

She spent the rest of the afternoon shopping and making dinner. Bouil-labaisse. She was glad of the time it took to sauté and to scrub; it meant she did not have to be with Henry and Eliot. And the dinner was a success. But while Henry praised Louisa, Eliot sat in silence, playing with the mussel shells. Then Henry turned his attention to his son. They spoke of old outings, old neighbors. They laughed, she was disturbed to see, most heartily about a neighbor's wife who had gained a hundred pounds. They imitated the woman's foolishness in clothes, the walk that forgot the flesh she lived in. They talked about their trips to Italy, to the Pacific Northwest.

Louisa saw there was no place for her. She cleared the table and washed the dishes slowly, making the job last. They were still talking when she rejoined them at the table. They had not noticed that she had left.

Henry mentioned the meeting he would have to go to after supper. He was the chairman of a citizens' committee to stall a drainage bond. Louisa was annoyed that Henry had not told her he would be away for the evening, had not told her she would be alone with Eliot. Perhaps he had guessed she would not have come if she knew.

"I think it's good that you and Eliot will have the time alone. You'll get to know each other," said Henry when he was alone with her in the bedroom, tying his tie.

After Henry left, she took her book down into the living room, where Eliot sat watching a Country-and-Western singer on television. She was embarrassed to be sitting in a room with someone at seven-thirty on a Saturday night, watching someone in a white leather suit who sang about truck drivers.

"When did you first become interested in country music?" she asked.

"A lot of my friends are into it."

She opened her novel.

"You don't like me much, do you?" he said, after nearly half an hour of silence.

His rudeness was infantile; no one but a child would demand such conversation. All right, then, she would do what he wanted; she would tell the truth, because at that moment she preferred the idea of hurting him to the idea of her own protection.

"I don't think you deserve your father."

The boy stopped lounging in his chair. He sat up—she wanted to say, like a gentleman.

"Don't you think I know that?" he said.

She turned her legs away from him, in shame and in defeat. How easily he had shown her up. He could work with honesty in a way that she couldn't. He reminded her that he was, after all, better bred; that she was what she had feared—someone who had learned the superficial knack of things but could be exposed by someone who knew their deeper workings. She did not know whether she liked him for it; she thought that she should leave the house.

"I'm sorry," she said. "I had no right to speak to you like that."

"The real secret about my father is that nobody's good enough for him. But he keeps on trying. His efforts are doomed to failure."

Did he say that? "His efforts are doomed to failure." Of course he did. He was, after all, the son of his father. And she saw that he had to be what he was, having Henry for a father. She saw it now; such a moderate man had to inspire radical acts.

"Forgive me," she said. "I was very rude."

He was not someone used to listening to apologies. She wanted to touch his hand, but she realized that for people connected as they were, there was no appropriate gesture.

"Once I was in Alaska, riding my bike through this terrific snowstorm. And I had a real bad skid. I fell into the snow. I think I musta been out for a couple of minutes. I thought I was going to die. When I came to, I could hear the sound of my father's typewriter. I could hear him at that damn typewriter, typing letters. I was sure I was going to die. I was sure that was the last sound I'd hear. But someone came by in a pickup and rescued me. Weird, isn't it?"

She could see him lying in the snow, wondering whether he would survive, thinking of his father. Hearing his typewriter. Was it in love or hatred that he had heard it? She thought of Henry's back as he wrote his letters, of the perfect calm with which he arranged his thoughts into sentences, into paragraphs. And what would a child have thought, seeing that back turned to him, listening to the typewriter? For Henry needed no one when he was at his desk, writing his letters for the most just, the most worthy, of causes. He was perfectly alone and perfectly content, like someone looking through a telescope, like someone sailing a ship. She thought of this boy, four inches taller than his father, fifty pounds heavier, wondering if he would die, hearing his father's typewriter. But was it love or hatred that brought him the sound?

She began to cry. Henry's son looked at her with complete disinterest. No man had ever watched her tears with such a total lack of response.

"I'll say good night, then. I'm taking off in the morning. Early. I'll leave about four o'clock," he said.

"Does your father know?"

"Sure."

"And he went to the meeting anyway?"

"It was important. And he's going to get up and make me breakfast."

"What about tonight?"

"What about it?"

"Don't you want to stay up and wait for him?"

"He'll be late. He's at that meeting," said Eliot, climbing the stairs.

"I'll wait up for him," said Louisa.

"Far out," said Eliot—was it unpleasantly?—from the landing.

———

She read her novel for an hour. Then she went upstairs and looked at herself in the mirror. She took out all the makeup she had with her: eyeshadow, pencil, mascara, two shades of lipstick, a small pot of rouge. She made herself up more heavily than she had ever done before. She made her face a caricature of all she valued in it. But it satisfied her, that face, in its extremity. And it fascinated her that in Henry's house she had done such a thing. Her face, no longer her own, so fixated her that she could not move away from the mirror. She sat perfectly still until she heard his key in the door.

THE NEIGHBORHOOD

*M*y mother has moved from her house now; it was her family's for sixty years. As she was leaving, neighbors came in shyly, family by family, to say good-bye. There weren't many words; my mother hadn't been close to them; she suspected neighborly connections as the third-rate PR of Protestant churches and the Republican Party, the substitute of the weak, the rootless, the disloyal, for parish or for family ties. Yet everyone wept; the men she'd never spoken to, the women she'd rather despised, the teenagers who'd gained her favor by taking her garbage from the side of the house to the street for a dollar and a half a week in the bad weather. As we drove out, they arranged themselves formally on either side of the driveway, as if the car were a hearse. Through the rearview mirror, I saw the house across the street and thought of the Lynches, who'd left almost under cover, telling nobody, saying good-bye to no one, although they'd lived there seven years and when they'd first arrived the neighborhood had been quite glad.

The Lynches were Irish, Ireland Irish, people in the neighborhood said proudly, their move from the city to Long Island having given them the luxury of bestowing romance on a past their own parents might have downplayed or tried to hide. Nearly everybody on the block except my family and the Freeman sisters had moved in just after the war. The war, which the men had fought in, gave them a new feeling of legitimate habitation: they had as much right to own houses on Long Island as the Methodists, if not, perhaps, the old Episcopalians. And the Lynches' presence only made their sense of seigneury stronger: they could look upon them as exotics, or as foreigners and tell themselves that after all now there was nothing they had left behind in Brooklyn that they need feel as a lack.

Each of the four Lynch children had been born in Ireland, although only the parents had an accent. Mr. Lynch was hairless, spry, and silent: the kind of Irishman who seems preternaturally clean and who produces, possibly without his understanding, child after child, whom he then leaves to their mother. I don't know why I wasn't frightened of Mrs. Lynch; I was the sort of child to whom the slightest sign of irregularity might seem a menace. Now I can place her, having seen drawings by Hogarth, having learned words like *harridan* and *slattern*, which almost rhyme, having recorded, in the necessary course of feminist research, all those hateful descriptions of women gone to seed, or worse than seed, gone to some rank uncontrollable state where things sprouted and hung from them in a damp, lightless anarchy. But I liked Mrs. Lynch; could it have been that I didn't notice her wild hair, her missing teeth, her swelling ankles, her ripped clothes, her bare feet when she came to the door, her pendulous ungirded breasts? Perhaps it was that she was different and my fastidiousness was overrun by my romanticism. Or perhaps it was that she could give me faith in transformation. If, in the evenings, on the weekends, she could appear barefoot and unkempt, on Monday morning she walked out in her nurse's aide's uniform, white-stockinged and white-shod, her hair pinned under a starched cap, almost like any of my aunts.

But I am still surprised that I allowed her to be kind to me. I never liked going into the house; it was the first dirty house that I had ever seen, and when I had to go in and wait for Eileen, a year younger than I, with whom I played emotionlessly from the sheer demand of her geographical nearness and the sense that playing was the duty of our state in life, I tried not to look at anything and I tried not to breathe. When, piously, I described the mechanisms of my forbearance to my mother, she surprised me by being harsh. "God help Mrs. Lynch," she said, "four children and slaving all day in that filthy city hospital, then driving home through all that miserable traffic. She must live her life dead on her feet. And the oldest are no help."

Perhaps my mother's toleration of the Lynches pointed the response of the whole neighborhood, who otherwise would not have put up with the rundown condition of the Lynches' house and yard. The neighbors had for so long looked upon our family as the moral arbiters of the street that it would have been inconceivable for them to shun anyone of whom my mother approved. Her approvals, they all knew, were formal and dispensed *de haut en bas*. Despising gossip, defining herself as a working woman who had no time to sit on the front steps and chatter, she signaled her approbation by beeping her horn and waving from her car. I wonder now if my mother liked Mrs. Lynch because she too had no time to sit and drink coffee with the other women; if she saw a kinship between them, both of them bringing home money for their families, both of them in a kind of widowhood, for Mr. Lynch worked two jobs every day, one as a bank guard, one as a night watchman, and on Saturdays he drove a local cab. What he did inside the house was impossible to speculate upon; clearly, he barely inhabited it.

My father died when I was seven and from then on I believed the world was dangerous. Almost no one treated me sensibly after his death. Adults fell into two categories: they hugged me and pressed my hand, their eyes brimming over with unshed tears, or they slapped me on the back and urged me to get out in the sunshine, play with other children, stop brooding, stop reading, stop sitting in the dark. What they would not do was leave me alone, which was the only thing I wanted. The children understood that, or perhaps they had no patience; they got tired of my rejecting their advances, and left me to myself. That year I developed a new friendship with Laurie Sorrento, whom I never in the ordinary run of things would have spoken to since she had very nearly been left back in the first grade. But her father had died too. Like mine, he had had a heart attack, but his happened when he was driving his truck over the Fifty-Ninth

Street Bridge, at five o'clock, causing a traffic jam of monumental stature. My father had a heart attack in the Forty-Second Street Library. He died a month later in Bellevue. Each evening during that month my mother drove into the city after work, through the Midtown Tunnel. I had supper with a different family on the block each evening, and each night some mother put me to bed and waited in my house until my mother drove into the driveway at eleven. Then, suddenly, it was over, that unreal time; the midnight call came, he was dead. It was as though the light went out in my life and I stumbled through the next few years trying to recognize familiar objects which I had known but could not seem to name.

I didn't know if Laurie lived that way, as I did, in half-darkness, but I enjoyed her company. I only remember our talking about our fathers once, and the experience prevented its own repetition. It was a summer evening, nearly dark. We stood in her backyard and started running in circles shouting, "My father is dead, my father is dead." At first it was the shock value, I think, that pleased us, the parody of adult expectation of our grief, but then the thing itself took over and we began running faster and faster and shouting louder and louder. We made ourselves dizzy and we fell on our backs in the grass, still shouting "My father is dead, my father is dead," and in our dizziness the grass toppled the sky and the rooftops slanted dangerously over the new moon, almost visible. We looked at each other, silent, terrified, and walked into the house, afraid we might have made it disappear. No one was in the house, and silently, Laurie fed me Saltine crackers, which I ate in silence till I heard my mother's horn honk at the front of the house, and we both ran out, grateful for the rescue.

But that Christmas, Laurie's mother remarried, a nice man who worked for Con Edison, anxious to become the father of an orphaned little girl. She moved away and I was glad. She had accepted normal life and I no longer found her interesting. This meant, however, that I had no friends. I would never have called Eileen Lynch my friend; our sullen, silent games of hopscotch or jump rope could not have been less intimate, her life inside her filthy house remained a mystery to me, as I hoped my life in the house where death had come must be to her. There was no illusion of our liking one another; we were simply there.

Although I had no friends, I was constantly invited to birthday parties, my tragedy giving me great cachet among local mothers. These I dreaded as I did the day of judgment (real to me; the wrong verdict might mean that I would never see my father), but my mother would never let me refuse. I hated the party games and had become phobic about the brick of vanilla, chocolate, and strawberry ice cream always set before me and the prized bakery cake with its sugar roses. At every party I would run into the bathroom as the candles were being blown out and be sick. Resentful, the mothers would try to be kind, but I knew they'd felt I spoiled the party. I always spent the last hour in the birthday child's room, alone, huddled under a blanket. When my mother came, the incident would be reported, and I would see her stiffen as she thanked the particular mother for her kindness. She never said anything to me, though, and when the next invitation came and I would remind and warn her, she would stiffen once again and say only, "I won't be around forever, you know."

But even I could see there was no point trying to get out of Eileen Lynch's party. I didn't say anything as I miserably dressed and miserably walked across the street, my present underneath my arm, a pair of pedal pushers I was sure Eileen wouldn't like.

Superficially, the Lynches' house was cleaner, though the smell was there, the one that always made me suspect there was something rotting, dead, or dying behind the stove or the refrigerator. Eileen's older sisters, whose beauty I then felt was diminished by its clear sexual source, were dressed in starched, high dresses; their shoes shone and the seams in their stockings were perfect. For the first time, I felt I had to admire them, although I'd preferred their habitual mode of treatment—the adolescent's appraisal of young children as deriving from a low and altogether needless caste—to their false condescending warmth as they offered me a party hat and a balloon. Eileen seemed unimpressed by all the trouble that had been gone to for her; her distant walk-through of Blind Man's Bluff and Pin the

Tail on the Donkey I recognized as springing from a heart as joyless as my own.

Throughout the party, Mrs. Lynch had stayed in the kitchen. After the presents had been opened, she appeared, wearing her nurse's uniform and her white hose, but not her cap, and said to all of us, "Will ye come in and have some cake, then?"

It was the cake and ice cream I had known from all the other birthday parties and I closed my eyes and tried to think of other things—the ocean, as my mother had suggested, the smell of new-mown grass. But it was no good. I felt the salty rising behind my throat: I ran for the bathroom. Eileen's guests were not from my class, they were a year younger than I, so I was spared the humiliation of knowing they'd seen all this a dozen times before. But I was wretched as I bent above the open toilet, convinced that there was nowhere in the world that I belonged, wishing only that I could be dead like my father in a universe which had, besides much else to recommend it, incorporeality for its nature. There was the expected knock on the door. I hoped it would be Mrs. Lynch instead of one of Eileen's sisters whose contempt I would have found difficult to bear.

"Come and lay down, ye'll need a rest," she said, turning her back to me the way the other mothers did. I followed, as I always had, into the indicated room, not letting my glance fall toward the eating children, trying not to hear their voices.

I was surprised that Mrs. Lynch had led me, not into the child's room but into the bedroom that she shared with Mr. Lynch. It was a dark room, I don't think it could have had a window. There were two high dressers and the walls were covered with brown, indistinguishable holy images. Mrs. Lynch moved the rose satinish coverlet and indicated I should lie on top of it. The other mothers always turned the bed down for me, and with irritation, smoothed the sheets. Mrs. Lynch went into the closet and took out a rough brown blanket. She covered me with it and it seemed as though she were going to leave the room. She sat down on the bed, though, and put her hand on my forehead, as if she were checking for fever. She turned the light out and sat in the chair across the room in the fashion, I now see, of the paid nurse. Nothing was said between us. But for the first time, I understood what all those adults were trying to do for me. I understood what was meant by comfort. Perhaps I was able to accept it from Mrs. Lynch as I had from no other because there was no self-love in what she did, nothing showed me she had one eye on some mirror checking her posture as the comforter of a grief-stricken child. She was not congratulating herself for her tact, her understanding, her tough-mindedness. And she had no suggestions for me; no sense that things could change if simply I could see things right, could cry, or run around the yard with other children. It was her sense of the inevitability of what had happened, and its permanence, its falling into the category of natural affliction, that I received as such a gift. I slept, not long I know—ten minutes, perhaps, or twenty—but it was one of those afternoon sleeps one awakes from as if one has walked out of the ocean. I heard the record player playing and sat up. It was the time of the party for musical chairs.

"Ye'd like to join the others then?" she asked me, turning on the light.

I realized that I did. I waited till the first round of the game was over, then joined in. It was the first child's game I can remember enjoying.

My mother didn't come for me in the car, of course. I walked across the street so she and Mrs. Lynch never exchanged words about what had happened. "I had a good time," I said to my mother, showing her the ring I'd won.

"The Lynches are good people," my mother said.

I'd like to say that my friendship with Eileen developed or that I acknowledged a strong bond with her mother and allowed her to become my confidante. But it wasn't like that; after that time my contacts with the Lynches dwindled, partly because I was making friends outside the neighborhood and partly because of the older Lynch children and what happened to their lives.

It was the middle fifties and we were, after all, a neighborhood of second-generation Irish. Adolescence was barely recognized as a distinct state; it was impossible to imagine that adolescent rebellion would be seen as anything but the grossest breach of the social contract, an incomprehensible

one at that. *Rebel Without a Cause* was on the Legion of Decency con-
demned list; even Elvis Presley was preached against on the Sunday mornings before he was to appear on the *Ed Sullivan Show*. So how could my
neighborhood absorb the eldest Lynch kids: Charlie, who left school at
sixteen and had no job, who spent his afternoons in the driveway, souping up
his car. Or Kathy, who'd got in trouble in tenth grade and then married,
bringing her baby several times a week, assuming that Eileen, at ten, would
be enchanted to take care of it. She wasn't of course, she viewed the child
with the resentful gaze she cast on everything in life and refused to change
its diapers. Rita, the third daughter, had gone to beautician school and
seemed on her way to a good life except that she spent all her evenings
parked with different young men in different cars—we all could see that
they were different, even in the darkness—in front of the Lynch house.

I was shocked by the way the Lynches talked to their parents. In the
summer everyone could hear them, "Ma, you stupid asshole," "Pop, you're
completely full of shit." "For Christ sake, this is America, not fucking
Ireland." Once in the winter, Charlie and Mrs. Lynch picked Eileen and
me up from school when it was raining a grey, dense, lacerating winter rain.
In the backseat, I heard Mrs. Lynch and Charlie talking.

"Ye'll drop me at the supermarket, then."

"I said I'd pick these kids up. That was all."

"I just need a few things, Charlie. And I remember asking ye this
morning and ye saying yes."

He slammed the brakes on and looked dangerously at his mother. "Cut
the crap out, Ma. I said I have things to do and I have them. I mean it
now."

Mrs. Lynch looked out the window, and Charlie left us off at the Lynch
house, then drove away.

People said it was terrible the way the Lynches sat back, staring help-
lessly at their children like Frankenstein staring at his monster. My
mother's interpretation was that the Lynches were so exhausted simply
making ends meet that they didn't have the strength left to control their
children, and it was a shame that children could take such advantage of

their parents' efforts and hard lot. The closest she would come to criticizing them was to say that it might have been easier for them in the city where they didn't have the responsibility of a house and property. And such a long commute. But it was probably the kids they did it for, she said. Knowing how she felt, nobody said "shanty Irish" in front of my mother, although I heard it often on the street, each time with a pang of treachery in my heart as I listened in silence and never opened my mouth to defend.

Everyone for so long had predicted disaster for the Lynches that no one was surprised when it happened; their only surprise was that it happened on such a limited scale. It was a summer night; Charlie was drunk. His father had taken the keys to the car and hidden them so Charlie couldn't drive. We could hear him shouting at his father, "Give them to me, you fucking son of a bitch." We couldn't hear a word from Mr. Lynch. Finally, there was a shot, and then the police siren and the ambulance. Charlie was taken off by the police, and Mr. Lynch wheeled out on a stretcher. We later found out from Joe Flynn, a cop who lived down the street, that Mr. Lynch was all right; Charlie'd only shot him in the foot. But Charlie was on his way to jail. His parents had pressed charges.

Then the Lynches were gone; no one knew how they'd sold the house; there was never a sign in front. It was guessed that Mr. Lynch had mentioned wanting to sell to someone in the cab company. Only the U-Haul truck driven by Kathy's husband and the new family, the Sullivans, arriving to work on the house, told us what had happened. Jack Sullivan was young and from town and worked for the phone company; he said he didn't mind doing the repairs because he'd got the house for a song. His father helped him on the weekends, and they fixed the house up so it looked like all the others on the street. His wife loudly complained, though, about the filth inside; she'd never seen anything like it; it took her a week to get through the kitchen grease, she said, and they'd had to have the exterminator.

Everyone was awfully glad when they were finally moved in. It was a relief to have your own kind, everybody said. That way you knew what to expect.

WATCHING THE TANGO

*O*ne should not *watch* the tango. Or at least not in a theater like this, one so baroque and so well cared for, so suggesting plutocrats and oil money or money made from furs: Alaska, some cold climate, underpopulation, paying women to come out. They watch the tango, these two lovers, because they have heard from friends that it is good to watch these dancers, and seats were available on quite short notice. And they must do things on short notice, for they are illicit lovers; he is married, and her job has those long hours: it is hard to get away. They are longing for the lights to go out so they can hold hands. Someone they know is in the row behind them; they must wait for darkness.

They do not know what to expect but they have, of course, associations with the tango. Underlit and fundamentally quite dirty dance halls in parts of some large city fallen now into decay. The lights go out. They hear the sounds of an accordion, and over-rich violins. He takes her hand, plays tunes on the palm of it. Her eyes close out of pleasure and she feels herself sink down and yet be buoyed up. And it encourages her to give herself up to these impossible joke instruments, their tasteless sounds.

The dancers come onto the stage. They are not young. First the men dance with each other. And the women, to the side, each dance alone in circles, as if they didn't notice, didn't care. Then suddenly, like the crack of a whip, the couples come together. Mere formality is seen to be the skeleton it is; limbs intertwine, the man's hand on the woman's back determines everything: the stress is all. The dancers are seductive, angry, playful, but it does not matter. All their gestures are theatrical, impersonal: the steps matter, and the art, which is interpretive. None of the couples is the same.

What are these women doing with their middle age? Theirs is not a body type familiar to us North Americans. Long and yet heavy-limbed, with strong, smooth athletes' backs, the high arched feet of the coquette, these bodies have not kept themselves from the fate of those of the simply indolent. Beneath the skirts, covered with beads and sequins, are soft stomachs, loose behinds. Can it be that when they are not here dancing these women are lounging, reading illustrated Spanish romances that look like comic books: heavy-lidded blondes succumbing, ravished, their words appearing over their heads in balloons like the words of Archie and Veronica? Are they eating chocolates, these women, these dancers? How late do they sleep?

It is impossible to invent for them an ordinary life. Of course they sleep all day. And where? Their bedrooms are quite easy to imagine. Dark and overfull: the hair pomade, the bottles of gardenia, jasmine; the pictures of the dying saints. The dolls stiff on the dresser tops, their skirts lace or crocheted, look out upon the scene like smug and knowing birds. What have they witnessed? Tears and botched abortions, abject and extravagant apologies, the torpid starts of quarrels, joyous reconciliations unconvincing in the light of day. The light of day, in fact, must never enter. The dark shiny curtains stay closed until late afternoon. Outside the closed door the house life goes on like another country. Some old woman—mother, servant, it hardly matters—dusts and polishes the furniture with oil that smells of roasting nuts. She does not knock to say "Still sleeping? Rise and shine!" She does not dare. She is professionally quiet.

The woman who is watching the tango takes her lover's hand and brings it to her lips. He does not know exactly why, but she can see that he has understood the springs of such a gesture. Sorrow. "You all right?" he whispers. "Yes." She is thinking: we will never dance together among friends. It makes her want to cry: she so envies the spectacle of these couples before them, so free of responsibility. They sleep late, they make love, they dance among their friends. But they do not look happy.

Happiness seems as irrelevant to them as sunlight, medicine, or balanced meals. Yet they do not suggest the criminal. They are infinitely, reverently law-abiding. You can see how they would love a dictator. But what is this: a woman dancing amorously with another woman? And a man, seething with anger, dangerously dancing by himself? What now? Here he comes with a knife. Of course he kills her. More in love than ever with her dead, he carries her offstage, kissing her all the while with a real tenderness.

They had talked before at supper, the two lovers, about violence between women and men. The statistics, she said to him are up: more women now are violent to men. Oh good, he said, like lung cancer. How far we've come. Still, many more men are violent to women than women are to men, she said. And men can kill women with a blow of the fist. Don't forget that, she told him. Thanks, he said. I'll keep it in mind. Once he told her that he had hit a woman. She was completely on his side.

A short, dyed blonde appears on stage holding a microphone. The lovers, listening, do not know Spanish, yet they understand this woman has been betrayed. By whom? She is at least in her mid-fifties. The sex she suggests is quite unsavory. Money may have changed hands. Did a young man in tight black pants grow tired of the way he had to earn his free time? So he could be out gambling with his pals while the singer sang her heart out. Worse, with a young girl who made fun of her. The singer is right; it is terrible. She knows better. But she will make the same mistake again. The woman watching thinks of the singer dying her secret hairs, grey now, perhaps with a small brush. The thought of it raises in her a terrible pity. She begins to be afraid of growing old.

Intermission now. In the red lobby with its stone festoons, the lovers must pretend to be talking casually. In fact, every word he says increases her desire, and she doesn't want to go back to the theater, to the dark, where she cannot see his face, so beautiful and so arousing to her. But there is nowhere else to go. Adulterous, they are orphans. They sit in restaurants; they walk around the streets.

His friends come up. Almost never when the lovers are together do they speak to anyone except themselves. It is odd; the woman feels they are speaking in a foreign language. "We have visited Argentina," the man who is her lover's friend says, and it sounds to her like a sentence in a textbook. The four of them hear the bell and walk together down the aisle back to their seats.

A new couple has joined the dancers. Older, heavier, afraid of risks, as if they know there are things not easily recovered from, not ever, they move funereally and with no sense of play. But their somberness has not destroyed the others' spirits. Over in the corner are the madcap couple, jumping, laughing like jitterbuggers. He loudly slaps her behind. The male dancer to their left has an expression of balked chastity. "That one's a spoiled priest," the woman tells her lover. "I've seen that face on thousands of rectory walls." "And the old guy owns the nightclub," says her lover. "He has my marker for seventy-five grand." The dancers are becoming individuals, which makes them to the woman, oddly now, less interesting. She feels that, knowing them, she has to take them seriously. And she doesn't want that. She wants to lose herself in the cheap music and to dream about her lover's body.

The finale brings out all the dancers' passion to assert their differences. The musicians, too, are ardent. The woman watching with her lover thinks: the lights will go on, we will leave each other for the hundredth time. Thousands of times more we will kiss each other blandly at the train station, in case his neighbors are around.

He says, "Their children probably don't dance the tango. Maybe no one will when they are dead."

"We will," she says. "We'll do it for them."

They take hands with the lights on. Suddenly gallant and protective, they see everyone—the dancers, the musicians, the sad singers—all of them valorous, noble, worthy and capable of the most selfless love.

"We'll do it one day," she says. "One day we'll dance the tango."

They walk outside the theater holding hands with the rash courage of new converts, soldiers, gamblers, pirates, clairvoyants. The rain keeps them beneath the theater marquee where they kiss as if it didn't matter or as if it were the only thing that did. They see one of the dancers arguing with someone—his real wife?—a sparrow in a kerchief and brown shoes. Impatiently, he opens his umbrella, leaves her there—she has no coat, no pocketbook—and walks away. She stands with the self-conscious stoicism of one who knows she has no choice. A minute later he returns, beckons, and she runs to the umbrella. He is wearing patent leather shoes. His dancing shoes? They will be ruined.

"Let's go now," the watching woman says to her lover. She doesn't want to see the other dancers coming out. She doesn't want to have to worry.

AGNES

O*W*ell, it's the same old story. It's the woman pays. You see it every time," said Bridget, closing her pocketbook with a click, Nora could see, of dreadful satisfaction.

"Anybody could have seen it coming. But you don't, I guess," said Nettie.

"And whose fault was it but her own?" Bridget asked.

"Poor soul, there was few enough moments of joy she had on earth. And God have mercy on the dead. There'll be no more talk of it in my kitchen," said Kathleen.

Nora looked up at her mother, thinking her a coward to make the conversation stop. She had contempt for every one of them, her two aunts and her mother. And her father too, pretending he was sorry about Agnes' death. For they had never liked her, any of them, although at least her mother had been kind to her. Nora had not liked Ag herself.

Ag was a disappointment, for she was the only woman any of them knew who lived in sin, and she made such a dowdy appearance. Really, Nora felt, and anyone with sense would have agreed with her, if you were going to be somebody's mistress, you should look—how? You should be overdressed and overly made up with loud dyed hair that was itself a challenge, a large bosom and a shocking, sticking-out behind, a waist you drew attention to with tight, cinched belts. You should smoke cigarettes and leave them in the ashtray marked with your dark lipstick, piles of them so people would count them when you were gone, and make remarks. But Agnes looked, Nora had always thought, like a wet bird, with her felt navy-blue hat in winter, her straw navy-blue hat in summer, with her damp hands that she kept putting to her face as if she were afraid that if she didn't keep checking, she'd find her face had fallen off.

Sometimes, though, the difference between Ag's fate and her appearance raised in Nora a wild hope. Ag looked as damaged as Nora with her one short leg knew herself to be. But Ag provided a suggestion that it could be possible to live a life of passion nonetheless. How could this be anything to Nora but a solace? At thirteen, she dreamed identically to her girlfriends. Rudolph Valentino would carry her off somewhere, his eyes gone vague and menacing with love. He would hold her at arm's length, staring at her face, unable to believe in his good fortune. They would lie down together on soft sand. He would not have noticed her leg, and when she tactfully brought it up he would laugh, that laugh that could have been a villain's but was not, and say, "It is as nothing with a love like ours."

Sometimes in the middle of this vision, Nora grew embarrassed at herself and angry, and her anger grew up like a bare spiked tree against an evil sky; it grew and spread until it became the only feature in the landscape. "Fool," she called herself, for everybody knew that no one would forget her leg, it was the first thing anybody saw about her, it was the thing the merciful looked past, remarking on her hair, her eyes; the thing that most people could not get past, so that they did not look at her. She would never be beloved, carried off. She would take a commercial course, forget the academic that the teachers told her she belonged in, forget that stuff, for she would always be alone, and when her parents died she would live in the house alone. She would always support herself so she would never have to rely on her four brothers. At such moments, a last resort but one she dared to trust, Ag's face would swim up among the others in her mind. For Nora knew her Uncle Des could have had anybody, but he'd stuck with Ag. Ten years he'd stuck with her, and all that time she'd asked for nothing. Supported him and said okay when he said he would never marry, that he had no patience for the priests and couldn't be tied down. Still he stayed with her, and the example of Ag and her uncle suggested to Nora that if she could bring a man to see that she would ask for nothing, she too could have a passionate life.

But in the end, there was no comfort in it, for the life so obviously weakened Ag and made her hungry for respectability. Ag was no help to her, and Nora grew resentful of the cruelly false hint Ag did not know she proffered. She could only just bring herself to be civil to Ag, and she allowed her parents to believe that she judged Ag's morals as harshly as her Aunt Bridget did.

Now she felt bad about not having liked Agnes, and it was typical of Agnes, she was great at making everyone feel bad. She came into a room like the end of the party: no one could enjoy themselves with her around; nobody could relax. She should have seen it and kept away. But she didn't see it, of course, and kept on coming. You could say, perhaps, that it was Uncle Des's fault: he should never have brought her in the first place, acting as if it was respectable. But she came more than he did: three times to his one, although the sisters always knocked themselves out asking him to come and knocked themselves out when he got there.

Nora knew her Uncle Desmond was a bootlegger. She'd heard the word before. It was a queer word, she thought, "bootlegger," it sounded innocent like "shoemaker" or "fireman," far more innocent than names of other jobs: "chauffeur," "handyman," that men in her family without much comment seemed to hold. But because of Des there were odd night stirrings, brisk events involving whispers and rushed trips downstairs to the coal cellar and then up again and downstairs in a greater rush, and Nora being told to keep the children back, but told not one thing else. And then the arguments, the terrible dangerous anger when her father came home and was told: Des had to hide some of his liquor in the cellar, he could be killed or be arrested, there was not another blessed place.

Edmund Derency paced, he literally pulled his hair, he told his wife her brother was a thief, a wastrel, and he didn't give a tinker's damn for her or for her family, and they would lose it all, lose everything for him, and because of his damn laziness and trickery it all would go for nothing, the trip over and the years of work so they could have what they had now: the house, a girl in high school, jobs in the government you kept forever unless they found out about something like this, and then it was all gone. Look at the house, Kathleen, he said, take a good look at it, remember it so you can think of it when us and all the kids are living on the street because of your damn brother and his damn fast tricks.

But then it was over, Des was back with money in his pocket and a gift for everyone, a radio big as a piece of furniture that even her father could not resist. Nor could he keep up his grudge against Des, spectacularly handsome in his shirt sleeves, the sight of him a gift, like a day at the beach for all the children issued fresh, as if it was the thing they all deserved, they knew it now, but had been all along afraid to wish for. When Des put his hands on Ed Derency's shoulders and said, "God, Edmund, I'd have shot myself in the foot rather than do this to you and Kath. If there had been a God's blessed way out of it. But they were on my neck, and I don't need to tell you of all people what that could have meant."

"Not another word, Des. What else would family be for? God knows they're trouble enough at the best of times, if you take my meaning."

There were the two of them, drinking her Uncle Desmond's whiskey, the very bottles Nora's father had threatened to smash up with an axe, winking, their arms around each other, men together, as if women and all that had to do with them—the children and the houses and the family meals—were just a bad joke that had been forced upon their kind. Nora hated them for that, she hated what was clearer to her daily: the adult world of false seeming, lies and promises you couldn't trust an inch. There was Des, just having made a joke, or laughed at one, about the weight of women on the world, singing "I'll Take You Home Again, Kathleen" while her mother played the piano for him, tears dropping on her fingers while she played. And the aunts crying in their chairs and Agnes sitting there patting her eyes with a twisted-up handkerchief as if she were afraid that if she made a noise or if her tears fell on the furniture she would be a nuisance. Nora hardened her heart against her uncle, against all of them, and turned away when he sang the song he used to sing to her when she was little: "With someone like you, a pal good and true/I'd like to leave them all behind."

She thought with anger how she once had loved it, what a fool she'd been, a fool he'd made her, and the family'd allowed. He knew that he had lost her, and he made his eyes go sad. "There's no more time for your old uncle now you're a young lady, is there?"

How could anybody look so sad? He needed all her comfort. She was about to say, "Oh, Uncle Des," and put her arms around him, smell the smell of his tobacco and the starched collar he always wore. But something in his look gave him away, some insecurity. He looked around the room, hedging his bets, looking toward the younger children, giving up: they were all boys. But in that moment he had lost her, and she shrugged her shoulders and said, "I have lots to do. With school, you know, and all."

Afterwards she was glad she had done it. For that was the last time he had come with Agnes; it all happened not long after that: he must have known. Must have known when they made him sing "I'll Take You Home Again, Kathleen" a second time, and he looked at all of them, especially at Agnes though, and said, bringing his fist down on the radio, "We'll all go back. I swear it to you. It's the one reason I'm in this rotten business. If I make a killing, it's back home in triumph for the lot of us. First class. We'll turn them green."

He hadn't meant a word of it. Two weeks later he was on the train to California with his brand-new wife.

"Well, it's ridiculous, he's never even brought the girl around. How could he have just upped and married somebody we've never met? You must have read it wrong, the letter. Let me have a look at it," said Bridget.

She read the piece of paper—hotel stationery—as if she were a starving person looking in a pile of rot for one intact kernel. Then, Nora could see, she hated herself for her fool's work and looked around her for someone to blame.

" 'Twas fast, like, you'd have to say that," Nettie said timidly. "Perhaps they had to."

"I'd say Des would know better than that," said Edmund Derency, "I'd say that for him."

The sisters turned upon him then, their eyes hard with the fury of shared blood.

"You never knew him," Kathleen said with tight lips to her husband. "There's something he's keeping from us. The woman could be sick, dreadfully sick. Or dying, and he would want the three of us to know."

Ed Derency threw down his newspaper. "She's a rich girl whose family threw her out for marrying a greenhorn. That's as sick as she is."

"And how will he support a wife in California? He'd got nothing put away. Too generous," said Kathleen.

"And Agnes Martin to count on with the money she got wiping the noses of the Yankee brats," said Edmund.

"She worked for the finest families in New York, Ed Derency, don't you forget it," Bridget said.

"Since when are you on Ag's side?" he asked.

"What will happen to Ag now?" said Nettie.

"I hate to think of it," said Edmund.

"No one's asking you to think of it," Bridget said. "It's none of your affair. Someone should phone her."

"I'll telephone her," said Kathleen, rising as if she'd waited to be asked. "I'll invite her for Sunday dinner."

Nora ran upstairs to the bathroom, shut the door behind her and ran the water in the sink as loudly as she could. She dreaded the thought of Ag and wished her mother had the courage to cut her off. There was nothing they could do for her, nothing that anyone could do. She hoped Ag knew that and would have the sense to stay away. But then she knew Ag wouldn't, and her vision of Ag sitting in the living room and hoping for a scrap of news hardened Nora's heart. She'd be damned if she'd be nice to Ag; if Ag had pride, she'd stay away. But if she'd had the pride, she'd never have taken up with Uncle Desmond and embarrassed every one and put herself in this position so she would be hurt. She'd be better off dead, Nora said to herself, enjoying her cruel face in the mirror.

———

When Ag arrived, she looked no different; if she'd spent nights weeping, it had left no mark. She talked of Desmond's marriage, his departure, reasonably, as if it were something they had discussed together and agreed to.

"He pointed out to me," Ag said, "that really he had no choice but to marry her. 'She's not like you and me, Ag,' he said. 'She was brought up with the silver spoon. I couldn't do it to her, leave her in the lurch. She stood up to her parents for me. She lost everything. She wasn't like the two of *us*. She really had something to lose.' "

Ag said this proudly, with a pride Nora had never seen in her when she'd had Desmond actually with her. And Nora hated her because Ag didn't see how she'd been taken in. Desmond had gone off with another woman, had given her everything that Ag had wanted from him, and Ag acted as if he'd given her a gift. Disgust welled up in Nora, and at the same time fear; she wanted Ag to know what had happened to her, but she didn't want anyone to say it. She was petrified every second that Bridget would open up her mouth.

But the visit passed with not much more than the usual discomfort; Ag had always been so troublesome a presence that her new estate hardly made a difference.

"Do you think we've seen the back of her at last?" asked Bridget.

"There's no one else for her on holidays and things. In charity, I'd say we'd have to ask her," Kathleen said.

"Charity my foot," said Ed.

"You talk big, Ed Derency, but you'd be the last to turn her out. Or have her sitting by herself on Christmas."

"It's just February, Kath. Let's see what the year brings," said Nora's father, but Nora couldn't tell whether or not he meant it kindly. She could see that they felt relieved that Agnes hadn't come apart over Desmond's leaving; their relief had made them quiet. They discussed Ag's folly, her gullible swallowing of the story Des had fed her, less than they might have, or than they'd discussed anything else she'd ever done. They were quiet because they were cowards, and they couldn't say a word about what had happened without putting Desmond in a light which even their love couldn't render flattering.

======

Agnes phoned whenever Desmond wrote her.

"Well, at least he keeps in touch with her, that's something," Kathleen said.

It was from Ag and not from Desmond that they learned Desmond's wife had had a baby. Desmond's letters were about weather, about his new job in a haberdasher's, about how a customer who worked in Hollywood had said that Des should have a screen test. Not a word about his wife, as if she were a temporary measure, and the important things in life were weather, scenery, the movie industry, the cut of clothes. It was only from Ag that they learned how he met his wife. Des was her father's bootlegger; her father was a big lawyer in New Jersey. Tenafly, Agnes had said. No one could tell Nora how it happened: that he went from chatting the girl up, leaning his foot on the running board of some big car, and then the next thing, they were on the train to California. Was it that it was obvious to everyone but her how it had happened? Or was it that she was the only one who had the sense to know that the time in between was the real clue, the real important time, the time that held what she and Agnes needed to know: what had happened that had made Des give this woman easily the thing Ag wanted and would never get, or ask for, or after a while think of as any possibility at all.

Agnes was cheerful at the news of Desmond's baby's birth. She had become, Nora could see, more family to him than his own family. Her new responsibility gave her a pride of place that she had never had, as if she'd landed a good job at last and reveled in the title. Nora saw that all this made the sisters hate her, and she knew that Agnes didn't have the sense to see. Proudly, without apology, she brought them news of him as pretext for a visit. She came often, for Desmond called her often for advice: she was a children's nurse, and Des said, Ag reported proudly, his wife had never been around a baby in her life.

"I even wondered if I should go out there. Lend a hand, you know. Poor thing, she sounds so overwhelmed. You see it all the time. She's very young, you know."

Bridget put her full tea cup heavily down in her saucer. They all knew she was about to say something terrible, but for this once no one tried to shift the conversation to distract or stop her. Nora saw that they wanted Bridget to do the dreadful thing, to hurt Ag, that they—her mother and Nettie, with their famous reputations, in her mother's case for being kind, and in her aunt's for being too cheerful to think a bad thing about anyone —wanted now for Agnes to be hurt. Nora saw that only she did not want it, but she was afraid, not strong, a child, and to prevent it you had to be stronger than all that hating of the three of them, than all that wish to hurt. She saw them look at Bridget, and saw her take it as a sign.

"She's young, all right, but you're not, Agnes. Old enough, I'd say, to know better. Stay out of where you're not wanted. The minute she finds out about you, she'll stop you herself. Have a little pride for once in your life. Tell him you're not his free advice bureau. Tell him to pay some greenhorn girl himself."

After Bridget had said what they had wanted her to say, Nora could see that they were sorry. She saw Nettie desperately looking at Kathleen to say something to smooth things over.

"Of course she didn't really mean that she was going to go out there, Bridget. It was just a way of talking, like. A way of saying that she wished them well."

Ag neither confirmed Kathleen's words nor denied them: she had sense enough to let the matter drop, to let Bridget sniff silently, convinced that she was right, but too much of a lady to press home her point.

———

In the end what bothered Nora most was how right Bridget had been. Desmond's wife found out about Ag and brought all communication to an end.

She had come upon a letter Des was writing to Agnes. "She's awfully pretty, Ag, but very young and doesn't understand a thing. It's very often now I long for our good old chats." Underneath this, which had been written in Des's formal copper plate, was scrawled in a back-slanting script: "I have found this in my husband's desk, and having informed him of my discovery, he has agreed that from this moment all communication between you two must cease. There is a child to be considered after all." And she had signed her name: Harriet Browne O'Reilley. Underneath her signature, as if she were continuing a conversation, Ag had scratched: "This is the thing I cannot bear." And then she hanged herself.

Nora made herself imagine it: the letter with the three different handwritings, the things that Ag had done between the time she'd put the pen down and the time she'd tied the dressing-gown sash around her neck and kicked the chair away. She imagined Ag had done some ordinary things: made tea, perhaps, or washed out stockings. She knew Ag had never been upset or agitated: killing herself must have seemed to her simply the next thing to be done, like boarding a bus or shopping for a pair of shoelaces. "This is how it is," she must have said. "And I will do this now." Nora could see just how it was, Agnes's small efficient movements canceling her pain. Each night Nora would think of Ag before she went to sleep. She didn't want anyone else to think about her. She resented that she had not been the one to find her. It should have been Nora, not a neighbor breaking down the door with the police, afraid because they hadn't seen Ag leaving the apartment. It should have been herself, not the police, who'd called up Des in California. It should have been she, not her mother, who took the instructions from Des about the disposition of the body. No, not that: Des should not have been consulted. Nora should have made the plans. She would have stood up to the priest who refused Ag a Christian burial. She would have made up a story to fool him; she would have found a way to hide the circumstances of Ag's death. She would have seen to it that Ag had a proper funeral, that everyone came to pay respects and brought in Mass cards and took holy pictures with Ag's name on the back of them to put into their prayerbooks so that they'd remember her at Mass.

She would have done far better than her mother, who set out for the police station, her eyes apologetic and her posture cringing and came back having made the arrangements with an undertaker who was Presbyterian to have the simplest coffin and to send the bills to Des. She understood her mother's anger, and her shame, but her mother had got it wrong, she was angry and ashamed for the wrong thing, as Ag had died for the wrong thing, and left it to the wrong person to pick up all the pieces.

Kathleen said nothing about Ag when she came home from making the arrangements, and it was months before the family said a word about her. When Agnes's name came up in family conversation, Nora could see everybody take Des's part; it was easy, she thought with contempt, to know what they would say. They wanted to make a lesson from it, sew it up, as if it could be useful to their lives. Whereas the truth was only she had anything to learn of it. The lesson was not anything the women thought. It was much worse than anything they mentioned. The truth was that Ag was right to hang herself, except she should have done it earlier. The truth was women like that were better off not being born, and if you saw you had a girl child growing up like that you'd be best drowning it straight off, holding its head under the water till the breath went out of the doomed creature, so you'd save it all the pain and trouble later on.

THE MAGICIAN'S WIFE

*U*nlike most of her friends, Mrs. Hastings did not think of herself first as the mother of her children. She was proudest of being Mr. Hastings' wife. So that in their old age it grieved her to see her husband known in the town as the father of her son, Frederick, the architect, who was not half the man his father was, for beauty, for surprises. Frederick had put up buildings, had had his picture taken with mayors outside city halls, with the governor outside office buildings. She ought to have been proud of Frederick, and of course she was, really, and he was very good to them; they would not be half so well off without him. She valued her son as she valued the food she had cooked, the meals she had produced, very much the same since the day of her marriage.

Her husband had added to his salary by being a magician. Not that he hadn't provided perfectly well for them; still it was something else that life would have been meaner without, the money he had made on magic. How had it first started? That was one of the arguments she had with his mother. His mother said he had always been that way, putting on magic shows in the barn as a boy. But she knew it hadn't started that way; she remembered the way it had. It was on their honeymoon. They saw a vaudeville show in Chicago, and there was a magician, the amazing Mr.

Kazmiro, whose specialty was making birds appear. That night on the way to the hotel, Mrs. Hastings could see her husband brooding over something. When he brooded his eyes would go dull, the color of pebbles, and she could see him rolling the idea from one side of his brain to another as you would roll a candy ball from one side of your mouth to the other if you had a sore tooth. In the morning (it shocked her, how handsome he was in his pajamas) he said, "May, let's go shopping." They went down to the area behind the theater where the shops sold odd things: white makeup in flat little tins, wigs for clowns or prima donnas, gizmos comedians used. It was in one of those stores that he bought his first trick; she remembered it was something with balls and hoops and wooden goblets with false bottoms. She never looked too closely at his tricks—not then, not ever. It had shocked her how much the trick cost, ten dollars, but she had said nothing. It was her honeymoon. She never said anything about the expense except to ask what it was about these things that cost so much money. Her husband said it was a highly skilled business, that each of his tricks was the work of craftsmen. But that was how he got started, she remembered, on the fourth day of their honeymoon. No matter what his mother said, it had nothing to do with his life before he got married, his magic.

=====

Once he had performed for the Roosevelts. It was 1935 and one of the Roosevelt grandchildren was recovering from measles. The boy was crotchety and there was nothing you could do to please him, one of the servants had said, one who had seen Mr. Hastings entertaining at the County Fair in Rhinebeck. It was a wicked night, she remembered. It thundered and flashed lightning so that the lights flickered on and off. When the telephone rang, they thought it was a joke, some lady calling to ask if Mr. Hastings would care to come over to Hyde Park and do a small performance for a sick child. Her husband and children had thought it was a joke, for one minute. Of course her husband would be called to entertain the President, of course the car, the big black car driven by a man in a uniform, would come for him. She remembered how her husband had talked to the chauffeur, as if he had been brought up to order servants about. She remembered what her husband had said, not looking at the man in the uniform, but not looking at his feet either, looking straight ahead of him. She remembered he had said, "Do you mind if I bring my wife?" and the chauffeur had said, "As you wish, sir," and opened the door. That was the gallantry of him, so that she would get to meet Franklin Roosevelt, and Eleanor, who was as plain as she looked in her pictures and had a voice that was an embarrassment; but she was, as Mrs. Hastings said to the people whom she told about it, "Very gracious to us, and a real lady."

=====

All the vivid moments of her life had been marked by her husband's magic. Not only the Roosevelts—although how would she ever have met the Roosevelts if she had not married Mr. Hastings?—but the moments that heightened the color of everyone's ordinary life. There was a show for each of her birthdays and anniversaries, for each important day of each child's life. On one occasion Frederick had sulked and said, "It's my party and everyone's paying attention to *him.*" And she had told him he should thank his lucky stars not to have a father like everyone else's, dull as dishwater, and that any other boy would give his eyeteeth to have a father who could do magic. And Frederick said—where did he get those eyes, those dull, brown, good boy's eyes, they weren't hers, or his father's— Frederick said, "Not if they really knew about it."

Frederick was not nearly so handsome as his father, particularly when his father was doing magic. Mrs. Hastings remembered the look of him when he was all dressed up, with his hair slicked back and his mustache. He looked distinguished, like William Powell. She knew all the women in the town envied her her husband, for his good looks and his beautiful manners and his exciting ways. Once Mrs. Daly, the milkman's wife, said, "It must be hard on you, him spending all his spare time practicing in the basement." It was well-known that Mr. and Mrs. Daly had had separate bedrooms since the birth of their last child. Mrs. Hastings wanted to tell

Mrs. Daly about the trick her husband had played on her in bed one night, pulling a pearl from the bodice of her nightgown, putting it in his mouth and bringing out a flower. But that was exactly the kind of detail Mrs. Daly wanted, which Mrs. Hastings had no intention of giving her. So she turned to Mrs. Daly and said in her high-falutin' voice—her husband said, "Okay, Duchess," when she used it on him—"He always shows me everything while he's working on it," which was partly true, although he would never show her anything until he was sure it worked. But it was true enough for someone like Mrs. Daly, who slept in a single bed near the window, true enough to knock her off her high horse.

How could she be lonely up in the kitchen with the knowledge of him below her doing things over and over with scarves and boxes and cards and ribbons. She could imagine the man she loved, alone, away where she could not see him, practicing over and over the tricks that would astound not only her but every person they knew. Why would she prefer conversations at the kitchen table about money or food or what who wore when? She thought it a great and a kingly mercy that he kept his job as a machinist, which he hated, instead of quitting to work full time as a magician, which he sometimes talked about. When he talked about it, a little flame of fear would go up in her, as if someone had lit a match behind one of her ribs. But she would say, "Do whatever you want. I have faith." What she liked really, though, was that during the day he went to his job, like anyone else's husband, but he spent his nights doing magic. He would come up the stairs every night in triumph, and every night he wanted her because, he said, she was the best little wife a man ever had; and every night she wanted him because she could not believe her good fortune, since she was, compared with her husband, she knew, quite ordinary.

And the years had passed as they do for everyone, only for her it was different. Her years were marked not only by the birth and aging and ceremonies of children, but by the growth of her husband's art. After 1946, for example, he gave up the egg and rope tricks and moved into scarves and coins. His retirement was nothing that he feared. He did not go around like other men, taking a week to do a chore that could have been done in an hour. Nor did she go around like other women, saying, "I can't get him out of my hair; he doesn't know what to do with himself." She loved being the wife of a retired husband as she had never loved being the mother of young children. She loved hearing him take long steps from one end of the basement to the other, loved the times she could hear him standing still, could hear, she thought, his concentration coming up to her through the ceiling, could see it seeping through the floorboards like waves of visible heat. She would never, never interrupt him, but she always knew when it was the last second of his work and she would hear his step on the stairway, would hear him say, "Got any beer?" And she would say, "I've had it waiting." It was the happiest time of her life, the years of his early retirement.

But then his eyes began to go. At first it was rather beautiful, the way his eyes misted over. It was like, she said to herself, a lake the first thing in the morning. He wore thicker glasses with a pink tint which the doctors said were more restful. They would have made any other man look foolish, but not her husband, with his fine, strong head, his way of holding his shoulders. Even at his age his looks were something other women envied her for. She could see the envy in the way they'd look at her as she walked with him in the evening.

She began to notice how queerly he held things, the funny angle at which he held the newspaper. Now she would hear him in the basement, snorting with frustration, using words that she imagined he used only on the job, not words for her or the house. And worst of all, she could hear him drop things; sometimes she would hear things break. She would pretend to be sewing or reading when he came looking for the broom or the dustpan.

The doctors said nothing would reverse the process, so, as time passed, there were more and more things he couldn't do. But the miracle of it was that the losses did not enrage him as, she knew, they would have enraged her. He simply accepted the loss of each new activity as he would have accepted the end of a meal. Finally one night he said to her, "Listen, old girl, you're my only audience now. I'm blind as a bat, and one thing nobody needs is a half-blind magician."

Did she like it better that he did his tricks only for her now, in the living room? Or had she liked it better sitting in the audience, watching the wonder of the people around at what he could produce from the most surprising places. On the whole she thought she liked it better watching the stupefaction, the envy. But it was in her nature, that preference. She had not as nice a nature as his. It was his nature to take her hand and say, after he had done a trick she had seen five hundred times, perhaps, and was not tired of, "I only make magic for *you* now." Making his almost total blindness into a kind of gift for her, a perfect glass he had blown and polished.

On the whole she blamed Frederick for what happened on the Fourth of July, although she knew the idea had come from the grandchildren. Sometimes her husband would take them down to the basement with him to show them some of the equipment. Sometimes he would do tricks for them, the simpler ones that he had done almost from the beginning and knew so well that he didn't have to see to do them. She understood the children's enchantment with him and his magic; he was a perfect grandfather, indulgent, full of secret skills. Of course she understood their pride —there was no one like him. But she didn't understand Frederick's going along with their damn fool idea. His great virtue had always been his good sense. Why did he put his father up to it, without even asking her?

It was tied up with the grandchildren and the way they were so proud. They wanted their friends to see that their grandfather was a magician, so they egged him on to give a show at the Fourth of July Town Fair. Finally Frederick got behind them.

At first she thought it would be all right because of the look on her husband's face when he talked about it, because she knew what gave him that look: the prospect of once again astonishing strangers. Nothing could make up for the loss of it, and it was something she could not give him. Sitting in that living room, honored as she was by the privacy of this intimate performance for her only, no matter how much she loved him, she had seen it all before.

=====

And so she had to tell him what a good thing it was, how proud she would be, what a miracle he was in the lives of his grandchildren. At first she thought he would do only old tricks, and she felt safe. The audience would love him for his looks and because he was Frederick's father. She pressed his suit herself, weeks before; she pressed it several times just for practice. She looked through all her dresses to find the one that would most honor him. Finally she decided on her plainest dress, a black cotton with short sleeves. It was an old woman's dress but, being without ornament, the dress of an old woman who knows herself to be in a position of privilege. She would braid a silver ribbon into her long hair.

As the weeks went on, all ease was drained from her, a slow leak, stealing warmth, making the center of her chest feel full of cold air as if she had just walked into a cave. It was not the old tricks, the ones he almost didn't need eyes for, that he was doing. He was trying to do the newer, more complicated ones. She knew because of the household things he asked for: ribbon now instead of string, scarves instead of cotton handkerchiefs. When he showed her the act, as he always did before the performance, she saw him fumble, saw him drop things that he did not see so that the trick could not possibly go right. But she saw, too, that sometimes he was unaware that he had not done the trick properly. Sometimes the card was not the right card, the scarf the wrong color. All the life in her body collected in one solid disk at the center of her throat when she saw him foolish like that, an old man. But she would not tell him. It was not something that she could do, to say to him: your best life is entirely behind you—you are an old man. She could not even suggest that he do the simpler things. It was not in her; it had never been in her, and she understood what he was doing. He was risking foolishness to get from his audience the greatest possible astonishment, the greatest novelty of love.

She could not sleep the night before, looking at his sweet white body, the white hairs on the chest that still had the width and the toughness of the young man she had married. She poured boiling water over her finger so she had to go to the fair with her hand in a bandage. That annoyed Frederick, who said, "Today of all days, Mother."

Frederick was looking very foolish. He was wearing red, white and blue striped pants and a straw boater which, with his thinning hair, his failure of a mustache, was a grave tactical error. His father came down wearing his white suit, blue shirt, red bow tie and provided, by his neat, hale presence, all the festivity Frederick had worked so hard to embody.

They had set up a stage on the lawn of the courthouse. First some of the women in the Methodist choir sang show tunes. Then the bank president's daughter, dressed like Uncle Sam, did her baton routine, then somebody played an accordion. Then Frederick got up onstage. All his business friends whistled and stamped and made rude noises. She was embarrassed at the attention he was bringing to himself.

"Now I don't want to be accused of nepotism," he said. (It must have been some joke, some business joke; all the men laughed rudely as she imagined men laughed at dirty jokes.) "But when you have a talent in the family, why hide it under a bushel? My father, Mr. Albert Hastings, is a magician *extraordinaire*. He had the distinction of performing before Franklin Delano Roosevelt. And as I've always said, what's good enough for the Roosevelts is good enough for us."

The men guffawed again. Frederick stretched out one of his arms. "Ladies and gentlemen, the amazing Hastings."

Albert had been backstage all the time. She was glad he had not been with her to sense her fear, perhaps to absorb it. A woman behind her tapped her on the shoulder and said, "You must be very proud." Mrs. Hastings put her finger to her lips. Her husband had begun speaking.

It was the same patter he had used for years, but there was a new element in it that disturbed her: gratitude. He kept telling the audience how good it was to allow him to perform. *Allow* him? He would never have spoken like that, like a plain girl who has finally been asked to dance, ten years ago, five even. She hoped he would not go on like that. But she could see that the audience loved it, loved him for being an old man. But was that the kind of love he wanted? It was not what she thought he was after.

One of the grandchildren was onstage helping him. He made some joke about it, hoping that no one would doubt the honesty of his assistant. For the first trick the child picked three cards. It was a simple trick and over quickly. The audience applauded inordinately, she thought, for it was a simple trick and he used it first, she knew, simply to warm them up.

The second trick was the magic bag. It appeared tiny, but out of it he pulled an egg, an orange, grapes, and finally a small bottle of champagne. "I keep telling my wife to take it to the supermarket, but she won't listen," he said, gesturing at her in the first row of the audience. She got the thrill she always had when he acknowledged her from the stage. She began, for the first time, to relax.

The next trick was the one in which he threaded ribbons through large wooden cards. He asked his grandson to hold the ribbons. It was important that they be held very tightly. She could see her husband struggling to see the holes in the cards through which the ribbon had to be threaded. She could see that he had missed one of the holes, so when he pulled the ribbon, nothing happened. It was supposed to slip out without disturbing the cards. But he pulled the strings and nothing moved. He looked at the audience; he gave it an old man's look. "Ladies and gentlemen, I apologize," he said.

Then they applauded. They covered him with applause. How she hated them for that. She could feel their embarrassment and that complicity that ties an audience together, in love or hatred, in relation to the person so far, so terribly far away on the stage. But it was not love or hate they felt; it was embarrassment for the old man, and she could feel their yearning that it might be all over soon. To hide it, they applauded wildly. She sat perfectly still.

If only the next trick would go well! But it was the scarf trick, the one he had flubbed in the living room. She felt as though she could not breathe. She thought she was going to be sick. She should have told him that it had not worked. She should not have been a coward. Now he would be a fool to strangers. To Frederick's business friends.

"Ladies and gentlemen, I have a magic box, a magic cleaning box. I keep trying to get my wife to use it, but she's a very stubborn woman."

She knew what was supposed to happen. You put a colored scarf in one side of the box and pulled a white one out of the other side. But in the living room he had pulled out the same colored scarf that he had put in. But she had not told him. And he had not seen the difference.

He did the same thing now. At least it was over quickly. He held up the colored scarf, the scarf he thought was white, and twirled it around his head and bowed to the audience. He did not know that the trick had not worked. The audience was confused. There was a terrible beat of silence before they understood what had happened. Then Frederick started the applause. The audience gave Mr. Hastings a standing ovation. Then he disappeared backstage with a strange, old man's shuffle she had not seen him use before.

Frederick got up on the stage again. He was saying something about refreshments, something about gratitude to the women who had provided them. She was shaking with rage in her seat. How could he go on like that, after the humiliation his father had endured? And it was his responsibility. How could he go on talking to the audience, about games, about prizes, when that audience had witnessed his father's degradation? Why wasn't he with his father, to comfort him, to cover his exposure, when it had been his fault, when it was Frederick, through thickheadedness, or perhaps malice, who had caused his father's failure in this garish public light?

"Let me get you some supper," said Frederick, offering his mother his arm. He was nodding to other people, even as he spoke to his mother.

She turned to her son in fury.

"Why did you allow him to do this?"

"Do what?"

"This performance. This failure."

"He got a big kick out of it. He's a good sport," said Frederick.

"Everyone saw him fail," said Mrs. Hastings through closed teeth.

"It's all right, Mother. He thinks he did fine."

"It was a humiliation."

He shook his head and looked at her but with no real interest. He walked slightly ahead of her, too fast for her; she could see him searching the crowd for anyone else to talk to. He looked over his shoulder at her with the impatience of a young girl.

"Shall I fix you a plate?" he asked.

"You'll do nothing for me after what you've done to your father."

He stopped walking and waited for her to catch up.

"You know, Mother, Father is twice the person you are," he said, not looking at her. "Three times."

She stood beside him. For the first time in his life, Mrs. Hastings looked at her son with something like love. For the first time, she felt the pride of their connection. She took his arm.

OUT OF THE FRAY

*S*he looked out of the window of a plane with pleasure for the first time in her life. The land gave way to water, and there was a minute when it was not possible to say where it left off and air began. The word ozone came to her mind, that comforting and fleshless territory where the mere act of breathing was a joy and every issue grew abstract. Now she could feel this, Ruth knew that she had changed her life.

Always before when any plane she flew on became airborne, she'd searched around for the stranger she would choose to die with. As a young woman, she'd picked people whose faces or clothes or postures indicated they would face death interestingly, or flippantly or with some wit. After she had children, she looked for someone who seemed as if he would keep his head—if the children were with her, she'd want the practical help of such a person; if she were alone she'd want to go over the details of her life insurance and discuss the prospects of half-orphans finding psychological wholeness in maturity. But now she was with Phil, and they were on their way to London. It was a business trip for him; he worked for a human rights organization whose headquarters was in London, and he suggested Ruth come along: it would be, he said, their last vacation before marriage. Soon he would be her husband. She remembered that when she was with her first husband, she'd still searched planes, and that memory made her squeeze Phil's arm, guilty that these stray pieces of information could so reassure her, that she needed reassurance. But it was an odd decision that they'd made, to marry. It struck everyone they knew as at best unnecessary, and it made them feel apart from other people. Like orphan children in a foreign country they'd become solicitous, protective, unnaturally alert. Phil felt something more, though, he was almost childishly proud of their decision, as if it were an original, brave idea. For the last month, he'd taken her to meet people he'd known in grammar school or worked with for six months in college. She felt it made the people cynical and bored, and she didn't blame them; he'd been married twice before and left a woman he had lived with. It would be for her a second marriage, and she had been reluctant to agree.

"How," she said, refusing him at first, "how can we do it, knowing what we know?"

"But what about the kids?" he'd said. "How can they go around saying 'that guy my mother lives with'?"

"You like 'my stepfather'?"

"I do," he'd said. "It sounds like something you can count on."

And she had wanted that, that the children could count on him, some-how, even if he and she broke up. If they were married, she could name him in her will as the person to have custody in case both she and her ex-husband died. She had quite amicable relations with her children's father; still, she felt it would be odd to get him to agree to naming her paramour as the person in charge of their children's fate. If she could say "my husband" to her former husband, she could put the idea to him in language that had dignity and weight. It was important to her, this relation between language and the facts that it encircled. She was a science writer. She'd wanted to be a scientist herself; genetics was the field she had chosen. But quickly she learned that she lacked the kind of imagination that real scientific distinction called up; what she was good at was taking the findings—often brilliant, often crucial—of men and women who could not communicate what they had found, and making of them something articulate and shapely and still true. And so it bothered her that, in marrying, she was making a promise she couldn't keep. She felt like a child crossing her fingers behind her back: she felt it for both herself and Phil. When she thought of their marrying, she saw them as children, standing before a judge, their fingers crossed behind their backs saying, "I promise I will never leave you." When what they meant was, "I will try."

Before they left for London, Phil had himself measured for a custom-tailored suit. My wedding suit, he'd called it. And he gave the children a hundred dollars each to buy new clothing for the wedding. Elena was fourteen; she was delighted with the prospect of new clothes. But Jacob was eleven; he told Phil he'd just broken his Walkman and asked if he couldn't use the hundred dollars for a new one instead. Phil never got angry with the children, but Jacob could see that he had hurt him and pretended he'd said what he said as a joke. When Phil pretended to believe him, Ruth felt herself fill with a surprising love that made the walls of her heart, which was a muscle after all, feel thin and stretched like a balloon filled up with water. She remembered thinking of heavy water, water with an extra molecule, made only artificially and never to be put in contact with living things. You could poison plants by watering them with heavy water; it could be dangerous if drunk.

Was Philip dangerous? She couldn't understand how a man so lovable, so tactful and so generous of heart had left three women. It was an odd position she was in in her relation to his past. She didn't want to seem merely inquisitive, although there was an element of gossip in her desire to know the details of her predecessors. But there was more: there was something much worse. What she really wanted was to have him paint pictures so unflattering that they were little murders: then she could bury the mutilated carcasses herself and never fear. But she knew the way of it, everyone did: people began, in great hope, love affairs, and then things soured and went bad. And so she and Phil spoke remarkably little about the women in his life, and his friends had been more than reticent. After three disasters, she suspected they had lost the energy for one more round of reassurances: she was infinitely better than the others, they could see that now for the first time Phil was really happy, they were glad she was around.

━━━

They were driving through London in a taxi, the exciting route past Marble Arch. The massive green of Hyde Park, the enlivened whiteness of the buildings made Ruth feel daring. "We're really here," she said to Phil. "We've made it."

"We always make it, darling," he said. "And we always will."

She kissed him on the mouth so that he would not feel her doubting.

"Tell me again how you met Sylvie," she said. They were on their way to visit Sylvie MacGregor, who was divorced from Jack MacGregor, Phil's oldest friend.

"It must have been, what, I guess 1965. Jack and I had just come from the San Gennaro Festival. I'd won two prizes, throwing rubber balls and knocking over ducks or one of those games. I'd won a bottle of wine and a breakaway cane. For some reason we decided to drive up to Tanglewood. Well, I know why we did it, we were trying to pick up girls. Tanglewood is a terrific place to pick up girls. So I was walking with this cane. And when Sylvie saw me, she said I must be tired, did I want to sit on her blanket with her and her friend. I pretended to be a cripple for the whole day— I didn't want to embarrass her. It's no wonder she chose Jack instead of me.

"Three months after that she'd married Jack; Jack and I were both working for Lindsay then. In the fall of 1967, Jack went across the country with the McCarthy campaign, and late the following January he told Sylvie he'd met someone else and was leaving. Sylvie tried to kill herself. She called me just in time. I went with her to Roosevelt Hospital in the ambulance and let her come back to my apartment. It was just after my first divorce."

Ruth imagined that apartment, ugly in the willed, self-punishing style of the abodes of men who have left women. But, he told her, Sylvie brought it around wonderfully. She made him meet her at furniture stores, look carefully at swatches of fabric. She arranged for everything: the curtains, the deliveries. "But she didn't go too far," he said. "She never made me feel she was taking over, she made me feel it was my place."

"And were you lovers?"

"No. One night I suggested it, and she said, 'That's not the kind of thing I want.' I was actually a little relieved. She'd be quite something to take on: all that devotion. One of the reasons she was so devastated by Jack is that she'd given him everything, she'd had no reserve.

"She really fell apart," said Phil, "and people were ridiculous about it. They thought she was exaggerating. You know, that was the time everyone was leaving everyone. But only Sylvie got suicidal. And then she made this terrible decision: to grow old. All our friends were wearing long skirts or tight jeans, and she began wearing tweeds and cashmeres, putting her hair in a chignon. She couldn't stay in New York, it was no place for her, nobody understanding her, and her always being afraid of running into Jack or the new woman. She's Belgian, but she didn't want to go back. So she decided on London.

"I remember the night she left. I took her to the airport. We were three hours early—you know how I am—so we had too many drinks, which she said she wanted; she wanted to sleep the flight through. But when she landed in Heathrow, she got the news: Bobby Kennedy had been shot. She got hysterical in the airport; when you meet her you'll see how extraordinary that must have been. It was as if someone had taken her marriage to Jack, which she'd decently buried, dug it up and hacked it to pieces publicly. She phoned me, really out of control. I told her to come right back and stay with me. But she said she wouldn't. 'I just wanted to hear a friendly voice,' she said, 'And now I must get started.' "

"And she did," said Ruth, "she did get started."

"In a way, yes, of course she did. She got a flat in Clapham and had a small piano moved in. Three days a week she took lessons—she'd never touched the instrument in her life before—with some terribly hard-up young student at the conservatory. Then he got married and went to Sweden, and she began taking lessons with Miss Taub.

"You'll meet Miss Taub, no doubt," Phil said. "She must be seventy if she's a day. She and Sylvia became best friends almost immediately, and she took Sylvie into her circle, although Sylvie's the youngest of the group by twenty years. And she has this job, she runs some sort of institute for the blind. So she's become a kind of fixture on the South Bank, this beautiful, rather remote woman, taking old women and blind people to concerts. You'll see, we'll have at least one night with Miss Taub, and possibly a blind person. I never know what to do with those occasions."

"Why?"

"Well, I always feel that my physical health and whatever youth I have is a kind of affront to them. Besides, I'm always afraid I'm going to step on the guide dog's tail and start him howling in the middle of something *pianissimo.*"

"Phil, guide dogs don't howl. They're used to people stepping on their tails."

"It would be just my luck to get one that's hypersensitive."

They drove out of the impressive part of London; just into Clapham it was easy to imagine people living ordinary lives, taking their shoes to the shoemaker's, getting quick meals from Indian take-outs, going to movies because they were too tired to read. Ruth wondered what Sylvie had looked like when Phil had first known her. She remembered the first thing Phil had told her about Sylvie, something her ex-husband had said, that she had always wanted to be an old woman, and she'd turned herself into one so she could have the life she wanted. Ruth had been puzzled by Phil's tone in telling her: he'd sounded angry. She had assumed that he was angry for the whole estate of men: in refusing to fight against aging, in embracing it prematurely, Sylvie was taking herself out of the game. "I won't play," she'd said, and left the other players feeling foolish. Yet Phil considered her one of his dearest friends.

"You know," he said as they approached her street, "You can ask Sylvie anything about me."

Ruth didn't say what she was thinking, that the problem was that she knew too much about Phil already, that the only real information she wanted was impossible to get: she didn't want more history, she wanted guarantees. You will be happy now, she wanted someone to say, I promise. Perhaps that was what she'd wanted from Sylvie, but her first glance as Sylvie opened the door told her she wouldn't get it. Sylvie had taken pains to show that her allegiance was with a past which was more real, more vivid to her, than the thin present in which she felt herself required now to live.

Her flat was based on the idea of home of single women who had come to London from the Continent after the war. Modestly, wisely, they had bought the first luxuries available in the early fifties; as if they didn't want to seem too brash they concentrated on light browns and cream colors. Accents of gold might show themselves from time to time—some braid on a throw pillow, a detail of a tapestried chair. Pale green lamps threw their genteel and muted lights on objects neutral as shells. Only occasionally a porcelain box, a cigarette case, a small dish for nuts or candy would cry out that it was un-English and suggest some difficult, exciting European life that had been left for good.

At first Ruth thought that Sylvie had chosen her clothing along the same lines, and as a kind of camouflage to beauty. But then she looked more closely and saw that those careful clothes—the dun-colored blouse, the olive-green loose skirt, the beige shoes with a thin chain on the instep—represented Sylvie's real understanding of the nature of her beauty. Ruth wondered if, like a tall woman who wears high heels, Sylvie underscored her unfashionableness to turn it into an asset. She was, after all, nearly fifty, and by choosing to dress older than she was, there was no need for her to acknowledge that she was no longer young. Ruth felt *arriviste* in her red flowered skirt, blue shirt, jade beads, an outfit she'd been pleased with in the hotel mirror.

Sylvie offered them drinks and brought out little plates of sandwiches.

She disappeared again and again into the kitchen, bringing out dishes of odd, Germanic foods: pickled or salted, all desirable because they looked distinctly un-nutritious. She seated herself across from Ruth, her spine an inch or two away from the chair back, and said, "Now you must tell me all about your children." But Ruth grew tongue-tied; her children seemed out of place in the flat. You wouldn't like them, Ruth thought, catching Sylvie's bright and overeager eye. You'd think them spoiled and greedy and uneducated.

"It's so hard to describe one's children," she said, defeatedly. "One never knows if one's being at all realistic."

"Anything you said about them would sound like bragging," Phil said. "Only it would be the truth."

"How enchanting," Sylvie said. "Phil's a born father, Ruth, don't you think?"

"None of the potential mothers seemed to think so," Phil said. "I was game."

The personal tone seemed almost obscene to Ruth among the artifacts of Sylvie's flat; she blushed for Phil's misjudgment. But Sylvie went on to talk about the other wives, the other women, as if it were the most natural thing in the world. The conversation led naturally to people they had known, and Ruth could see Sylvie straining not to talk about old times, times Ruth had not been a part of, but her efforts to update their talk made Ruth feel childish, as if the grownups had kindly taken the time to ask her how she liked her school. She'd been through this before, meeting Phil's friends, but it was different with Sylvie. The smooth surface of Sylvie's life, her presentation of herself, left no foothold for Ruth. She jumped up eagerly when Phil said they must leave for dinner; then she felt her action made her appear greedy, and she told Phil to sit down again, they needn't rush. But Sylvie arose then, slowly, as if she were walking out of the ocean, and said "No, let's go now. It's horrible to be late, don't you think so, Ruth?"

"No, Ruth is unable to be on time," said Phil. "If she happens to be early, she'll do something—wallpaper the bathroom or begin to learn to play the flute—anything to avoid the terrible fate of being on time."

"How extraordinary, Phil, and you so anxious always about lateness," Sylvie said. "This must be love at last."

They walked into the street wrapped in a garment of bonhomie that Phil, Ruth saw, believed was genuine and beautiful and that to her was a hair shirt.

———

Phil had been right; Sylvie had made arrangements for them first to have dinner, then to go to the Schubert *lieder* in the Purcell room with Miss Taub. One of the people from the Institute for the Unsighted had been asked but, Sylvie explained, at the last moment she had got the flu.

"Ah, here's Miss Taub," said Sylvie when they approached the restaurant. "She makes rather a fetish of being early, but through the years I've managed to indulge her when I can. Tonight she's had to wait."

Miss Taub kissed Phil and gave her hand to Ruth. It was appropriate, of course; she'd known Phil, and it was her first meeting with Ruth. Of course, it was appropriate, but it was one more brushstroke, Ruth felt, in the group portrait: the two older women, eminently civilized, being courted safely, tenderly by Phil, and Ruth apart, spread out and representing Nature. Sylvie floundered visibly in trying to keep the conversation non-exclusionary, entertaining, smooth. Then, all at once, she gave Ruth a look of pure unhappiness. "See, I am drowning," the look said, "and it is your fault." At once Ruth saw that she had been impossible. The pain in Sylvie's eyes was genuine. Its disproportion drew out the maternal side of Ruth: she would not let this woman, who had so clearly suffered, suffer more. She sat up straight, then leaned her elbows on the table. She talked about her children and asked Miss Taub's advice about their music lessons. Phil turned on Ruth his look of bliss. She knew that they had triumphed, but the triumph had been brought about by Sylvie who had let herself appear, to this unpleasant stranger, intimately weak.

"Bonne chance," Miss Taub said, as they put her in a taxi. "I know we will meet again."

And Ruth hung on her lover's arm, because the words seemed like a blessing and a talisman, and in her gratitude for them she felt suddenly weak as if she could, without Phil's arm, fall down or faint.

=======

Sylvie had invited them to lunch Saturday at her flat, but she phoned in the morning to ask if she could take them, instead, to a restaurant near her office. The institute librarian, she explained, was sick, and many of the members could use the library only on Saturdays. She could leave one of the members in charge while they lunched, but they could not be leisurely, she said, not half so leisurely as they'd have liked.

Phil had a meeting in the morning; he told Ruth that he would meet her at the institute at one o'clock. But when Ruth arrived, Sylvie told her Phil had telephoned; the meeting would be indefinitely long, and they would have to lunch without him.

Ruth looked around her in a kind of panic. The blind people walked around the room, so even-paced and so sagacious she could have gone down on her knees. And Sylvie walked slowly, certainly, among them, touching some of them on the shoulder, saying their names, as a queen might walk among her castle staff. She introduced Ruth to the man who would sit at the desk while they lunched.

"How lucky you are to have our Sylvie to lunch," he said, his smile courtly beneath his merely damaged gaze.

"Yes, I'm only sorry my friend is tied up and can't join us," Ruth said, then felt she'd been tactless. "I mean, it's terrible that on a day like this he has to work."

"Your friend?" laughed Sylvie. "Your fiancé, you mean. They will be married, Ted, within two weeks."

"Taking your honeymoon before," he said, but he could not sound worldly. Ruth smiled, then realized he couldn't see her, so she laughed too loudly. Some people sitting at the tables looked toward her with the self-righteous stares of interrupted readers. That the stares were sightless was irrelevant, the censure was the same, and Ruth apologized to Sylvie and to the man Ted, whom she had wanted to praise by her laughter.

"Not at all," he said. "There's nothing worse than a library prig."

"Take your time," he said to Sylvie, who said she would. But when she got outside, she said to Ruth, "Ted's such a dear, and wonderfully intelligent, but if a crowd should gather at the desk, he simply couldn't cope."

As they walked, Ruth wondered if Sylvie suspected, as she did, that Phil had invented his overlong meeting so that the two women could be alone. For herself, she felt he had erred badly; the small ease she had gained with Sylvie at dinner days before had vanished. She felt, as they walked, that she followed in Sylvie's majestic wake, an undistinguished tug behind a schooner.

After they had ordered, Sylvie asked her about her work, apologizing for her ignorance in science. Then, without transition she said, "Have you ever met my husband, Jack MacGregor? Phil still sees him, I believe."

"Yes, but he lives in California, and I haven't met him yet."

Ruth was shocked by Sylvie's question and embarrassed to hear her call Jack "my husband." They had been divorced seventeen years; Jack had teenage children by the woman he'd left her for.

"We never write, it's such a shame. We've quite lost touch. I'm utterly dependent upon Phil for news of him. Strange, isn't it? You'd think that one would keep in touch with someone so important in one's past. It's lucky I have Phil, or Jack could die without my knowing."

Sylvie patted the corners of her mouth with her stiff napkin, then folded her hands as if to say, "What is it exactly that you want to know?" Ruth tried to read the beautiful, pale face, but it was blank and formal. A poker face, Ruth thought, and then realized at once how it was between them. She sat across from Sylvie like an inexperienced player before a seasoned gambler. Sylvie had, Ruth saw now, the professional's immaculate composure. The formality of every gesture was a weapon and a code. Concealment was the métier, the game untitled and the stakes unnamed. The purpose of the game itself became known only gradually. It was to get the green player to reveal her hand. Then the professional, seemingly prepared to throw down everything, would discard, in fact, only selected single cards —the obvious, the garish pictures—which could distract the green player from the game's real feat: everything valued or thought important had been kept back.

Ruth felt herself dig in, take root, grow obdurately stable. She asked Sylvie about Belgium, her childhood, her emigration to America. It seemed to Ruth that Sylvie quite purposefully drained all these topics of interest in order to return the conversation to its natural center: Phil. But Ruth knew that she could resist, for lunch was not meant to go on too long. They were both grateful to leave each other. When they parted, they did not kiss.

Ruth watched Sylvie walk down the street, unhurried and assured. And yet her back was angry, and she thrust her neck a shade uncomfortably forward as she walked. Phil well might say that she was happy, but watching her progress, Ruth saw the effort and the cost. She understood that Sylvie's life had been finished when Jack left her; she walked now as one dead. A blow that others might recover from, she never would; the damage that was temporary for some had been for Sylvie quite final. And the recovery of others, somehow, made it worse. It put everyone into a falsifying light, for if Sylvie's response was just, then others were deficient; if they were sane and sensible, then her life was a waste.

She walked around the squares of Bloomsbury feeling for no reason that she must kill time. The chestnuts held their flowers jealously, like precious candelabras that had been in the family for years. Some roses were beginning, others would be over in a day. The image of Phil's body kept floating before her eyes, and then parts of his body only: the torso, the back, the legs. She began running to the hotel, terrified that when she got there the room would be empty. It was not. She found Phil on the bed, reading a six-week-old copy of the *New Statesman;* others were spread out on the floor around the bed. He was touched and gladdened by her eagerness, though she suspected he mistook its causes and believed Sylvie had eased her mind about his past.

———

They would spend their last evening with Sylvie. Phil apologized when he told Ruth, but it seemed to be the only night Sylvie was free, and they had a piece of luck: they could get tickets for *Antony and Cleopatra.* "Fine," Ruth said. "Really, that's wonderful." She was thinking that she wanted to be home with her children. Their presence was a forced balance to her always. If they were here, she thought, the figure of Sylvie might not have loomed so menacingly, so symbolically; with the children along, she felt she might have been less cruel.

"I've always liked the character of Enobarbus," Phil said, after the play as they drank gin on Sylvie's settee. "I'd like to have seen him played by Ray Bolger."

They made up their ideal cast of *Antony and Cleopatra,* and the time went pleasingly and fast. But Ruth could sense behind it all, like a perfume at once menacing and seductive, Sylvie's dread that they would leave. She kept thinking up little stratagems so they would linger: she wrote down things she'd love for them to send her from New York; she asked questions about the children to which she already knew the answers. She kept offering them different foods, and when they refused, running into the kitchen to see what else she had to offer. But in the air there began to arise another scent: the thin, high one that was merely Phil's anxiety about packing, about missing planes. Both women knew that was the scent that must be followed, and they rose at once.

"Next time I see you, you will be married," said Sylvie, holding Ruth's hands. "I wish you every happiness," she said, handing them a gift. It was a miniature of a woman, blond and blue-eyed, in a low-cut yellow dress. "It is from my family."

Phil had tears in his eyes as he thanked Sylvie, but Ruth could only wonder what gift Sylvie had given the other women as they parted. Were they all treasures from her family? Had Phil taken them with him when he left the women? Were they even now in his apartment, in his office, objects that she hadn't questioned, that he'd got in just this way?

"Things change, my friend, but we are constant," Sylvie said, as she kissed Phil goodbye.

She smiled at Ruth as she looked over Phil's shoulder, and Ruth felt herself forced to return the smile in kind.

———

She sat in a chair across the room and watched Phil as he slept. Usually she was a sounder sleeper than anyone she slept with. She wondered whether any man had watched her as she watched Phil now; she could not imagine it.

The light that came from the streetlights made the room seem unchangeable: an object in history, a work of art. Phil's back was to her, and his posture made him boyish. The fine shoulders were the shoulders of a boy, the few dark hairs made a pattern she wanted to follow with her lips. She could not bear any more to be merely looking, and she wondered if she lay against him if she would wake him up. She decided to take the chance; he seemed deeply asleep. She took her nightgown off because she wanted to feel the softness of her breasts against the hard curve of his back. He did not waken. She moved away, back to the chair. She wanted to be watching him again.

She understood that if he left her it would be like death and wondered when it happened how she would go on.

THE THORN

*f I lose this, she thought, I will be so far away I will never come back.

When the kind doctor came to tell her that her father was dead, he took her crayons and drew a picture of a heart. It was not like a valentine, he said. It was solid and made of flesh, and it was not entirely red. It had veins and arteries and valves and one of them had broken, and so her daddy was now in heaven, he had said.

She was very interested in the picture of the heart and she put it under her pillow to sleep with, since no one she knew ever came to put her to bed anymore. Her mother came and got her in the morning, but she wasn't in her own house, she was in the bed next to her cousin Patty. Patty said to her one night, "My mommy says your daddy suffered a lot, but now he's released from suffering. That means he's dead." Lucy said yes, he was, but she didn't tell anyone that the reason she wasn't crying was that he'd either come back or take her with him.

Her aunt Iris, who owned a beauty parlor, took her to B. Altman's and bought her a dark blue dress with a white collar. That's nice, Lucy thought. I'll have a new dress for when I go away with my father. She looked in the long mirror and thought it was the nicest dress she'd ever had.

Her uncle Ted took her to the funeral parlor and he told her that her father would be lying in a big box with a lot of flowers. That's what I'll do, she said. I'll get in the box with him. We used to play in a big box; we called it the tent and we got in and read stories. I will get into the big box. There is my father; that is his silver ring.

She began to climb into the box, but her uncle pulled her away. She didn't argue; her father would think of some way to get her. He would wait for her in her room when it was dark. She would not be afraid to turn the lights out anymore. Maybe he would only visit her in her room; all right, then, she would never go on vacation; she would never go away with her mother to the country, no matter how much her mother cried and begged her. It was February and she asked her mother not to make any summer plans. Her aunt Lena, who lived with them, told Lucy's mother that if she had kids she wouldn't let them push her around, not at age seven. No matter how smart they thought they were. But Lucy didn't care; her father would come and talk to her, she and her mother would move back to the apartment where they lived before her father got sick, and she would only have to be polite to Aunt Lena; she would not have to love her, she would not have to feel sorry for her.

On the last day of school she got the best report card in her class. Father Burns said her mother would be proud to have such a smart little girl, but she wondered if he said this to make fun of her. But Sister Trinitas kissed her when all the other children had left and let her mind the statue for the summer: the one with the bottom that screwed off so you could put the big rosaries inside it. Nobody ever got to keep it for more than one night. This was a good thing. Since her father was gone she didn't know if people were being nice or if they seemed nice and really wanted to make her feel bad later. But she was pretty sure this was good. Sister Trinitas kissed her, but she smelled fishy when you got close up; it was the paste she used to make the Holy Childhood poster. This was good.

"You can take it to camp with you this summer, but be very careful of it."

"I'm not going to camp, Sister. I have to stay at home this summer."

"I thought your mother said you were going to camp."

"No, I have to stay home." She could not tell anybody, even Sister Trinitas, whom she loved, that she had to stay in her room because her father was certainly coming. She couldn't tell anyone about the thorn in her heart. She had a heart, just like her father's, brown in places, blue in places, a muscle the size of a fist. But hers had a thorn in it. The thorn was her father's voice. When the thorn pinched, she could hear her father saying something. "I love you more than anyone will ever love you. I love you more than God loves you." *Thint* went the thorn; he was telling her a story "about a mean old lady named Emmy and a nice old man named Charlie who always had candy in his pockets, and their pretty daughter, Ruth, who worked in the city." But it was harder and harder. Sometimes she tried to make the thorn go *thint* and she only felt the thick wall of her heart; she couldn't remember the sound of it or the kind of things he said. Then she was terribly far away; she didn't know how to do things, and if her aunt Lena asked her to do something like dust the ledge, suddenly there were a hundred ledges in the room and she didn't know which one and when she said to her aunt which one did she mean when she said ledge: the one by the floor, the one by the stairs, the one under the television, her aunt Lena said she must have really pulled the wool over their eyes at school because at home she was an idiot. And then Lucy would knock something over and Aunt Lena would tell her to get out, she was so clumsy she wrecked everything. Then she needed to feel the thorn, but all she could feel was her heart getting thicker and heavier, until she went up to her room and waited. Then she could hear it. "You are the prettiest girl in a hundred counties and when I see your face it is like a parade that someone made special for your daddy."

She wanted to tell her mother about the thorn, but her father had said that he loved her more than anything, even God. And she knew he said he loved God very much. So he must love her more than he loved her mother. So if she couldn't hear him her mother couldn't, and if he wasn't waiting for her in her new room then he was nowhere.

When she came home she showed everyone the statue that Sister

Trinitas had given her. Her mother said that was a very great honor: that meant that Sister Trinitas must like her very much, and Aunt Lena said she wouldn't lay any bets about it not being broken or lost by the end of the summer, and she better not think of taking it to camp.

Lucy's heart got hot and wide and her mouth opened in tears.

"I'm not going to camp; I have to stay here."

"You're going to camp, so you stop brooding and moping around. You're turning into a regular little bookworm. You're beginning to stink of books. Get out in the sun and play with other children. That's what you need, so you learn not to trip over your own two feet."

"I'm not going to camp. I have to stay here. Tell her, Mommy, you promised we wouldn't go away."

Her mother took out her handkerchief. It smelled of perfume and it had a lipstick print on it in the shape of her mother's mouth. Lucy's mother wiped her wet face with the pink handkerchief that Lucy loved.

"Well, we talked it over and we decided it would be best. It's not a real camp. It's Uncle Ted's camp, and Aunt Bitsie will be there, and all your cousins and that nice dog Tramp that you like."

"I won't go. I have to stay here."

"Don't be ridiculous," Aunt Lena said. "There's nothing for you to do here but read and make up stories."

"But it's for *boys* up there and I'll have nothing to do there. All they want to do is shoot guns and yell and run around. I hate that. And I have to stay here."

"That's what you need. Some good, healthy boys to toughen you up. You're too goddamn sensitive."

Sensitive. Everyone said that. It meant she cried for nothing. That was bad. Even Sister Trinitas got mad at her once and told her to stop her crocodile tears. They must be right. She would like not to cry when people said things that she didn't understand. That would be good. They had to be right. But the thorn. She went up to her room. She heard her father's voice on the telephone. *Thint,* it went. It was her birthday, and he was away in Washington. He sang "happy birthday" to her. Then he sang the song that made her laugh and laugh: "Hey, Lucy Turner, are there any more at home like you?" because of course there weren't. And she mustn't lose that voice, the thorn. She would think about it all the time, and maybe then she would keep it. Because if she lost it, she would always be clumsy and mistaken; she would always be wrong and falling.

———

Aunt Lena drove her up to the camp. *Scenery.* That was another word she didn't understand. "Look at that gorgeous scenery," Aunt Lena said, and Lucy didn't know what she meant. "Look at that bird," Aunt Lena said, and Lucy couldn't see it, so she just said, "It's nice." And Aunt Lena said, "Don't lie. You can't even *see* it, you're looking in the wrong direction. Don't say you can see something when you can't see it. And don't spend the whole summer crying. Uncle Ted and Aunt Bitsie are giving you a wonderful summer for free. So don't spend the whole time crying. Nobody can stand to have a kid around that all she ever does is cry."

Lucy's mother had said that Aunt Lena was very kind and very lonely because she had no little boys and girls of her own and she was doing what she thought was best for Lucy. But when Lucy had told her father that she thought Aunt Lena was not very nice, her father had said, "She's ignorant." *Ignorant.* That was a good word for the woman beside her with the dyed black hair and the big vaccination scar on her fat arm.

"Did you scratch your vaccination when you got it, Aunt Lena?"

"Of course not. What a stupid question. Don't be so goddamn rude. I'm not your mother, ya know. Ya can't push me around."

Thint, went the thorn. "You are ignorant," her father's voice said to Aunt Lena. "You are very, very ignorant."

Lucy looked out the window.

When Aunt Lena's black Chevrolet went down the road, Uncle Ted and Aunt Bitsie showed her her room. She would stay in Aunt Bitsie's room, except when Aunt Bitsie's husband came up on the weekends. Then Lucy would have to sleep on the couch.

The people in the camp were all boys, and they didn't want to talk to her. Aunt Bitsie said she would have to eat with the counselors and the K.P.'s. Aunt Bitsie said there was a nice girl named Betty who was fourteen who did the dishes. Her brothers were campers.

Betty came out and said hello. She was wearing a sailor hat that had a picture of a boy smoking a cigarette. It said "Property of Bobby." She had braces on her teeth. Her two side teeth hung over her lips so that her mouth never quite closed.

"My name's Betty," she said. "But everybody calls me Fang. That's on account of my fangs." She opened and closed her mouth like a dog. "In our crowd, if you're popular, you get a nickname. I guess I'm pretty popular."

Aunt Bitsie walked in and told Betty to set the table. She snapped her gum as she took out the silver. "Yup, Mrs. O'Connor, one thing about me is I have a lot of interests. There's swimming and boys, and tennis, and boys, and reading, and boys, and boys, and boys, and boys, and boys."

Betty and Aunt Bitsie laughed. Lucy didn't get it.

"What do you like to read?" Lucy asked.

"What?" said Betty.

"Well, you said one of your interests was reading. I was wondering what you like to read."

Betty gave her a fishy look. "I like to read romantic comics. About romances," she said. "I hear you're a real bookworm. We'll knock that outa ya."

The food came in: ham with brown gravy that tasted like ink. Margarine. Tomatoes that a fly settled on. But Lucy could not eat. Her throat was full of water. Her heart was glassy and too small. And now they would see her cry.

She was told to go up to her room.

———

That summer Lucy learned many things. She made a birchbark canoe to take home to her mother. Aunt Bitsie made a birchbark sign for her that said "Keep Smiling." Uncle Ted taught her to swim by letting her hold onto the waist of his bathing trunks. She swam onto the float like the boys. Uncle Ted said that that was so good she would get double dessert just like the boys did the first time they swam out to the float. But then Aunt Bitsie forgot and said it was just as well anyway because certain little girls should learn to watch their figures. One night her cousins Larry and Artie carried the dog Tramp in and pretended it had been shot. But then they put it down and it ran around and licked her and they said they had done it to make her cry.

She didn't cry so much now, but she always felt very far away and people's voices sounded the way they did when she was on the sand at the beach and she could hear the people's voices down by the water. A lot of times she didn't hear people when they talked to her. Her heart was very thick now: it was like one of Uncle Ted's boxing gloves. The thorn never touched the thin, inside walls of it anymore. She had lost it. There was no one whose voice was beautiful now, and little that she remembered.

EILEEN

*T*here's some that just can't take it," Bridget said. "No matter what they do or you do for them, they just don't fit in."

"You certainly were good to her, Kathleen," said Nettie, "when she first came over. No one could have been better when she first came over."

"That was years ago," Kathleen said. "We never kept up with her."

Nora thought of Eileen Foley when she had first come over, twelve years ago, when Nora was eleven and Eileen, twenty-one. They'd had to share a bed, and Kathleen had apologized. "There's no place for her, only here. I don't know what they were thinking of, sending her over, with no one to vouch for her, only the nuns. The Foleys were like that, the devil take the hindmost, every one of them. You'd see why she wanted to get out."

But Nora hadn't minded. She liked Eileen's company, and her body was no intrusion in the bed. Her flesh was pleasant, fragrant. Though she was large, she was careful not to take up too much room. They joked about it. "Great cow that I am, pray God I don't roll over one fine night and crush you. How'd yer mam forgive me if I should do that."

And they would laugh, excluding Nora's brothers, as they excluded them with all their talk about the future, Eileen's and Nora's both. It was adult talk; the young boys had no place in it. It was female too, but it was different from the way that Nora's mother and aunts, Bridget and Nettie, spoke, because it had belief and hope, and the older women's conversation began with a cheerful, skeptical, accepting resignation and could move— particularly when Bridget took the lead—to a conviction of injustice and impossibility and the inevitable folly of expecting one good thing.

They talked every night about what had happened to Eileen at work. She was a cook at a school for the blind run for the Presentation sisters. It was in the Bronx. In Limerick, she'd worked at the sisters' orphanage; she was grateful they had recommended her over here. She was proud of her work, she liked the people, worshipped the nuns that ran the place. She said she would have loved to be a nun, only for her soft nature. She was right about herself; she had a penchant for small luxuries: lavender sachets to perfume her underclothes, honey-flavored lozenges that came in a tin box with a picture of a beautiful blond child, a clothesbrush with an ivory handle, a hatpin that pushed its point into the dull black felt of Eileen's hat and left behind a butterfly of yellow and red stones. She would take these things out secretly and show them first to Nora, so that Nora felt that she possessed them too and considered herself doubly blessed: with the friendship of one so much older and with the passion of her observation of these objects she could covet, and could prize but need not own.

The nuns, Eileen told Nora often, had a terrible hard life. They slept on wooden pallets and were silent after dark; they woke at dawn, ate little and were not permitted to have friends. Not even among each other; no, they had to be particularly on their guard for that. "Particular friendships, it's called," Eileen told Nora proudly. "They're forbidden particular friendships." She told Nora she'd learned all this from Sister Mary Rose who ran the kitchen. It was not her praise that mattered to Eileen, though, but the words of Sister Catherine Benedict, the superior.

"She came up to me once, that quiet, I didn't know she was behind me. I was cutting up some cod for boiling, you know the blind ones have to have soft foods, as they can't cut, of course—and Sister must have been watching me over my shoulder all the time. 'You are particularly careful,

Eileen Foley, and the Blessed Mother sees that, and she will reward you, mark my words. A bone left in a piece of fish could mean death for one of the children, so to cut up each piece with the utmost care is like a Corporal Work of Mercy for the poor little souls.' "

Eileen said that Sister Catherine Benedict had come from Galway city. "You could tell she comes from money. But she gave it up. For God." At Christmas time, Sister had given Eileen a holy picture of her patron saint, Saint Catherine of Siena and on the back had signed her name with a cross in front of it. Nora and Eileen would look at the picture; it seemed to them a sign of something that they valued but could not find or even name in the world that they inhabited; excellence, simplicity. One day, Eileen promised, she would bring Nora to the home so that she could meet Sister Catherine for herself. But it never happened, there was never time.

Because, really, Eileen hadn't lived with the Derencys very long, six months perhaps. Nora tried to remember how long it was; at twenty-three the seasons of an eleven-year-old seemed illusory: what could possibly have happened then to mark one month from another, or one year? Each day of her adulthood seemed like the dropping down of coins into a slot: a sound fixed, right and comforting accompanied her aging, the sound of money in the bank. Childhood was no gift to a cripple, she'd often thought, with its emphasis on physical speed, with those interminable hours which required for their filling senseless, interminable games of jumping, running, catching, following, scaling, shinnying, those various and diffuse verbs that spelled her failure. Even now, in her well-cut suit, her perfumed handkerchief shaped like a fan tucked in her pocket, the gold compact she had bought herself with her first wages, even now she could think of those childhood games and bring back once again the fear, the anger, the thin high smell that was the anguish of exclusion. Even now, though her success at Mr. Riordan's law office was breathtaking, even now she could bring back the memory of her body's defeat.

Even now, at twenty-three, as she stood in the kitchen drinking black coffee while her mother cooked and her aunts lounged over their boiled eggs, even now Nora could feel the misery. She thought of Eileen and of the pleasure it had been to have her; one of her few physical pleasures as a child. She thought about Eileen's abundant flesh that seemed to have much more in common with a food than with an object of sexual desire: the white flesh of an apple came to mind or milk, a peach in its first blush of ripeness, the swell of a firm, mild delicious cheese. Nothing dark, secretive or inexplicably responsive seemed to be a part of Eileen's body life. And Nora prized Eileen because it seemed to her that Eileen was as definitely cut off from coupling as she, although she could not quite say why. For it was Nora's body's brokenness that always would exclude her from the desiring eye of men, whereas with Eileen it was excessive wholeness that would turn men's eyes away: nothing could be broken into, broken up.

Six months it must have been, thought Nora, that she lived here. After that she moved into the convent. She felt embarrassed, she'd confessed to Nora, to be living with the family. She'd offered money for her board, but Kathleen had refused it. And she hated the remarks that Bridget made about her family. Family passion and its underside, the family shame, could make Eileen's high color mottle, and her perfect skin appear sickish and damp. She knew what her family was, but after all, she said, they tried their best, their luck had been against them.

"You make your own luck," Bridget had said when Nora tried, just after Eileen had left them, to defend the Foleys. She'd mentioned their bad luck. "Every greenhorn in America came here through nothing but bad luck. If it was good luck that we had, we'd be back home in great fine houses."

"Still there's some like the Foleys that God's eye doesn't shine on," said Kathleen.

"God's eye, my eye, 'tis nothing wrong with them but laziness and drink, the same old song, and no new verses added," Bridget said.

"But what about the mother?" Nettie said. The two sisters looked sharply at her, warning her to silence.

"That was never proved," said Kathleen.

"What was never proved?" eleven-year-old Nora had asked.

"Time enough for you to be knowing that kind of story. Hanging about the way you do, you know far too much as it is," Bridget said.

I know more than you'll know when you're a hundred, Nora wanted to say to her aunt, whom she despised for her bad nature and yet feared. She felt that Bridget blamed her for her leg, as if, if she'd wanted it, she could be outside running with the other children. There was some truth in that, there always was in Bridget's black predictions and malevolent reports. It was the partial truths in what she said that made her dangerous.

It was only recently that they'd explained about Eileen's mother. Nora tried now to remember what the circumstances might have been that would have made the sisters talk about it. She could not. It wasn't that they'd seen Eileen, they hadn't, not since Nora's high school graduation which was six years ago now. They had known the Foleys' house, so it was real to them, the news, when it came from her cousin Anna Fogarty, who had stayed on at home. Mrs. Foley, Eileen's mother, who everyone had thought was queer, had burned the house down and she herself and her youngest baby, a boy of six months, had both perished. Everyone believed that she had set the fire. Nora felt she saw it, the fixed face of the mother as her life burned up around her, the green skeleton of the boy baby, left to be gone over like the ruined clothes, the spoons, the pots and pans.

Eileen's father had married again, which just showed, Bridget said, the foolishness of some young girls. All the sisters thought of marriage as a sign of weakness: they made only partial exceptions for themselves. But the young girl who'd married Eileen's father seemed to prove the sisters' point. She'd left her family where she had considered herself unhappy, thinking she was moving out to something better. The parish had helped Jamesie Foley build a new house: that had turned the young girl's head. But what she got for her pains was a drunken husband and a brood of someone else's children whom she tormented until Eileen couldn't bear to see it and left to work in the orphanage in Limerick, where the nuns, knowing her wishes, got the place for her in their house in New York.

The sisters in both convents knew her dreams were for her brother Tom. Tom was twelve years younger than Eileen, the youngest living child. He was wonderfully intelligent, Eileen told Nora, and had an angel's nature. Every penny of her salary she could she put into the bank to bring him over; that was why she took the sister's offer of her living in the convent instead of with the Derencys, she could save her carfare. That was what she said to the Derencys, but Nora knew there was more to it. Her pride, which couldn't tolerate Kathleen not taking any money. Nora could tell that Eileen worshipped Kathleen. And it troubled her that there was nothing she could do for Kathleen when Kathleen did so much for her.

====

As Kathleen's life had blurred, Nora's had been pressed into sharp focus. She had wanted to become a teacher, and her teachers encouraged her. Austere and yet maternal Protestants, romantic from the books they read, they treasured the pretty crippled girl with her devotion to the plays of Shakespeare and to Caesar's Gallic Wars, to anything, in fact, that they suggested she should read. Nora had been accepted at the Upstate Normal School on the basis of her grades and of her teachers' letters. But none of them had mentioned Nora's deformity; she'd been born with one leg shorter than the other. She realized they hadn't known, the moment she arrived, nervous to the point of sickness, driven by her nervous mother. How shocked those men were, in the office of the Dean, when they beheld her with her high shoe and her crutch. They blamed the teachers. "No one has informed us . . . You must see, of course, it's quite impossible . . . We must think first about the safety of potential children who might be in your charge. Imagine if there were a fire or a similar emergency . . ." They talked as if they were reading what they said from a book. They did not look at her. They said that it was most regrettable, but they were sure she understood, and understood that it was no reflection—not-a-tall—on her. They were just sorry she had had to make the trip.

   She drove back with her mother in shamed silence, as if she'd been left at the altar and in all her wedding finery was making her way home. That was the way her father behaved, as if she had been jilted. He said he and some of his friends whose names he wouldn't mention would drive themselves up there and teach a lesson to those Yankee bastards. It was a free country, he said; you didn't get away with that kind of behavior here. He was very angry at his wife.

"Did you say nothing to them, Kathleen? Did you just walk out with your tail between your legs like some bog trotter thrown off the land by an English thief? Was that the way of it?"

Nora saw her mother's shame. She knew her father was just talk; he would have done no better. She herself had remained silent, and she bore her own shame in her heart. She would not let her mother feel the weight of it.

"I think, you know, Dad, it's a blessing in disguise. I'd make three times the money in an office. You were right, Dad, all along. I should have taken the commercial course."

"I was not right. You went where you belonged, there in the academic. You've twice the brains of any of them. Reading Latin like a priest. French too. I'm that proud of you."

She wanted to tell him that her education had been nothing, foolishness, Latin she was already forgetting, French she couldn't speak, history that meant not one thing to her, plays and poems about nothing to do with her life. She felt contempt, then, for her teachers and the things they stood for. She felt they'd conspired against her and made her look a fool. They could have fought for her against the men who sat behind the desks there in the office of the Normal School. But they did not fight for her, they kept their silence, as she had and as her mother had. And they had counted on that silence, those men in that office; it gave them the confidence to say the things they said, "regret" and "understanding" and "upon reflection." They had counted on the silence that surrounded people like Nora and her family, fell upon them like a cloak, swallowed them up and made them disappear so quickly that by the time Nora and her mother had stopped in Westchester for a cup of tea they could forget that they had ever seen her.

She determined that she would be successful in the business world. She finished senior year with the high grades she had begun with: she owed her parents that. But her attention was on the girls she knew who worked in offices: the way they dressed and spoke and carried themselves. She would be one of them; she would be better than any one of them. She would take trains and manicure her nails. Every muscle in her body she would devote to an appearance of efficiency and competence, with its inevitable edges of contempt.

Her one regret was that she had to ask her father for the money for her business-school tuition. He was glad to give it to her, she could tell he felt that he was making something up to her, making it all right. She was first in her class in every subject. Easily, within a week of graduation, she was hired by the firm of MacIntosh and Riordan, where she thrived.

She almost became the thing she wanted. She grew impatient with home life, in love with the world that required of her what she so easily, so beautifully could give. The years of all the anger which her family had not acknowledged or allowed she put into a furious, commercial energy. Soon Mr. Riordan had only to give her a brief idea of the contents of a letter; she herself composed those sentences that shone like music to her: threatening or clarifying, setting straight. This new person she had become had no place in her life for Eileen Foley, or for her brother Tom, whom she had finally brought over after six hard years.

He was fifteen when he arrived in New York; two years younger than Nora, but he was a child, and she a woman of the world. Eileen brought him to the Derencys to ask advice about his schooling; she was determined he be educated, although everyone advised against it, even Sister Catherine Benedict. And certainly Bridget advised against it.

"Vanity, vanity, all is vanity," she said, and everyone grew silent. Any kind of quote abashed them all.

"Well, what would you say, Nora, with your education?" Eileen asked.

It was a terrible word to Nora, education, all that she had had violently, cruelly to turn her back on, all that had betrayed her, caused her shame. Yet even in her bitterness, she saw it need not be the same for Tommy Foley. He would not want what she had wanted, Latin and the poetry, the plays. He would want, and Eileen wanted for him, merely a certificate.

What he would learn would never touch him; therefore it would never hurt him. He wanted, simply, a good job.

Nora felt her mother's eyes hard on her, wanting her to give encouragement to Eileen. She understood why. Eileen's desire for her brother's prospering was so palpable, so dangerous almost, that it should not be balked.

"Why not try?" said Nora in her new, sharp way. Her parents did not know she'd begun smoking; if she'd dared, it would have been a perfect time to light a cigarette.

═══

Eileen was constantly afraid that her ambitions for her brother would be ruined by the influences of the neighborhood. For her they were contagious, like the plague; the greenhorn laziness, the fecklessness, the wish for fun. Nora's success made Eileen worshipful; she grew in Nora's presence deferential, asking her advice on everything, ravenously listening to every word she said, and urging Tom to listen, too.

Nora knew enough of the world not to overvalue the position that the Foleys had invented for her. She knew her place; it was a good place, near the top. And yet she knew that she would never be precisely at the top. She saw in the hallway of the office building where she worked a hundred girls like her. She was not the best of them; her bad leg meant she could not make the picture whole. She could not stride off, her high heels making that exciting sound of purpose on the wooden floors. She could not rise purposefully from her typewriter and move to the file cabinet, closing the drawers like a prime minister conferring an ambassadorship, as Flo Ziegler or Celie Kane, the partners' secretaries, did. To really play the part she coveted required speed and line, like a good sailboat. Nora knew that her high shoe, her skirts cut full and long to hide it, detracted from her appearance of efficiency. Her work, the quickness of her mind might earn the highest place for her, but she would always be encumbered and slowed down by what John Riordan, a kind man, called her "affliction." Even so, even though she would never be at the very top, she knew herself above

Eileen and her brother; there was no place for them in her new life, except the place forced free by charity.

She tried to joke Eileen out of her subservience, reminding her of when they had shared Eileen's secret trove of almonds, nougat, crystallized ginger. But perhaps she didn't try wholeheartedly; her daily striving to achieve her dream of herself exhausted her; there was a kind of ease in lying back against the bolster of Eileen's adoration. Eileen had an idea of the game Nora was playing, even if she was mistaken about the nature of the stakes. Nora's parents and Aunt Nettie had no knowledge of the game. But Bridget did; she was contemptuous and mocking; when she saw Nora ironing, with passionate devotion, her blouses, handkerchiefs or skirt; when she came upon Nora polishing her nails, she sniffed and walked by, loose and ill-defined in her practical nurse's uniform, trailing the scorn of her belief in the futility of every effort Nora made.

Eileen kept hinting that Nora should be on the lookout for a place in Mr. Riordan's office that Tommy could fill. She'd heard about boys who started in law offices as messengers and worked their way up till eventually they studied on their own, sat for the bar exam and became lawyers.

"Well, I've heard of it. I've never seen a case myself," said Nora, smoking cynically. "You'd have to have an awful lot of push."

And this was what Tom Foley lacked completely: push. Pale, with hair that would never look manly and blue eyes that hid expression or else were supplicating, he was nearly silent except when he and Eileen talked about home. He could go then from silence to a frightening ebullience about some detail of their childhood: a cow with one horn only, a dog that barked when anybody sang, pears that fell from a tree once as they sat below it, soft, heavy as footballs, damaging themselves before they hit the ground. Then he would grow embarrassed at his outburst, would blush and look more childish than ever. It was quite impossible; she didn't understand why Eileen couldn't see it, he was not the office type and never would be. Right off the boat Eileen had put him with the Christian brothers; he lived there while Eileen lived with the nuns. In the summer on her week's vacation they went to a boarding house three hours from the city in the mountains, a house run by an Irish woman they had known from home. But Tom had never spoken to a soul outside his school except in Eileen's company, and Nora doubted that he could. She'd never mentioned him to Mr. Riordan, it would not work out and in the end would just make everyone look bad.

She suspected Eileen resented her for not doing anything for Tom. They stopped seeing one another; when the family got the news of Eileen they hadn't heard a word from her in longer than a year. She phoned to tell them Tommy had died. He'd got a job working for Western Union, as a messenger to start, but his bosses had said he'd shown great promise. He was delivering a wire and had walked by a saloon. There was a fight inside, and a wild gunshot had come through the window. The bullet landed in his heart.

Eileen said this in the kitchen drinking tea with Nora and her mother and her father and her aunts. As she spoke, her cup did not tremble. They had no way of knowing what she felt about the terrible thing that had happened; she would give no sign. She met no one's eye; her voice, which had been musical, was flat and tired. What they could see was that the life had gone out of her flesh. What had been her richness had turned itself to stone; her body life, which once had given her and all around her pleasure, had poured itself into a mold of dreadful bitter piety. She talked about the will of God and punishment for her ambitions. It was this country, she said, the breath of God had left it if it ever had been here. Money was God here, and success, and she had bent the knee. Her brother had died of it.

So she was going home, she said. She cursed the day she ever left, she cursed the day she'd listened to the lying tongues, the gold-in-the-street stories, the palaver about starting over, making good. It was the worst day of her life, she said, the day she'd come here. But she wanted them to know that she was grateful for the way they'd helped her when she first was over; she would not forget. She told them she was going back to her old job at the orphanage in Limerick. She said that she would write them, but they all knew she would not.

When she walked out the door, they felt one of the dead had left them, and they looked among themselves like murderers and could find no relief. When Bridget tried to blame Eileen or blame the Foleys, no one listened. They could hardly bear each other's company.

Nora went upstairs to her room and lay down on her bed, still in her work skirt. It would be terribly wrinkled; before the night was over she would have to press it. But not now. Now she lay back on her bed and knew what would be her life: to rise from it each morning and to make her way to work. Each morning she would join the others on the train, and in the evening, tired out but not exhausted, and with no real prospects that could lead to pleasure, with the others she would make her way back home.

NOW I AM MARRIED

I am the second wife, which means that, for the most part, I am spoken *to*. This is the first visit of my marriage, and I am introduced around, to everyone's slight embarrassment. There is an unspoken agreement among people not to mention *her*, except in some clear context where my advantage is obvious. It would be generous of me to say that I wish it were otherwise, but I appreciate the genteel silences, and, even more, the slurs upon her which I recognize to be just. I cannot attempt to be fair to her: justice is not the issue. I have married, and this is an act of irrational and unjust loyalty. I married for this: for the pleasure of one-sidedness, the thrill of the bias, the luxury of saying, "But he is my husband, you see," thereby putting to an end whatever discussion involves us.

My husband is English, and we are staying in the house of his family. We do not make love here as we do at my mother's. She thinks sex is wicked, which is, of course, highly aphrodisiac, but here it is considered merely in bad taste. And as I lie, looking at the slope of my husband's shoulder, I think perhaps they are right. They seem to need much less sleep than I do, to be able to move more quickly, to keep their commitments with less fuss. I wish I found the English more passionate; surely there is nothing so boring as the re-enforcement of a stereotype. But it is helpful to be considered southern here: I am not afraid to go out on the street as I am in Paris or Rome, because all the beautiful women make me want to stay under the sharp linen of my hotel. No, here I feel somehow I have a great deal of color, which has, after all, to do with sex. I can see the young girls already turning into lumpish women in raincoats with cigarettes drooping from their lips. This, of course, makes it much easier. Even my sister-in-law's beauty is so different that it cannot really hurt me; it is the ease of centuries of her race's history that gave it to her, and to this I cannot hope to aspire.

Yesterday we went to a charity bazaar. One of the games entailed scooping up marbles with a plastic spoon and putting them through the hole of an overturned flower pot. My sister-in-law went first. Her technique was to take each marble, one at a time, and put it through the hole. Each one went neatly in. When it was my turn, I perceived the vanity of her discretion and my strategy was to take as many marbles as I could on the spoon and shovel them into the hole as quickly as possible. A great number of the marbles scattered on the lawn, but quite a few went into the hole, and, because I had lifted so many, my score was twelve; my sister-in-law's five. Both of us were pleased with our own performance and admiring of the rival technique.

I am very happy here. Yesterday in the market I found an eggplant, a rare and definite miracle for this part of the world. Today for dinner I made *ratatouille*. This morning I took my sister-in-law's basket and went out, married, to the market. I don't think that marriage has changed me, but for the first time, the salespeople appreciated, rather than resented, the time I took choosing only the most heartwarming tomatoes, the most earnest and forthright meat. I was no longer a fussy bachelorette who cooked only sometimes and at her whim. I was a young matron in stockings and high heels. My selections, to them, had something to do with the history they were used to. They were important; they were not for myself.

I had wanted to write this morning, but I had the responsibility of dinner, served at one. I do not say this in complaint. I was quite purely happy with my basket and my ring, basking in the approval of the shopkeepers and the pedestrians. I am never so happy writing. It is not that the housewife's tasks are in themselves repugnant: many of them involve good smells and colors, satisfying shapes, and the achievement of dexterity. They kill because they are not final. They must be redone although they have just been finished. And so I am shopping rather than polishing the beautiful Jacobean furniture with the sweet-smelling lavender wax. I am doing this because I am dying, so that I will not die.

1 . MARJORIE

Bring her in for a cup of coffee, I said to him. I saw you on the street, and you were so happy looking. Not me and my husband. Dead fifteen years, and a bloodier hypocrite never walked. I pretended I was sorry when he died, but believe me, I was delighted. He was a real pervert. All those public-school boys won't do anything for you till they're beaten; don't let them tell you anything about the French, my dear.

I was just in France. I was kind of like an *au pair* girl to this communist bloke, only he was a millionaire. Well, they had a great house with a river behind it, and every day I'd meet the mayor of the town there, both of us throwing our bottles from the night before into the river. They had men go round with nets to gather up the bottles and sell them. They know how to live there. The stores are all empty here. Not that I'm much of a cook. We start our sherry here as soon as we get up. Your coffee all right? Have a biscuit. I'll have one too. I shouldn't . . . look at me around the middle. I'm getting to look quite middle-aged, but there's some life in me yet, I think, don't you?

Look at your husband sitting there with his blue eyes just as handsome. Fancied him once myself, but he hadn't time for me. Keep an eye on him, dear, he's got young girls in front of him all day. Oh, I don't envy you that job. They must chase after him all the time, dear, don't they? Cheer up, a little jealousy puts spice in a marriage, don't you think?

Well, there's a real witch hunt out for me in this building. I've taken in all the boys around the town that've got nowhere to go. Just motherly.

All of them on drugs, sleeping out every night. Well, my policy is not to chivvy and badger them. Tried marijuana myself once but I didn't get anything out of it because I didn't smoke it properly. But they all have a home here, and I do them heaps more good than some virginal social worker with a poker you know where. Of course the old ladies around here don't like it. Mrs. Peters won't forgive me since I was so drunk that night and I broke into her house and started dancing with her. A poor formless girl she's got for a daughter, afraid of her own shadow. Starts to shake if you as much as say good morning to her. Thirty-five, she is, if she's a day. Pious, that one. I've seen her chatting up the vicar every evening. You know what *she* needs. My husband was a parson. He was plagued with old maids. I'd'uv been delighted if he'd rolled one down in my own bedroom just so's he'd leave me alone. Bloody great pervert, he was. And sanctimonious! My God! He looked like a stained-glass window to the outsiders. And all the old biddies in the town following him around calling him Father. Not me. I'd like to tell you what I called him.

Anyway, all the old bitches here think they can get me thrown out, but they're very much mistaken. This building happens to be owned by the Church of England, of which my husband happened to be a pillar. My pension comes from there, you know. Well, my dear, of course they can't throw one of the widows of the clergy out on her sanctified arse, so I'm really quite safe for the moment.

That's why I wouldn't get married again. I wouldn't give up that bloody pension for the life of me. I'll see they pay it to me till I die, the bloody hypocrites. 'Yes, Mrs. Pierce, if you'd conduct your life in a manner suitable to a woman of your position.' Bugger 'em, I say. They're all dust, same as me.

No, I'm quitting Charlie. I've been with him five years, but I must say the rigamarole is becoming trying. His wife sits home with their dachshunds, Wallace and Willoughby, their names are—did you ever hear anything so ridiculous—and occasionally she'll ring up and say 'Is Charlie Waring there?' and I'll say 'Who? You must have the wrong number.' Five years. It's getting ridiculous.

I think I'll take myself down to the marriage bureau. Thirty quid it costs for a year, and they supply you with names till you're satisfied. Of course at my age what d'ye have left? And I'd want somebody respectable, you know, not just anybody. Of course, you meet men in pubs, but never the right sort, are they? My dear, you wouldn't believe what I come home with some nights, I'm that hard up.

Anyway, Lucinda's sixteen, and she's already on her second abortion. How she gets that way I don't know. She simply walked out of school. Told one of the teachers off when she ordered her to take off her makeup. She said to her, 'My mother doesn't pay you to shout at me.'

Dried-up old bitches those teachers were. Of course, in point of fact it's not me or her that's paying, it's the Church, but just the same, I see her point. You're only young once, so why not look your best. They'll never want her more than they want her now, right. Isn't it true, they won't let us near a man till we're practically too old to enjoy one. Well, I've got her a Dutch cap now, though I don't suppose she'll use it. I never did. That's why I've got five offspring. I'm sure I don't know what to do with them. Anyway, she's answering telephones for some lawyer three hours a day, and I'm sure he's got her flat on her back on his leather couch half the time. Smashing-looking Indian chap. But it's pocket money for her. And we don't get along badly, the way some do. I give her her own way, and if she gets into trouble we sort it out somehow. I suppose she'll get married in a year or so, only I hope it's not an ass or a hypocrite. Bloody little fool I was at her age. My dear, on my wedding night I didn't know what went where or why. Don't ask how I was so stupid. Of course my mother was a parson's wife, too, and I think she thought if she said the word sex the congregation would burn her house down. Dead right she *was*.

Well, you certainly are an improvement over the other one he was married to. My dear, she thought she could run everyone's life for them. Knew me a week, and she came over one morning and said, uninvited, 'Marjorie, you should get up earlier. Why don't you watch the educational programs on the telly?' 'Bugger off,' I said, and she never came near me again.

Well, I have to go off and see one of my old ladies. This one keeps me in clothes, so I've got to be attentive. Let me tell you, if you could see how respectable I am in front of her, my dear, you wouldn't believe. Well, I take her cashmere sweaters and hope the constable won't see me on the way out. One visit keeps Lucinda and me in clothes for a year. I don't care, it cheers her up, the poor old bugger. Hope someone'll be as good to me when I'm that age. But I'll probably be a cross old drunk, and I bloody well won't have any spare Dior gowns in my closet, that's sure.

You don't mind if I give your husband a kiss goodbye. Lovely. Oh, perhaps I'll just take another one. Fancied him myself at one time. Well, you're the lucky one, aren't you? Come over again, perhaps you could come for a meal, though what I could cook nowadays I'm sure I don't know. I don't suppose that would set well with the family. Can't say that I blame them, they have to live here. Well, slip in some time on the QT and I'll dig you out some tea. Make it afternoon though, dear, I don't like mornings, though I'm ever so glad of your company.

2 . DORIS

I don't go anywhere by myself now. Three weeks ago I got a car but I took it back. I was so lonely driving. That was the worst. I think I'm afraid of everybody and everything now. I'm always afraid there's men walking behind me. I won't even go to post a letter in the evening. I was always afraid of the dark. My mother knew I was afraid of the dark, so she made me sleep with the light off. She said if I kept on being afraid of the dark, God wouldn't love me.

Of course, it's all so different now George is gone. People are like things, d'ye know what I mean? They're very nice, of course, and they do care for me and call, but it's all, I don't know, shallow like. Of course I do prefer the company of men. Not that I run down my own sex, but men are gentler, somehow, don't you think? The first month after George was gone all I could think about was who could I marry now. But now I look back on it I shudder, d'ye know what I mean. George bein' so so sick and all

that we didn't have a physical relationship for many years. And men like
to be naughty. Sometimes, though, I do enjoy a man's companionship.
After George lost his leg, he said, 'I can't give you much in the way of the
physical, Mother.' But we were terribly close, really. Talked about everything. He *would* insist on having his chair here by the door so's he could
see everybody coming in. I used to kid him a lot about it. Winter and
summer, never come close to the fire. He'd sit right there by the door,
winter and summer. And Gwen would sit on the settee at night and never
go out. I used to say to her, 'Gwen, you must go out. Go to the cinema.'
But she was afraid, like, to leave her father. Even though I was here. She
was afraid if she went out he'd be gone when she got back.

Of course it was very hard on the children. It'll take them years to sort
it out, I suppose. Perhaps they'll never sort it out. Gwen went down to
eight stone. Bonnie she looked, but I was worried. Then she got these
knots like, in her back, and she stopped going to work altogether. Said she
couldn't face the tubes anymore. She hated it; bein' smotheredlike, she
said, it was terrifying. But I think she wanted to be home with Daddy so
we let her come home.

Colin has a lovely job now. Got a hundred blokes under him. But they're
afraid he'll go back to university and quit so they don't pay him properly.
He almost took a degree in logic, but he broke down after two years. You
should see his papers. Lovely marks on 'em. His professors said if he sat
right down, he'd come away with a first. But he got too involved, if you
know what I mean. Forgot there was a world around him.

He's had a lot of lovely girls, and I guess he's had his fling, but I don't
think he'll ever marry. After George died, he said, 'I don't know how to
put it, Mum, but I'm just not that interested in sex.' Once a few years ago
he came out to the breakfast table. He was white as a ghost; I was worried.
He said, 'Dad, may I have a word with you?' I said, 'Do you want me to
leave the room?' He said, 'No, of course not, Mum.' Then he told George
he didn't sleep at all that night. He said he felt a kind of calling. He was
terrified, he said; he was sure God was calling him to his service. Well,
George held his tongue, and so did I. He asked Colin what it felt like, and

Colin said, 'Don't ask me to describe it, Dad.' He had a lot of sleepless nights, and we called the vicar, and he took him to the place where the young men go for the priesthood, and Colin said that he liked it, but when the time came he never did go.

Him and his father were great pals. Colin, of course, was studying Western philosophy, and he was very keen on it and George just as keen on the Eastern. Oh, they would argue, and George would say, 'Just read this chapter of the book I'm reading,' and Colin would say, 'I'm not interested, Dad.' Then after George died he took all his books away with him to Bristol. I said, 'I thought you weren't interested.' He said, 'I really always was, Mum.'

Lynnie's going to be a mother in September. I'm not really keen on being a grandmother. I'm interested in my daughter; she's an adult. I'm not interested in babies. I've never seen anyone like her for being cheerful, though. That girl cannot be made miserable, not even for an hour. I'm sure it'll be a girl, the way she holds her back when she walks, straight, like. I suppose I'll be interested in it when it's born.

George had a kind of miraculous effect on people, though. One time our vicar asked him to address a group of young people. Four hundred of them there was, packed the house with chairs, they did. And up on the stage one big armchair for George. One night I made them all mugs of tea, there must have been fifteen of them here on the floor. Half of them admitted they were on drugs. Purple hearts, goofballs, whatever they call them nowadays. And when they left here they said they were all right off them now.

Of course he had this good friend, the bachelor vicar, Arthur. Like a father to him George was. A very intelligent man, but a terrible lot of problems. Spent all his time here, he did. He'd stay here till two o'clock on Sunday morning and then go home and write his sermons. Said George all but wrote his sermons for him. Once he told me he was jealous of George having me and me having George. Said it was the one thing he could never have. And him a wealthy man. His father has a big engineering firm in Dorset and a great house. Three degrees he has, too. But I think he's really like they say, neurotic. He *cannot* express his feelings. Me and George, we told each other everything. We kept no secrets. Not Arthur, though. He's taken me out to dinner twice since George died but I like plain food, d'ye know what I mean, and he took me out to this Japanese restaurant with geisha girls and God knows what. Well they gave me so much I sent half of it back, and they said was there something Madame didn't like, and I about died of shame. I think old Arthur's knocking, but I'm not at home to him. Of course he's a wonderful priest, the kids in the youth group love him. He cried during the whole funeral service. I was so mortified. And he will not mention George's name. He says he can't forgive God for taking George.

I used to feel that way but I don't any more. When George was in so much pain, like, I'd go to the Communion rail and shake my fist at Christ on the cross and say, 'What d'ye know about suffering? You only suffered one day? My George has suffered years.' I don't feel that way now. I think there's a reason for it, all that pain, even. George died without one drug in his body, he had that much courage.

Well, I guess I'll be getting you a bath. It's good you've come. You'll never regret the man you've married. George thought the world of him. We've only water enough for one bath. So one can take it tonight and one tomorrow. George and I used to bathe in the same water, but I think we were different from most.

I feel like I've known you all my life. I knew you'd be like this from the letters. Old friends they were, my man and yours. You're not like the first wife. She was a hard one, that one. Ice in her veins.

Perhaps I'll come and visit you in America. I have a job now at the hospital and three weeks holiday in July. Perhaps I'll come out to visit you. But what would I do, the two of you out working. I hate to impose, you know. We used to have friends, widows they were, and we'd invite them over and they'd say, 'Oh, no thanks, we'd be odd man out.' I never knew what they meant, but now I know. Look at me talking. I can't even go to Epping by myself, and Lynnie made the trip when she was eight. Perhaps if you found out all the details for me. Wouldn't it be something!

It's good having someone in the house at night. I usually sleep with all the lights on, I'm that frightened on my own. I think I'm getting better with the job and all. But sometimes I'm very empty, like, and cold.

3. ELIZABETH

I like living here on my own. Dear lord, who else could I live with? Like old Miss Bates, she lived with another teacher, for, oh, twenty years it must have been. They bought a dear little house in the Cotswolds to live in for their retirement. Lived there a year and up pops some cousin who'd been wooing Miss Campbell for forty years, and off they go and get married. Well, Amelia Bates was furious, and she wouldn't speak to Miss Campbell, and they'd been like sisters for twenty years. Well poor Miss Campbell died six months later, and there's Amelia Bates on her own in that vast house full of regrets and sorrow.

Here's a picture of me in Algeria in 1923. Oh, I had a beautiful ride over on the ship, it took three days. Some people took the trip just to drink all the way, people are foolish. The first night I lay in my cabin and the ship was creaking so badly I was sure it was the end for me. I went up top, and the waves were crashing around the deck and they said, 'You'd better go down below, Miss,' and that's where I met Mr. Saunders.

Don't let the others in the family act so proud to you. When I found out that Ethel had cut you, ooh, I was so angry. I wrote her a very cross letter. Her mum and dad were separated for years and he was living with a half-caste woman in India and afraid to even write his wife a letter. Of course he should have left her and stayed with that other woman, but he didn't have that much courage. He's been miserable ever since. Poor old Lawrence, he's a decent old boy but terrified to death of Millie. You know she was just a governess for his family when he fell in love with her. She was good looking though, the best looking of all of us. Well, poor old Lawrence when he came to Mount Olympus (that was the name of my factor's house, dear. It fulfilled the ambitions of a lifetime for him) well, when he came to Mount Olympus to meet the family he came down with malaria and was sick in bed for a month. Had to have his meals brought up to him and his sheets changed three times a day. Well, after that there was no getting out of it, he was quite bound. Not that he thought of getting out of it then. People simply didn't in those days, and that's why so many of them were so unhappy. I'm sure things are much better now, in some ways, but nobody seems much happier anyway, do they?

Here is a picture of the family I worked for in India. Now even I had my mild scandal I suppose. It wasn't so mild to father. Millie came home from India and told dear father a great tale. Father wrote to Mr. Saunders and demanded that I be sent home. Then he wrote to me and said I must come back upon my honor as his daughter and an Englishwoman. We simply didn't answer the letters. Mr. Saunders hid them in a parcel in his desk drawer, and I simply threw mine in the fire. Then Mr. Saunders took the family back to England, and I went back to Mount Olympus. Father told me I must take a new name and tell everyone I was married, that I was the widow of an officer. I refused; I told him no one knew but him and Millie. Then we never spoke of it.

I started a kindergarten for the children in the town. Here is the picture of the first class, and here's one of your husband as a baby. Wasn't he golden? Then mother got sick, and I had to give it up. Nobody took it on after that, it was a pity, really. I regretted that.

Here's a picture of Cousin Norman. Doesn't he look a bounder? Wrote bad checks and settled in Canada. He's a millionaire today.

I'm giving you these spoons as a wedding gift. They belonged to my grandmother's grandmother. I think it's nice to have a few old things. It makes you feel connected, somehow, don't you think?

I only hope my mind holds out on me. I love to read, and I wouldn't care if I were bedridden as long as my mind was all right. Mother was all right for some time, and then when she was in her seventies she just snapped. She didn't recognize anybody in the family, and one night she came at Father with a knife and said he was trying to kill her. We had to put her in hospital then. It was supposed to be the best one in England, but it was awful. There were twenty women in a room not this size, and in the evenings you could hear them all weeping and talking to themselves. It would have driven me quite mad, and I was sane. Then she said the nurses were all disguising themselves to confuse her, and they were trying to poison her. And then she said they wouldn't let her wash, and she was dirty and smelled ill. Well, we finally took her back home, and father wouldn't let anyone see her. I gave up my position—I was working for that woman who writes those trashy novels that sell so well. And her daughter was an absolute hellcat—and came home. She'd call me every few minutes and say, 'Elizabeth, what will we do if anyone comes? There isn't a pock of food in the house.' And I would tell her no one would be coming. Then she'd say, 'Elizabeth, what will we do if anyone comes, the house is so dirty.' And it would go on like that. Sometimes she wouldn't eat for days, and sometimes she would stuff herself till she was quite ill. She died of a stomach obstruction in the end, but that was years later. Every night Father would go in to her and say goodnight and kiss her, and she would weep and say that she was wicked, that she was hurting us all. But sometimes she would just be her old self and joke with us after supper and play the piano and sing or read—she loved George Eliot—and we'd think she was getting better, perhaps. But the next morning she'd be looking out the window again, not talking to anyone.

I can't go near anyone who has any kind of mental trouble. When my friend Miss Edwards was so ill in that way she wrote and begged me to come, and the family wrote, and I simply couldn't. I get very frightened of those sorts of things. I suppose I shouldn't.

Here is a caricature my brother drew of the warden, and here is one of the bald curate and the fat parson who rode a bicycle. He was talented, our Dick, but of course he had a family to support, and that awful wife of his put everything on her back that he earned. And here is one of our father turning his nose up at some Indian chap who was trying to sell him a rug he didn't fancy.

Here I am in Malta, and here's one of me in Paris. Wasn't I gay then? When the Germans took over Paris, I wept and wept. I didn't want to go on. Have you been to Paris, dear? Beautiful city, isn't it? You feel anything could happen there. It wouldn't matter where you'd been or what you'd done, you could begin all over, no regrets or sorrows.

Here is a picture of your husband's mother, wasn't she beautiful? Turn your head like that, you look rather like her when you put your face that way. She would have loved you, dear, and she was a beautiful soul. She used to laugh and laugh, even during the war when we'd have to stay in the shelter overnight and we were terrified we wouldn't see the sunlight ever again. She'd tell us gay stories and make us laugh. She had a little bird, she used to call it Albert as a joke. She let him fly out all about the house on his own. And she taught the creature to say funny things; it was so amusing. She would be very happy for you, dear; she loved to see people happy.

I don't suppose I'll do any more traveling. I remember when I went to France last summer I said, 'Elizabeth, this is your last voyage,' and I felt so queer. But I have this house and my garden and Leonard's wife Rosemary and I go out every week and do meals-on-wheels—we take food around to the shut-ins, dear. I suppose they'll be doing that for me some day, but not for a while, I don't think. I like to be active and work in the garden. These awful pillow roses have taken over everything, and I haven't the heart to prune them. And then, when people come, it's so lovely, isn't it, I wish they could stay forever.

4 . SUSAN

It's good to have company. Sometimes I feel as though I haven't had a day off in three years since Maria was born. Geoffrey doesn't seem to want to be weaned; he's seven months. I suppose he will when he's ready. It's the only thing that quiets him. I'm beginning to feel very tired. And now Maria wants everything from a bottle, she wants to be a baby too. I suppose they'll stop when they're ready.

My days are very ordered, though. I remember when I was single and I lived in London I'd think what will I do with myself now? And then I'd just go out and walk down the street and I'd look in the windows at the china and the materials and then I'd stop somewhere and have a cup of tea and go home and read something. It's so difficult, isn't it, to remember what that kind of loneliness was like when you're with people constantly. It's like hunger or cold. But now my time is all mapped out for me. I give everyone breakfast and then I do the washing up and we go for a walk and it's time for lunch. It goes on like that. It's better now. When we lived in the high-rise building I felt terribly alone. There would be other push-chairs in front of other doors and occasionally I'd hear a baby crying in the hall but I wouldn't know whose it was and when I opened the door there was never anybody in the corridor, only that queer yellow light. And I hated the air in that building. It tasted so false in my mouth and we couldn't open up any of the windows. It was beautiful at night and I would hold the baby by the window and say, 'moon,' and 'star' and sometimes when they were both asleep Frederick and I would stand by the window and look out over the city at all the lights. The car horns were muted like voices at the ocean; it was very nice. I liked it then. But I did feel terribly lonely.

Sometimes I go up to the attic and I look at the piles of my research in egg cartons but I don't even take it out. I suppose I should want to someday. I suppose I should get back to my Russian. But it all hangs around me like a cloud and I feel Maria tugging at me, pulling at my dress like a wave and I think how much more real it all is now, feeding and clothing, and nurturing and warming and I think of words like 'research' and 'report' and even 'learning' and 'understanding' next to those words and they seem so high, so far away, it's a struggle to remember what they mean.

I love marriage, though, the idea of it. I believe in it in a very traditional way. My friends from graduate school come over, and they say I'm worn out and tired and I'm making a martyr of myself. I should make Frederick do some of the work. But it's the form of it I love and the repetition: certain tasks are his, some are mine. That's what these young people are all looking for, form, but it's a dirty word to them. I suppose I'm not that old, I'm thirty-two, that's young, I suppose, but I like feeling older. I wish

I were fifty. I like not having a moment to myself, it's soothing, and my life is warm and sweet like porridge. Before Geoffrey was born sometimes I'd spend the whole day and Maria was the only one I would talk to. She was two then and Frederick would come home, and he was so terribly tired, and I was too. We scarcely said a word to each other except how's the baby today or your shirt got lost at the cleaner's. It was the happiest time in my life. She wanted to know everything, and sometimes we'd spend whole mornings doing things like taking the vacuum cleaner apart or boiling water or walking up and down stairs. Then Frederick would come home and he'd want to talk about Talleyrand or something and I couldn't possibly explain to him how perfectly happy I was all day, taking everything out of my sewing basket and showing it to Maria, he would have thought I was stark, staring mad.

But I love that: sleeping next to someone you haven't spoken to all day and then making love in the dark with our pajamas on and even then going to sleep not having spoken. It soothes me, like wet sand. We couldn't have that without marriage, I mean marriage in the old way, with the woman doing everything.

Here's something for your lunch. I cook such odd things now, sausages for the children, tins of soup, sandwiches. But I always make this stew for us. I just boil up a hambone with lentils and carrots. I suppose you're a very good cook. I used to be, but now I don't like that kind of thing.

The babies have broken nearly all the china, so we use everything plastic now. Do you think it's terribly ugly? I do miss that nice thin china and glassware, I miss it more than books and the cinema. And the furniture's terribly shabby now. We'll wait until they're grown to replace it.

Don't worry about what people say. When I married Frederick even his mum wouldn't come, and people would run down his first wife, thinking they were doing me a favor, and all the time they were making it worse because I'd think if she was so bloody awful why did he marry her, and then I thought if he loved her and she's so dreadful and he loves me I must be dreadful too. And I kept going around in circles and hating Frederick and myself and some poor woman whom I used to think of as a perfectly harmless, remote monster. I could scarcely get out of bed in the morning, and people thought they were being kind. You must simply shore up all your courage to be silent. That's what I have done and sometimes I am so silent I like myself a great deal, no, more than that, I admire myself and that's what I've always longed for.

You shouldn't listen to me either, I'm probably half-mad talking to babies all day. Only there's something sort of enormous and grey and cold about marriage. It's wonderful, isn't it, being a part of it? Or don't you feel that way?

5 · GILLIAN

My mother had this thing about beauty, it was really very Edwardian the way she approached it. She had this absolutely tiny private income, and my father took off the absolute second I was born, and we hardly ever had any money, and my mother kept moving around saying these incredible things like 'It'll be better in the next town' and 'When our ship comes in' and things like that you expect to read in some awful trashy novel.

But she was a beautiful woman and she taught me these oddly valuable things, about scent and clothes and makeup. I'm trying to be kinder to her now I'm forty. I suppose one gets some kind of perspective on things, but what I really remember is being terribly, terribly insecure all the time and frightened about money and resentful of other girls who wore smart clothes and went off to university when they weren't as smart as I was. My mother used to dress me in the most outlandish outfits as a child, velvet and lace and what not. I hated it in school. I was forever leaving schools and starting in new ones, and I was perpetually embarrassed.

Well, when I married for the first time, I was determined to marry someone terribly stable and serviceable. As soon as I could I bought these incredibly severe clothes, they just about had buttons on them, and I married Richard. I was eighteen. I suppose it is all too predictable to be really interesting—and we lived in this fanatically utilitarian apartment, everything was white and silver, and I couldn't imagine why I felt cold all the time. Suddenly I found myself using words like beauty and truth, et cetera, and I went out and got a job so we could buy a really super house. I spent all my time looking at wallpaper and going to auctions, and the house really was beautiful. Then I met Seymour, and he was so funny and lugubrious—I just adored it. Here was this Jewish man taking me to little cabarets. The first time we went out, he said to me, 'You know, Gillian, girl singers are very important,' and I hadn't the faintest idea what he was talking about. Here was this quite famous psychologist who bought a copy of *Variety*—that American show-people's paper—every day, but it was very odd, the first time I met him, I thought how marvelous he'd be to live with.

And then, of course, I did a terribly unstable thing, I suppose. Shades of my mother only more so, and I divorced Richard and married Seymour. He gave all his money to his wife, and I let Richard keep everything of mine, and we started out without a penny. We slept in the car in our clothes, but we were terribly happy. So I got a job and we got another lovely house, only this was a really cheerful one, a very motherly home. Then I went back to school. I suppose it's hard for you to understand how important it would be for me: doing something on my own with my mind and speaking up and having people listen. I'd had too much sitting on the sidelines pushing the silver pheasant down the damask cloth and cradling the salt cellar while the men spoke to each other. So I told Seymour I simply had to go back to college, and he agreed with me for a while in theory, but when the time came he said to me 'What about the house?' But I was very firm, and I told him, 'The house will simply be a bit less beautiful for a while.' Then he understood how important it was to me, and he stood right behind me. We didn't do much entertaining for a while, but I did very well, really, everyone was surprised. I guess everyone else was much less smart than I expected.

Then I took a job teaching secondary school, and it was a disaster, really. There were all these perfectly nice people who wanted to grow up and repair bicycles, and I was supposed to talk about Julius Caesar and the subjunctive. It was all too absurd, really. I simply cared about the books too much to do it. I suppose to be a really good teacher you have to not care about the books so. Well, one day I simply didn't go back. I suppose it was awful, but there were plenty of people who wanted the job. I didn't feel too badly about it. Going in like that every day was making me so ill.

Now I've gone back to writing. I don't know if I'm any good. I don't suppose it matters, really. It's a serious thing, and that's important. I see everyone off in the morning and I go up to my study—the window looks out on a locust tree—and I write the whole day. The hardest thing is closing the door on Seymour and the children—but I do. I close the door on being a wife. I close the door on my house and all the demands. I suppose art demands selfishness, and perhaps I'm not a great artist, so perhaps it's all ridiculous and pitiable, but in the end it isn't even important whether I'm great or not—I'm after something, myself, I suppose; isn't that terribly commonplace? Only the soul, whatever that is—whatever we call it now—gets so flung about one is always in danger of losing it, of letting it slip away unless one is really terribly careful and jealous. And so it is important really and the only answer is, whatever the outside connections, one must simply do it.

═══

Who is right, and who is wrong? For years, I have waited for a sign, a sentence, periodic and complete. Now I begin to know there is loneliness even in this love. I begin to think of death, of solids. My friend, who is my age, is already a widow. She says that no one will talk to her about it. Everyone thinks she is tainted. They are frightened by her contact with dead flesh, as if it clung to her visibly. I should prepare for a staunch widowhood. I begin to wish for my own death, because I am happy now and vulnerable to contagion. A friend of mine who has three children tells a story about a colleague of his, a New England spinster. She noted that he had been out sick four times that winter; she had been healthy throughout. "But that is because I have a wife and three children," he said, "and I am open to contagion."

There is something satisfying about marriage at this time. It is the satisfaction of a dying civilization: one perfects the form, knowing it has the thrill of doom upon it. There is a craftsmanship here; I am conscious of a kind of labor. It is harder than art and more dangerous. Last night was very hot. I didn't want to wake my husband so I moved into the spare bedroom where I could thrash, guiltlessly. I fell asleep and then heard him wake, stir, and feel for me. I ran to the door of our bedroom. "You gave me a fright. I reached for you, and the bed was empty," he said. Now I know I am not invisible. Things matter. My feet impress a solid earth. I am full of power.

The most difficult thing is my tremendous pride. To admit that there are some things I do not know is like a degrading illness. My husband tries to teach me how to use a hoe, a machete. I do not learn easily. I throw the tools at his feet and in anger I weep and kick. He knows something I do not; can I forgive him? He is tearing down a wall; he is building a fireplace. I am upstairs in the bedroom, reading, dizzy with resentment. I come down and say, "I'm going away for a few days. Until you finish this." Then I cry and confess: I do not want to go away, but I hate it that he is demolishing and building and I am reading. It is not enough that I have made a custard and a beautiful parsley sauce for the fish. He hands me a hammer, a chisel, a saw. I am clumsy and ill with my own incapacity. When he tries to show me how to hold the saw correctly, I hit him, hard, between the shoulder blades. I have never hit another person like this; I am an only child. So he becomes the brother I was meant to hit. I make him angry. He says I should have married someone with no skills, no achievements. What I want, he says, is unlimited power. He is right. I love him because he is powerful, because he will let me have only my fair share. Stop, he says, for I ask too much of everything. Take more, there is more here for you, I tell him, for he is used to deprivation. We are learning to be kind to one another, like siblings.

Two people in a house, what else is it? I love his shoes, his shirts. I want to embrace his knees and tell him "You are the most splendid person I have ever known." Yet I miss my friends, the solitude of my own apartment with its plangent neuroses, the coffee cups where mold grew familiarly, the little grocery store on the corner with the charge account in my name only.

But I feel my muscles flex, grow harder, grow supple with intimacy. We are very close; I know every curve of his body; he can call to mind in a moment the pattern of my veins. He is my husband, I say slowly, swallowing a new, exotic food. Does this mean everything or nothing? I stand with him in an ancient relationship, in a ruined age, listening beyond my understanding to the warning voices, to the promise of my own substantial heart.

THE MURDERER GUEST

*I*t was like the dream she always had, the enemy soldiers running behind her, running in their brown wool uniforms. She was the only one; her family had escaped and had forgotten her. She had to bury their pictures so the enemy soldiers could not find them. Then she had to tell the soldiers she had no one—no father, no sister, no mother, no brothers. She must say to the soldiers, holding all the time in her heart the faces of those she loved, that there was no one, everyone she knew had died, she was entirely alone.

The air that night, the night that Mrs. Delehanty came, felt like the air in that dream. Her mother opened the front door and then stood away from it, as if she were afraid Mrs. Delehanty was going to fall into the house. Elizabeth's father said, "Well, then, Beverly," and kissed the woman who wore the green hat. And Elizabeth knew, she had been warned, that she must not act peculiarly. She must not let on by anything about her—her voice, the way she stood, the things she talked about. She must not let the woman know that she knew. Her mother had sat down on her bed after the telephone call and said to Elizabeth, "Suppose something terrible happened between me and Daddy. Suppose Daddy got sort of sick. Suppose he did something funny, and I was scared. And then I just did something. Wouldn't you want someone to be kind?"

"Yes," Elizabeth said. Her hair felt hot and wet against her face. She felt danger, and fever, the terror of becoming sick. She did not know what her mother meant.

"Well, Mrs. Delehanty, just in one minute . . . she didn't know what she was doing. Her husband was drunk. She had a big knife . . . she had been making supper."

"You wouldn't do that."

"Maybe anybody would."

"Not you. Not anyone we know."

"Mrs. Delehanty knows a lot of people. Now they want to act as if they don't know her. That's why she's coming here to stay with us for a while."

"Why?"

"She lived in Lincoln, Nebraska. And now none of her friends will talk to her. So she wants to move away."

"Here?"

"No, she'll just stay here for a while. Until she gets her bearings."

Bearings. Elizabeth saw the woman skating, falling, trying to get up.

———

The next day at lunch, Elizabeth's mother showed her pictures of Mrs. Delehanty as a girl. Mrs. Delehanty and Elizabeth's mother had gone to school together. There they were in their high school hats. How old they seemed to Elizabeth, and yet in these pictures they were only six years older than she was now, and it seemed a trick; it seemed to have something to do with the trouble Mrs. Delehanty was in, as if she ought to have known, wearing that hat, that bathing suit, that she was in for something. And Elizabeth thought, looking at the pictures, that it was a miracle her mother had been spared scandal, looking as she did at sixteen.

There was a trick to it, but Elizabeth did not know what it was. Was it that they had tricked their mothers into letting them wear high heels?

They were wearing high heels even with their bathing suits. As her mother turned the black pages of the album Elizabeth thought of her own flat shoes, how her legs and feet would look in a full-length photograph. She would look safe; she would look dependable. She would not look like the kind of person to whom terrible things would happen.

Vaguely she knew it could be otherwise, but why it was, she did not know. She had some sense that there were people whose lives were—she did not know what it was called—not like hers, not like her parents', but messy, somehow, not in order. Lives that were like the scandalous desk of Judith Lowery, who sat behind her in school. Judith was the poorest student in the class; Elizabeth, the best. Miss Grayson had decided it would be good "for both of you" if Judith and Elizabeth sat near each other throughout fourth grade.

Judith had one foreign parent. Her mother, so that was not good. Her mother was German. Sometimes Elizabeth tried to remember that the war had ended in the year of her birth, 1945, and ten years must not be a long time in the history of the world. She knew that, and yet, ten years was all of her life, and people talked about the war as if it were long ago. But when Elizabeth's mother talked about herself and Mrs. Delehanty in their bathing suits, Elizabeth could tell that her mother thought *that* wasn't very long ago at all. But she could see the date on the pictures—1936. And in 1945 the war had ended.

The war was with the Germans, and Judith Lowery's mother was German, and Mrs. Delehanty's life was like Judith Lowery's desk. Elizabeth remembered the time her mother had made her ask Judith Lowery to her birthday party. Her party was perfect; her mother had made a cake with merry-go-round horses around it and icing that was blue and pink and yellow. Perfect flowers. She had told her mother: You are a perfect mother to have made such perfect, perfect flowers out of icing, and a dress, light-blue dotted swiss with a sash, the sash she had always wanted. And people had brought perfect presents: clothes for her Ginny doll, a Little Lady Bath Set, a pin in the shape of a pink cat with blue glass eyes. But

Judith Lowery ruined the party by bringing the wrong present: two candy bars, German ones, wrapped in tinfoil. How quiet everyone had grown, until finally Susan Thomas, who was stupid but everyone called her cute, giggled. And then Elizabeth kissed Judith Lowery because at that moment she liked her better than Susan Thomas, and she remembered that Judith Lowery had been born in Germany.

Later Elizabeth heard her mother talking to Susan Thomas' mother about the present Judith Lowery had brought, and Susan's mother had said, "It's the mother. She doesn't know about our customs."

And then Elizabeth's mother said, "War bride."

And from then on, Elizabeth knew that something terrible had happened to Judith Lowery's mother. War bride. Elizabeth thought that meant Mrs. Lowery had had her head shaved. And that was why she always wore a kerchief. Elizabeth had seen that on television. It was a show she was not supposed to watch, but she watched it one night with a babysitter. The television said that German soldiers would shave women's heads and make the women walk home naked or wearing only shoes. Elizabeth was sure that had happened to Judith Lowery's mother.

So from then on, she decided to be nice to Judith. Because her mother had had her head shaved. She helped her with her schoolwork; she tried to show her how to play "Bluebird, Bluebird, in and out my window." Then one day Judith said to Elizabeth, "I have something good for you." She was smiling. It was not a nice smile; it made Elizabeth feel strange. At first she thought Judith was smiling like that because she wanted Elizabeth to have the box too much. It was a box the right size for a bracelet, and Elizabeth knew that Judith was giving her one of the heirlooms her mother had had to smuggle out of Germany. She opened the box, expecting jewels or treasure. But there was a small dead bird in the box, its eye open, its beak sharp and killing. Elizabeth dropped it and screamed. She could see Judith smiling. Miss Grayson ran over to them, and Elizabeth pointed to the bird box. Miss Grayson changed Judith's seat. She made her put her desk right up in the front of the room near the blackboard, away from the other children. And Elizabeth could see Judith staring at her every day with her small black eyes. And Elizabeth knew that Judith hated her, and what it was like in the war.

That was when she began to have the soldier dream, and now it felt like the dream when her parents opened the door and stepped back for Mrs. Delehanty.

Elizabeth's mother said, "You must be famished," and Mrs. Delehanty said no, and her mother said, "Of course you are," and she would fix some sandwiches. Elizabeth thought that was bad of her mother, leaving the room right away, because Mrs. Delehanty was her friend. Everybody wanted to leave the living room, Elizabeth thought, but only her mother had a reason. And she hated her mother for leaving her alone in the room with her father and Mrs. Delehanty. Her father kept starting to ask questions and not finishing them because he was afraid. Elizabeth saw her father dwindling in his own confusion, like spit going down the sink when you turned the water on. And she thought that her parents did not know what to do with their adulthood, her mother hiding in the kitchen humming, "When the red, red robin goes bob-bob-bobbin' along," her father sitting in his chair, starting questions all wrong, saying "How are things in Lincoln?" and then getting up to change the thermostat. She saw clearly the fixedness of her station, for there was nothing she could cook or cut, no dial for her to tinker with, for she was the child of the house and was in charge of nothing. Nothing was her special province, and yet she knew the right question. She knew what to ask, and would ask it, sitting perfectly still, her white socks crossing each other at the right place as she crossed her ankles.

"Did you have a good flight, Mrs. Delehanty?"

That was all anyone had to say; it was a question anyone could answer. But she was the only one who knew it, and Mrs. Delehanty looked at her with such gratitude that Elizabeth could never like her again.

"It was a smooth flight. It's terrific how quick it took."

That was all, but no one had been able to think of it. Cowards, thought

Elizabeth of her parents. Now her mother could come out of the kitchen and put the tray down in front of Mrs. Delehanty; now her father could rub his hands together and say, "What have we *here?*" Now they could do it. Because Elizabeth knew the right thing to say.

She watched Mrs. Delehanty eating; she watched the shape of the bites in the sandwich when Mrs. Delehanty put it down on the plate to have a sip of soda. And she watched Mrs. Delehanty's hands; she could see dirt under the fingernail of her left pinkie, a thin line of black like an eyebrow under the red of her nail. And she thought with real embarrassment that no one had asked Mrs. Delehanty if she wanted to wash up. She began to blush because she had not thought of it. But then, Mrs. Delehanty hadn't asked, so perhaps she never washed her hands.

Elizabeth tried to figure out whether she liked the way Mrs. Delehanty looked. She wore open-toed shoes, which Elizabeth liked but thought she should not. She wore a light-green dress with white buttons. It was the same green as the toilet paper in the upstairs bathroom. Elizabeth liked that green; it was like cooking apples or lettuce. And she tried to decide if she would choose that color for a dress, if she could choose her colors. Mrs. Delehanty's hair was fixed like Elizabeth's mother's, like everyone's mother's, and Elizabeth knew she would not ever wear her hair like that. She would let her hair grow long and then clip it at the top of her head with one barrette. She would do that for her daughter. She would do that much.

The adults talked about the weight they had gained, what they ate, the clothes they could not fit into.

"Elizabeth's a skinny malink, like I was," said Mrs. Delehanty, lighting a filter-tipped cigarette.

"What about your two?" said Elizabeth's father to Mrs. Delehanty.

Mrs. Delehanty began to cry.

"They're with their grandmother. His mother," she said, sobbing, searching in her handbag for a tissue.

Elizabeth knew she should hear no more; it would be bad for Mrs. Delehanty if she stayed there. She backed away and was upstairs before anyone could see her. She noticed that Mrs. Delehanty put her dirty tissue in the ashtray, in the middle of the ashes.

=======

She had taken off her clothes in the dark because it seemed the right thing to do under the circumstances. She prayed they would not talk loud; she prayed there would be nothing she would have to hear. For if their voices were a certain loudness, she would have to listen. She would have to strain; perhaps she would have to put her head on the floor so she could hear the voices through the ceiling. Sometimes her parents' voices would come through the floor to her, and she would have to hear things. The voices would come through, beautiful as clouds of heat, and a terrible hunger would come on her to hear her parents' voices as though it were the last time, as though, if she could not understand those words, if she went to sleep not understanding, she would never hear those voices again. She was afraid that if she did not strain to listen, she would lose them; if she did not hear her parents, they would be taken from her.

She heard her mother say, "Well, Stan could be like that."

And then her father, "It was the drink, not him."

And Mrs. Delehanty, "What could I do . . . the children."

She made it happen in her mind. She made herself be in the Delehanty's kitchen. She made herself see Mr. Delehanty, tall and blond the way he was in his bathing suit in one of the pictures in the album. She made him drunk, although she had never seen her father drunk. Her mother had once said, "Thank God your father knows his limits." But she knew what men were like. She made the man in the kitchen stumble. She made him say things that were loud and mean. She made him hit his wife.

And then she made herself be Mrs. Delehanty. She made herself afraid and then wanting to hurt. She said to herself, "Remember what you felt about Judith Lowery, about the bird. Remember how you wanted to hurt, how it would feel, lifting up the back of your tongue, making you feel the bones in the head and your back. How everything was heavy." And then she made herself be Mrs. Delehanty, picking up the knife.

Then they all laughed. Downstairs they laughed and coughed and started moving. They were coming up the stairs. Elizabeth closed her eyes. Her mother opened the door. She and Mrs. Delehanty stood above the bed. Mrs. Delehanty put her hand on Elizabeth's forehead. She moved a strand of hair off Elizabeth's face.

"God bless her, what I wouldn't give to sleep like that."

"Kids," said Elizabeth's mother. "They knock themselves out. Especially her. She's very high-strung."

"I was at that age," said Mrs. Delehanty as Elizabeth's mother closed the door behind them.

Elizabeth felt the spot on her head where Mrs. Delehanty had touched her. She felt sweat break out on her lip. She was afraid there was a mark on her head. She had to look. If there was something, she would have to get it off. But there was no mirror in her room. She went into the bathroom.

"You okay?" her mother shouted from the bedroom.

"I need a drink," said Elizabeth.

"Isn't it always the way?" said Mrs. Delehanty, who was standing near the closet of the spare room.

"Good night. I hope you sleep well," said Elizabeth to Mrs. Delehanty. There had been no mark on her head. But she had washed the spot and the hair on that side of her head was wet. It left a wet spot on the pillow.

In the night she dreamed again of soldiers in brown uniforms, of hiding her family's pictures, of saying, even as they tortured her, pushing her spine with the butts of their guns, that there was no one. She was all alone. In the dream they left a mark on her forehead to show she was a captive.

———

Mornings she woke first, always. How long it had been since she'd needed anyone to help her, and how much she liked it to be that way. It was the light she loved best, having the light to herself, and the hum of the refrigerator. She would open the refrigerator door and sometimes on a winter morning the light from the refrigerator would be the only light in the room. But if there was more sun, the light in the refrigerator would inhibit its bright, hard globe of coldness, deeper, full of secrets. It was the time she liked best, and the light that hit the floor sometimes in slats, like the light in China, where the people lived in houses made of paper.

She was standing on her toes to get the orange juice out of the freezer. Sometimes she hated getting the orange juice; the metal top would be completely dry and would stick to the tips of her fingers and for a moment she would panic; she was sure that when she tried to move her finger-tips she would not be able to; perhaps her frozen fingers would be left behind. She heard somebody's footsteps, and she was annoyed. She didn't like it when her mother came down, wakened by some outside stirring, or her father joined her, needing to be early at his job.

But when she turned around it was not her father, needing to be early, or her mother, but Mrs. Delehanty in her purple robe. Her slippers were rose-colored, puckered silk, with ribbons that needed tying at the wide arch.

Elizabeth put the orange juice down on the counter and said, "Good morning. Did you sleep well?"

"I don't sleep well," said Mrs. Delehanty. "Now I hardly sleep at all. I heard you downstairs, and I thought I'd come and make you break-fast."

"You didn't have to," said Elizabeth.

"I was up anyway."

"Usually I don't eat," said Elizabeth. The idea of food from that woman's hands made her feel ill. It was as if someone with a wet and dirty glove had put her hand inside Elizabeth's mouth.

"Your mother said you eat a big breakfast," said Mrs. Delehanty.

"Usually never now," said Elizabeth.

"Your mother said you love your scrambled eggs."

If Mrs. Delehanty cut something with a knife, there would be blood on it. The butter would be full of blood.

"I'll make you some scrambled eggs," said Mrs. Delehanty. Elizabeth could hear the wanting in her voice. It was a danger, as if she had said, "We will probably all be executed." And Elizabeth knew it was the truth about life: If someone wanted to do something so much, you would have to let them. That was what you had to do, especially if something bad had happened to the person who now wanted something.

She took bowls out for Mrs. Delehanty, and the eggs and forks. She saw that there were dark lines under all her fingernails. Dark from dirt. She saw the woman put her hand around the bottle of milk. Elizabeth would not look again, afraid that when she looked again the milk would have turned brown.

She stood in the kitchen, having killed her husband. It could have happened to anyone, Elizabeth's mother said. And now you had to give her what she wanted.

Elizabeth could see the bones of Mrs. Delehanty's back through her thin robe; the wings came out as she beat milk into the eggs. She took the knife and cut the butter. She put butter in the pan. Then she put the eggs on the bubbling butter. The eggs made a hissing noise, as always, like the whispers of cats. If she could just pretend it was her mother. Mrs. Delehanty did the same things at the stove Elizabeth's mother did. It would be just the same. Her mother had made eggs just that same way and had not killed her.

Mrs. Delehanty spooned the eggs onto the turquoise plate. A bit of the liquid ran across the surface. Then she buttered all the toast, from corner to corner, just as Elizabeth's mother would have done. She smiled at Elizabeth and put her hand on the top of Elizabeth's head after she placed the plate before her.

If I can eat this, I can save us all, Elizabeth thought. If I can eat this, we will all be spared. If I can eat this and not die. She prayed as she unfolded her blue paper napkin.

The woman stood behind her, waiting. Elizabeth could hear her anxious breathing in the empty kitchen. Elizabeth moved her plate a quarter of an inch across the table. She prayed for life and for deliverance. Her upper lip was beaded with new sweat. Something in her throat had closed. It was dry; it was a knot of bone, it would not move.

The woman stood behind her in the light that felt like light through heavy water.

"Eat it all," she said.

Elizabeth raised her fork.

THE OTHER WOMAN

She was lying in the spare room in the single bed at three in the morning. It was hot, and her sense of moral failure made her head go queer. She was not asleep, and yet you would have to say she was dreaming. Images behind her eyes buzzed and skipped as in a nightmare.

Two hours before, she had been lying in bed next to her husband. They were reading; sometimes her husband's hand would fondle her belly or scratch her thigh. He would read her a sentence from a book about England; she would look up from her magazine. They would read each other sentences; they would say, "You should read this."

She was reading a story about an adulterous affair. The woman had been left by her lover (who adored her), who went back to his wife. It was the sight of his children's hands as they slept, he had said, that made his decision for him. He loved the woman; he would go back to his wife. Because of the hands of his children as they slept.

She lay back, her arms behind her head, looking at her naked breasts and the curve of her waist. What does this body mean to me? she wondered, and ran her palms along the high bones of her pelvis. How peculiar it was, she thought, looking at her husband, that her body had the power to excite him, to make him lay down his book and turn to her, cupping her buttocks in his hands, wanting her like that. Her sense of the oddness of it all made her distant from him, but she began to feel his desire soothe her; it became a dwelling she could rest inside, and she thought as she met his desire with her own familiar body, How easy it is to be faithful! For it was not his body that excited her (it had never been men's bodies that had excited her), but the idea of him, of all that he was and was to her, that made her rise to meet him, desire for desire. It was the oddness of it all, and the familiarity.

He always became invigorated after sex, with a pure, inappropriate energy. She drew the quilt around her bare shoulders and settled down in the bed. It was sleep she wanted, sleep to flow over her. But she could see the muscles of his back twitching with impatience, like a horse's flanks sucking in and out. The magazine was still on the bed, and she threw it benevolently in his direction. "Read that story," she said. "You'll like it." And she brought the covers over her head so that she could be in darkness. She was content. He was engaged; she had earned the delicious feeling of cool sheets around her shoulders, of roundness, of being what we so rarely feel ourselves to be—in exactly the right place, doing what it is we are meant to do at that moment. The air conditioner hummed soothingly nearby; it was possible to sleep.

She became aware of the peculiar sensation that occurs when the interface between a dream and the world is violated. In her dream she was in a car, driving; outside the dream the bed was shaking with awkward, uneven spasms. She woke in a resentful confusion.

The sight she saw was the one that to her, even in a state of full wakefulness, was most finally disturbing. Her husband was weeping. He was a strong man, even in the obvious senses, and she depended on that. The strength of his body and its predictability were a center for her more random life.

In the years she had known him, he had been sick twice; he had wept four times. She remembered these incidents distinctly. When he wept, his weeping was torn out of his body. She could weep and be engaged in other activities; she could walk and weep or weep and pack a suitcase. But when he wept, his entire body was taken up with it, so that he needed her for physical support.

She sat up quickly and was annoyed by her breasts, bobbing so foolishly, so irrelevantly, as she moved to put her arms around him for comfort only. This now was the function of her body, and the other, earlier one, the one she was reminded of by her breasts, vexed her; it seemed peculiar that she had the same body for comfort as for excitement. It was as though she were divided in some final, harmful way.

She put her arms around him and put his head against her breast. She began to swim up past sleep and became aware that she did not know the reason for his weeping. She stroked his hair and spoke so quietly that her own voice was unfamiliar to her. But her words were coos and nonsense syllables—ancient language she had learned somewhere, in some life. For the moment, she did not want to ask him anything; she did not want to use her language for that.

She looked at his face and wiped his eyes with the sleeve of the night-gown that she had taken from under her pillow. She had never seen anyone look as he did—it was a look of such pure grief, a look of no extraneous emotions. His face looked ancient, as though it bespoke a great sorrow that had not spent itself in mourning. It was the face of a mother holding a dead child, of a wife whose husband has been drowned. One expected such a look from women, but this—this was her husband, a man, and that made it more terrible.

His sobs had stopped and he lay with his head against her in silence.

"My darling," she said. "What is it?"

"The story," he said.

"The story?"

She was surprised, for it was she who lived in stories and he who lived in the world.

"It was when the children were babies," he said. His children both were in their teens now, but still his children, and her husband's love for them, she had come to understand, was the deepest thing in his life. You could not say that it was a love that could come between him and her, because his love for her was outside that center of him, the center that was his love for his children. She had borne no children, and so she had no place in that center. It was as if he and his children stood somewhere at the bottom of a well, in a spot so dark, down so far, that she could not see it. It was not like his past, his divorce, which was another kind of darkness to her, because this with his children continued into her life, into all their lives. But it was a darkness she could live with, for they were children and she was a woman. That difference, she had come to understand, made it all right.

"It was when the children were babies," he said. "There was a woman. I never told you about her." And he began to weep again.

The area under her breast grew cold and stony. She wondered how he could leave his head there.

"I had never loved anyone so much," he said. "She was going to leave her family. We were going to go away. I had never loved anyone so much. I hated my wife; all that was nothing. And then I looked at the children, and I knew that nothing on earth could make me leave them."

"And the woman?" she said, almost sick with the effort it took her to go on holding him.

"She went back to her husband. That was the terrible part—how I failed her. I had never loved anyone so much."

He wanted her to weep with him, to sympathize, for her flesh to warm with his sorrow; and all she could think was, Why must you tell me this? You must not tell me this. How can you expect me to comfort you for this?

Suddenly he sighed, a great sigh, the release of a burden. "It was a very long time ago," he said exhausted, and he wept sleepily against her. But her body was tense with effort. She was his wife, and a wife must do this, must hold her husband in sleep and keep him from his sorrow.

But the idea of hurting him came to her mind like the thought of a delicious confection. She wanted to push him away from her, to let him lie there in the dark, wanting her, in shame, in need. She wanted to say, How you have hurt me! But she held him in her arms and stroked his head until she heard his gentle breathing. Once he was asleep, she could no longer endure the touch of his skin on her skin.

She put on her nightgown and went into the other room. She did not want to open the window for fear of waking him, so she lay in the hot, dusty air, conscious of sweat beginning to form arcs under her breasts. And she thought of her husband, who had loved a woman so much that after all these years her loss was his deepest sorrow. He would never weep like that for her. Often she had imagined her husband's response to her death. And she had always seen him accepting it as a part of their lives, going on, his mourning taking a practical turn. He would think of her, perhaps, in the garden.

For she had been his wife, and their love had known no obstacles. They had met, loved, been free to marry. Their love was even, sweet and temperate, like milk in a brown bowl on a shelf in a fragrant pantry. But, it seemed to her now, such a love might be too mild—toothless, without the edge of frustration to eat its way into his life. Like the other. And so he would never love her so much, so much as he had loved the other woman. Even when she died he would not mourn her so deeply. He could not, for their love had been born of ease and was happy. His love for the other woman had been born of sorrow, and so he would never love her so much as he had loved the other woman.

And how could he ask her for comfort? The coldness under her breast grew until her body was entirely filled with it. And through her mind, in anger, in exhaustion, beeped two sentences: He will never love me so much. How can he ask me for comfort?

She lay on top of the spread, stretching her limbs out as far away from her body as she could. Her sex was open—utterly vulnerable, she thought.

She began to fall into a sleep that was harsh, like rusted wires.

———

She heard the door open. Her husband came into the room, and even in the dark she could see that he was frightened; she could smell his fear in the darkness. But his fear did not move her; inside her were the cold light and the words that buzzed and skipped: He will never love me so much. How can he ask me for comfort?

"I had a terrible dream," he said. He was sweating. She did not tell him to continue, but he lay down beside her and said, "They were in a car. The children and the other woman. The car exploded. I woke up weeping. You weren't there."

"I was restless," she said. "I didn't want to wake you."

She wanted to get up and walk away from him—anywhere, outside into the air. But she stroked his hair and said in a voice that was thick with effort, "Come here. It was only a dream."

She thought surely he would discern the strain in her voice, in her hands. And she was torn between the desire for him to know what he had done to her and the desire to keep it from him, to absorb his sorrow into herself. But since she was a woman, her body had been bred to deceit. How easy it was for her, quite mechanically, with no connection to herself, to soothe her husband, to be a comfort to him. And he settled into her false comfort, pressing against her body for relief. She knew that he would never know what she was feeling, and knowing this, she had never loved him so little.

BILLY

I wasn't home when the call came saying that Billy had died. The woman left the message with my son. Extraordinary, really, to leave such a message with a boy, a ten-year-old. "Just tell your mother Bill McGovern died. I'm his landlady. We found her number in his room, it was the only one we found there. But there's nothing that she needs to do. We buried him already. Just to let her know." She said that Billy had become a hermit in his room. She told my son that they'd kept asking him to come downstairs, for holidays and things, but he'd always say no. "Just send me up a plate," he'd say.

My son reported all this flatly; he is the serious one of the three, the youngest; it was unfortunate the woman got him. He would worry. Worry that someone he never heard of died with his mother's phone number in his room. He is a modern child, the son of modern, divorced parents; he would imagine Billy was my lover. And so I wanted to tell him about Billy, to relieve him, for it would be awful for a boy like him to think of a dead person as his mother's lover. But I didn't know where to begin the story. Or how to tell it once I'd started. To make a story of a life, you had to shape it, and there was no shape to Billy's life, that was the problem. I thanked my son and sent him to his room to join his brothers.

I'd known Billy all my life. His mother was my mother's best friend. I loved Veronica McGovern. She brought into my childhood, books, classical records, prints of the Old Masters, and a hint that there was somewhere a world—which she had once inhabited and now only imagined—where people had intelligent conversations in low, untroubled voices, where no one ever worked too hard or got too tired. She flipped the switch of my imagination, lighting up those rooms that are a refuge from the anger and miscomprehension of the adult world. She saved me from the isolated fate of the bright, undervalued child. She spared me years of bitterness. But she ruined her son's life as certainly as if she'd starved him in infancy; he would probably have been much better off if she'd abandoned him at birth.

Veronica had always lied about her age; she was eleven years older than my mother, though we never knew it till her death. She'd married at eighteen and had Billy a year later; my mother had had me at thirty-one. So although Billy and I were technically in the same generation, he was twenty-two when I was born. I thought him handsome when I was growing up; some nights he didn't come home and Veronica wrung her hands and mentioned the name Roberta. It was such a serviceable name and yet the woman cast so lurid a glow. She lived in the Village; she was a dancer; when Billy was with her he didn't come home. I had no idea what Billy and Roberta did the nights that he was with her; I had no idea that it was *what* they did that caused Veronica's distress; I was young enough simply to see not sleeping in one's own bed as an emblem of danger.

Billy would come home after these nights at around lunchtime; my mother and I would be sitting at Veronica's kitchen table and at the sight of him we would fall silent. He shimmered with the glow of sex, though at the time I wouldn't have known to call it that. There was always a beat of silence when we saw him in the doorway, like the silence between merry-go-round tunes. Then he would say, "Hello, Mother." Veronica would light a Herbert Tareyton cigarette and tell him to bring a chair from his room. There were only three chairs in the kitchen, a setup left over from the days when Charlie McGovern, Veronica's husband, Billy's father, who died when I was nine, was still alive.

I'd grown up on tales of Charlie Mcgovern's binges and disappearances, and Billy had been pointed to as an example of what can happen when a single mother spoiled a child. My father disappeared when I was two; it was handy for my mother to have so ready an example. "Spoiled." It is a terrible word, suggesting meat gone iridescent, but in Billy's case, it has always seemed apt. My mother explained that Veronica had never said no to Billy. Life with Charlie devastated her and she wanted to keep Billy by her side. In return for his loyalty she indulged him and convinced him that the world was too gross to value him correctly; in time, he believed it an unfit place for him to walk in as a man.

I only knew Charlie McGovern as a drunk, but in the twenties he had been a millionaire. To a child in the early fifties, the twenties were like the fall of Rome, something much too distant to think of concretely or even to believe in. Had Veronica McGovern been a flapper? Impossible to connect that sweet, wounded, muted and above all genteel creature with the Jazz Age, but when she spoke about the early days of her marriage, it was all bathtub gin and the Black Bottom and rides in rumble seats and staying up till dawn. She mentioned that Charlie always bought her perfumed cigarettes and stockings with her name embroidered just at the top. Hearing about those stockings caused a river of electric joy to run through every nerve in my six, seven, eight-year-old body; it was one of those pieces of information children instantly know to be crucial, some essential clue to the incomprehensible maze of adult life, although they cannot place quite the significance of the small jewel so casually presented. I decided that at least I knew that Veronica and Charlie had once been in love, the love, perhaps, of people in the movies. But what had come of it? No two people could less suggest what my idea was of the love between men and women: Charlie so clearly embodying ruin in his bathrobe with its sash of fraying rope, Veronica, devoting her physical existence to concealing any hint of sex.

She clearly thought about how she looked: her impression of well-bred decay could not have been achieved by accident. I remember my shock when I realized as a quite young child that Veronica wore no brassiere. I fell asleep once in her lap and awoke with my arms around her torso. She must have sat perfectly still all the time I slept. Pretending to be still half asleep, I ran my fingers up and down her back as if it were a clavichord. I kept playing her back, not knowing what it was I missed. When I realized what it was it came to me to pity her, for it was pitiable that she had nothing to show for her womanhood, nothing like my mother's fine, high bolster of a bosom I had always been so happily able to trust. She wore 4711 Cologne—an androgynous scent in an age when the sexes shared almost nothing. Her shoes were a generation out of date: round-toed and laced and made to match some pre-war dream. She was personally fastidious, but when three of her bottom teeth fell out she couldn't bring herself to see a dentist, but filled in the gap with strips of wax.

And so, of course, it was shocking when Billy came home from a night with Roberta. I can see now that Veronica must have tried to incorporate her son's girlfriend into the fabric of her frail domestic life. She would ask about Roberta in a tentative, good-humored way, and Billy would reply in vague terms, but without bad spirits. I don't know if the women ever met, but Roberta must have tried in some ways to ingratiate herself, for I remember a birthday card she sent Veronica. On the front of the card, a smiling sausage said, "I wish you the happiest birthday ever." On the inside of the card, the same sausage, now fatter and smilier said, "And that's no Baloney!"

It seemed to me then that the birthday card was a clue to what was between Billy and Roberta, for Billy was by profession a cartoonist. He drew bosomy showgirls in the laps of sailors, or forlorn sex-starved *schlemiels* looking with longing at signs saying "Exotic Dancers." I don't know whether Billy made a living from cartooning before I was old enough to notice such things, but by the time I could understand, it was clear to me that he lived off his mother. She taught third grade in a public school in Harlem; she was a passionate teacher and she loved her work. I realize now that she never talked about her students' being black; given her nature, it is possible she didn't notice. When she came home from school, Billy was often still in bed. This *did* distress her. When she mentioned the fact to my mother, it was the only time I ever heard anything in her voice to suggest that something in her life had gone awry.

By the time I was twelve, Roberta was off the scene for good and Billy had hit the skids in earnest. He'd lost his looks; the dashing, slightly wicked ladies' man had turned into a fat mick with two days' growth of beard most of the days he cared to come out of his room. I don't know how often he left his room when he and his mother were alone in the apartment, but when my mother and I arrived, he was never visible, nor could he be counted upon to appear. When he did join us, he was affable and some-times witty, but his interest in us was limited, and he clearly longed to be back in his room.

The year I turned fifteen, I spent a week with Veronica and Billy while my mother was in the hospital for an appendectomy. I realized gradually that I'd become interesting to Billy; it was my first hint that I might in any way engage a grownup male. And although I could see that Billy was no prize in the particularities of his condition, his membership in the estate of adult malehood had its potency. I flirted with him—it was dreadful of me, of course, but then who ever thought of teenage girls as anything but savage. He took me bowling and bought me a beer. I didn't like it after the first few daring sips and asked for a Coke. He laughed and said I was a cheap date. I was alarmed and not a little bit insulted. I knew it was sex I was playing with, and not in its nicest aspects. I didn't know that calling someone a "cheap date" was a joke or a compliment; I was mistaken in the meaning of the words, but the unease I felt was right.

Billy and I walked out of the bowling alley, feeling the smoky blue air we'd just left behind to be the norm. Even the tainted air of the Bronx seemed too pure for Billy and me; I felt that we were seething with corruption. As we walked down the street, we ran into some of Billy's friends. They were as corpulent as he, and as ill-shaven; only it seemed they had been born to the bodies they were now inhabiting; it was clear to me that Billy had stepped down into his.

"Hey, Len, I want you to meet my girlfriend," Billy said, putting his arm around my shoulder.

Some genius made me go along with Billy; I was outraged at his suggestion, but I wanted to protect him from his friends. Clearly, if there were sides, I belonged on Billy's.

His friend Len, who wore a short-sleeved checked shirt and had a tattoo of an anchor on his forearm, snorted, "Guess you're robbing the cradle, for a change."

"I'm only kidding, Len," he said. "This is my mother's best friend's kid. I used to change her diapers."

These words angered me as his suggestion of our coupling hadn't. Both were false, but one falsehood elevated me to an honorific, if shameful position; the other simply reduced me to a child. And since I was much closer to being a child than a sexual adventuress, I resented Billy's revision. I wanted to tell them that it wasn't true that Billy'd changed my diapers, that he'd never done a helpful thing in his life. But Billy hadn't moved his hand off my shoulder, and I felt the urgency of his need for my loyalty thrum through his fingers. And so I looked sullen, but didn't move away.

"I bet you'd like to change her diapers now," Len snorted. His two friends snorted along with him, caricatures of simple-minded, fleshly-hearted sidekicks.

"Knock it off, Len," Billy said, stepping between the men and me, suddenly my gallant protector.

"Okay, Billy," Len said. "I didn't mean nothing by it. Just run along home to your mommy and forget it."

Then they were gone, moving away from us in a collective shift of bulk. For a moment, I was afraid Billy was going to cry.

"No one understands what it's like for me," he said, not looking at me. "Living with my mother. Living off her. I know I'm a mess but I can't help it. She made me a mess and the army finished the job. You know I'm on veteran's disability. You know that, don't you? I don't live off my mother. I pay my share of the rent. And don't you forget it," he said, shaking his finger at me.

"I won't," I said, in a frightened voice. I'd never lived with adult males; their rage was as foreign to me as space talk, and as terrifying.

"Listen, I'm sorry. I'm not myself these days. You know what I used to be like. Do I seem myself to you?"

"No," I said. I had no idea what could possibly be the right answer to that question.

"Let's go get a soda," he said. "I think you understand me. And by the way, don't say anything to my mother about meeting up with Len. She doesn't understand that kind of thing. You know, she was never in the army," he said, as if he were clearing up a misapprehension.

We went into an ice-cream parlor and both ordered hot fudge sundaes. Billy told me about his disability; it was lupus; he'd contracted it in Biloxi; he'd never even been sent overseas because of it. It meant he could never go out in the sun, he said; too much sun could make him look like a monster in half an hour. He never quite explained what would happen and I hadn't the nerve to ask.

"I like talking to you," he said. "You know how to listen. Always remember this: there's nothing more attractive to a man than a woman who really knows how to listen to him."

This was precisely the sort of information I most wanted; it made me willing to listen to him, to hang on through the long, self-pitying narrations to the bright, occasional sentence that would let me into the secret world of men. After a week, my mother came home from the hospital. Veronica was so grateful to me for "getting Billy out of himself" that she bought me a volume of Christina Rossetti. I'd asked for E. E. Cummings, but she said she'd wait till Christmas for that. Meanwhile, wouldn't I try Christina Rossetti, try to make a friend of her? I did as Veronica said, I read Christina Rossetti, but it was fifteen years before I could see her as anything but maudlin. Veronica kept her word, though, even after I told her I didn't like Christina Rossetti. She gave me Cummings' collected poems as a Christmas gift. I explained to her that I liked Cummings better because he wasn't a phony. I could have died when I saw the look on her face. Never had anybody looked so sad, so wounded, so unhopeful. And

I had done it. I could never take it back. I had done what Billy must have done a thousand times, and it disturbed me to feel so much kinship with him.

Soon after my time at Billy and Veronica's, I got my first boyfriend. It wouldn't have occurred to me to be grateful to Billy; I couldn't have known that it was his attentions that had given me the confidence to present myself as a desirable female. And so with the perfect heartlessness of a young girl in love for the first time, I couldn't bring myself to speak to Billy. I wouldn't go with my mother to Veronica's house. If Billy phoned and asked for me, I commanded my mother to say I was in the shower, or sick or sleeping. "Tell him I'm with my boyfriend," I said meanly to my mother, wanting at once to punish Billy for his presumptions, and to flaunt my status before his damaged countenance. Teenagers are pack animals; instinctively they turn on the wounded member and fall upon him, then run off. Occasionally, I would answer the phone when Billy called and I'd be forced into a conversation. Realizing the perfunctoriness of my presence, Billy would try to get my attention by telling dirty jokes. How completely he misunderstood our fragile, temporary bond! It wasn't the brute facts of sex I was interested in, had ever been interested in. What I'd valued in Billy's conversation was a clue to the rules of courtship. That courtship could potentially end in the kind of thing Billy told jokes about and could only outrage me. I was disgusted, and I lost what little faith I had in him as a source of information that could do me any good.

Veronica died when I was twenty; Billy, then, must have been forty-two years old. The cable between his house and ours was cruelly cut; he had no reason, really, to regularly get in touch with us. On holidays, his birthday, my mother made obligatory calls, but the news of his life was too dispiriting to encourage any but the smallest contact. For, as far as we could figure, he did nothing. He had no work, no friends. He said his mother had been right, his friends were no good. He said he felt better off just keeping to himself. We heard from neighbors of his that he'd grown obese, that he sometimes passed out at the local bar and had to be carried home—no mean feat since he was reported to weigh two hundred seventy-five pounds. The neighbors said he'd been told he was diabetic, so he was eating and drinking himself to death.

The last time I spoke to him was the night before my wedding. He'd been invited, but he hadn't sent back the little card that said——will—— attend. We were sure that he wouldn't come; perhaps we wouldn't have invited him if we'd thought there was a chance of his coming. We only heard from him when he was drunk; he'd call and talk about his mother with a sentimental tenderness the sources of which had never been obvious while his mother had lived. His relationship to her had been marked by a grudging deference that could turn to rudeness like the crack of a whip. And she had curved herself into a shape that would obtrude into his life as little as possible until he needed her reassurance that his failures were attributable not to his own deficiencies but to the sheer corruption of the brutish world.

Billy was the last person I wanted to speak to on the night before my wedding. I'd decided I hated my veil; I'd been hysterical for hours, and not in much mood to be polite. But I knew that this large and complicated wedding could only be paid for by my doing my bride's job of graciousness. Think of Veronica, my mother said, but what she meant was, think of all I've just done for you. And she *had* done everything, and done it well; it was surprising that she'd done it at all considering how much she disliked my fiancé.

I could tell Billy was drunk the moment he started speaking.

"I'll bet you're a pretty little bride," he said.

"All brides are pretty, Billy," I said impatiently.

"And what's the lucky man like?"

"Handsome, smart and madly in love with me."

"And what's he like in bed? Oh, I forgot, you're not supposed to know that. White for a virgin. White. But what color's the groom wearing?"

"Black, Billy. The men don't matter at a wedding."

"Just tell me one thing, honey. I just want you to tell me one thing. Did I ever have a chance?"

"A chance?"

"A chance with you. I mean, did you ever think about me?"

I felt filled up with disgust. To imagine that that gross, drunken creature thought of taking the place of my perfect, princely husband to be! I couldn't bear to talk to him another second.

"I've got to go, Billy. I've got a lot to do."

"Sure, honey. I'll call you up sometime."

"Sure, Billy, my mother has my new number."

===

But of course he never called, and I would never call him. He knew of my divorce; my mother made a round of what she felt were *de rigueur* informing calls; it took a year, but in the end she got through everyone in her address book.

I think of Billy now as I make dinner for the children. I think of him eating by himself on holidays, in furtiveness, in shame, off the landlady's plate. I wonder why he didn't kill himself straight out. What could life have been to him, what could his waking after noon each day have signaled but one more round of fresh defeats? I wonder, too, with the inevitable egotism of the living, if he thought of me after I was divorced, if he imagined a place for himself here, with my sons, in a house as fatherless as his had been. And I hate the thought of him thinking of me, of us, like that.

I would like to blame somebody. Billy or Veronica. Roberta or the landlady. I would like, even, to take the burden of his ruin on myself, to imagine that had I not stayed in their house when I was fifteen, his life might have been different. I would like to point to one specific moment, one incident embedded in his history and say: Here everything went wrong.

But I cannot find a moment solid, powerful enough to blame. It seems impossible that anything could have been other than it was. I call my sons for dinner. Irritable, I tell them they should make more friends. They are fourteen, twelve and ten: they regard my suggestion with various tones of incomprehension. Too soon after supper, it seems to me, they disappear into their rooms.

I realize I must say something to them. I don't want to; anger takes me over: I blame their father for his absence. Were he here now I could say "What should we do? What do I have to tell them?" There is no one to turn to. My mother is in her room now in the home run by the Visitation Sisters, in the plain, unyielding senile fog that has become her habitation, and will always be, until her death. There is no one but me to speak to the children. There is no one who knew Billy and knows them now but me.

The apartment seems too big although our problem in reality is that we are quite cramped. But the ceilings loom, the walls push out, refusing shelter, the no-wax linoleum glares up. I walk into their bedroom where they sit in the unreal half-light of TV, aquarium, beneath the ever-changing posters: now Police, Graig Nettles, Sting. I tell them I would like to talk to them, when they are ready. Astonishingly, they turn off the TV. They have been waiting.

"I wanted to tell you about Billy," I tell them. And I do say something, tell the outlines of his life, abstract the epochs, as if I were giving a lecture on prehistory: the Pleistocene, the Paleolithic. I speak about the army days, and his cartooning and the final, long demise.

"He sounds like a complete fuckup to me," says my oldest son. "A real loser."

"You're being a little hard," I say. "Things weren't easy for him." I neglect to fill in the details; it would not be tactful to speak to three fatherless boys about the devastations of a father's abandonment.

"So, things are hard for everyone. Big deal," my oldest son says. He is the unforgiving one. My strongest ally in refusing to forgive his father.

"Why do you think it happened to him?" asks my second son, the scientist.

"I don't know," I tell him. "That's what's hard to figure out."

But all this time I have known that the worried eyes of the youngest were fixed on us, needing reassurance, frightened of the spectacle of Billy's life, seeing it, of the three of them, most vividly.

"It couldn't happen to people like us, though, could it?" he asks. He is speaking for the group.

They gather from the far corners of their diverse positions here, with me in the still center. Do they want to know the truth? Will the truth help them?

I am thinking of Veronica. I think that what she did was tell the truth to Billy, but too early, and too much. The world is cruel, she told him, it is frightening, and it will hurt you. She told him this with every caress, with every word of praise and spoon of medicine. And he believed her. Well, of course he would. She was telling the truth; she was his mother.

I will not tell these boys the truth. To protect them, I will dishonor Billy. I will make him out a monster and a sport. I will deny his commonality to the three who sit before me, waiting for an answer. Not the truth, but something that will let them live their lives.

"No," I tell them. "It doesn't happen to people like you. Billy wasn't like you. He was not like you at all."

SAFE

I

*T*he morning starts with a child's crying. By arrangement I ignore it; by arrangement, my husband, who does not see the morning as I do —the embezzler of all cherished wealth, thief of all most rare and precious —gets the child and brings her to me. Still asleep, I offer her my breast, and she, with that anchoritic obsession open only to saints and infants, eats, and does not think to be offended that her mother does not offer her the courtesy of even a perfunctory attention, but sleeps on. There is a photograph of the two of us in this position. My eyes are closed, the blankets are around my chin. My daughter, six months old, puts down the breast to laugh into the camera's eye. Already she knows it is a good joke: that she is vulnerable, utterly, and that the person who has pledged to keep her from all harm, can do, in fact, so little to protect her. Is a person, actually, who can swear that never in her life has she awakened of her own accord. Yet, miraculously, she feels safe with me, my daughter, and settles in between my breast and arm for morning kisses. This is the nicest way I know to wake up. I have never understood people who like to be awakened with sex: what one wants, upon awakening is something gradual, predictable, and sex is just the opposite, with all its rushed surprises.

I carry my daughter into the bathroom. My husband, her father, stands at the mirror shaving, stripped to the waist. How beautiful he is. I place my cheek on his back and embrace him. The baby plays at our feet. In the mirror I can see my arms, my hands around his waist, but not my face. I like the anonymity. I take my nightgown off and go into the shower. Every time I take a shower now, I worry about the time when water will be rationed, when I will have to wash in a sink in cold water. My mother knew a nun who, after twenty-five years in the convent, was asked what gift she would like to celebrate her silver jubilee. She asked for a hot bath. What did that mean about the twenty-five years of her life before that? All her young womanhood gone by without hot baths. I would not have stuck it out.

I step out of the shower and begin to dry myself. I see the two of them looking at me: man and child, she in his arms. She stretches out her arms to me in that exaggerated pose of desperation that can make the most well-fed child suggest that she belongs on a poster, calculated to rend the heart, urging donations for the children of a war zone or a famine-stricken country. I take her in my arms. She nose-dives for my breast. My husband holds my face in both his hands. "Don't take your diaphragm out," he says. Just ten minutes ago, I fed my child; just last night I made love to my husband. Yet they want me again and again. My blood is warmed, then fired with well-being. Proudly, I run my hands over my own flesh, as if I had invented it.

11

The baby is predictable now. We know that she will want a nap at nine-fifteen, just after we have finished breakfast. I put her in her crib and wait until I hear her even breathing. Does she dream? What can she dream of, having lived so little? Does she dream of life inside my body? Or does she dream for the whole race?

My husband is in bed waiting for me. Deep calls to deep: it must have been sex they were talking about. I want him as much as ever. Because of this, because of what I feel for him, what he feels for me, of what we do, can do, have done together in this bed, I left another husband. Broke all sorts of laws: the state's, the church's. Caused a good man pain. And yet it has turned out well. Everyone is happier than ever. I do not understand this. It makes a mockery of the moral life, which I am supposed to believe in.

All the words of love, of sex and love, the simple words; have, take, come, now, words of one syllable. Behind my eyes I see green leaves, high, branching trees, then rocks that move apart and open. Exhausted, we hold each other, able to claim love. The worst thing about casual sex is not being able to express love honestly afterward. One feels it, but knows it to be false. Not really love. Yet, is it not inevitable to love one who has proffered such a gift?

We drift into sleep, knowing the baby's nap will not last long. She cries; the day begins for real. I am taking her into the city to see an old lover.

III

Of all the men I have been with, M—— found me consistently, astonishingly, pleasing. We had five months together in a foreign city, London, where he was almost the only one I knew. I was married then, to my first husband, who did not praise, who thought of me as if I were colonial Africa: a vast, dark, natural resource, capable, possibly, of civilization. As it turns out, I did not want his civilization—a tendency colonialists have discovered to their sorrow.

M—— is, as they say, well bred, but with him, the phrase has real meaning. Only centuries of careful marriages could have produced, for example, his nose. There are no noses like it in America, which got only the riffraff for its settlers, or those who must fear beauty as a snare. His nose is thin and long, the nostrils beautifully cut, the tip pointed down slightly to the full, decisive lips. He is the blondest man I have ever been with—this, in combination with his elegant, well-cut clothes, made him a disappointment naked. Really fair men always look foolish without their clothes, as if they ought to know better.

M—— likes to pretend that I have been married so many times he can't keep track. In letters, he tells me he imagines me inviting the milkman, the postman, the butcher into bed to thank them for their services. I write that there are no milkmen in America, the postman is a woman, and I buy meat in the supermarket. Don't quibble, he replies, suggesting my gynecologist, my lawyer, the man who does my taxes.

It is all praise, it is all a reminder of my power, and I thrive on it, particularly as we spoke last time we saw each other openly, about the pleasures of friendship without the intrusions of sex. I was newly married then, and he took no small pride in the court adviser/Dutch uncle tone he spoke in when he warned me against the dangers of infidelity. I told him he needn't worry; I had learned my lesson; I wanted to have a child. And besides my husband made me happier than I had ever been. So then you're safe, he said, as safe as houses. I didn't like the image: I knew the kind of houses that were meant: large and wide and comfortably furnished: it made me see myself as middle-aged, a German woman with thick legs and gray bobbed hair.

It is with a high heart that I ride down on the bus on a spring morning. The countryside is looking splendid: frail greens against a tentative blue sky, the turned earth brown and ready. M——'s nose is not his only benefice: his manners, too, are lovely. They are courtly, and I dream of my daughter meeting him at Claridge's one day for tea, when she is twelve, perhaps, and needing flattery. I look at her in my arms, proud of what I have come up with. This rosy flesh is mine, this perfect head, this soft, round mouth. And of course, I think we make a charming picture, rightly observed and I count on M—— for the proper angle.

The city pavements sparkle and the sun beams off the building glass. We get a taxi in a second—I am covered over with beneficence, the flattering varnish of good luck. But my luck changes and we are stuck in traffic for forty-five minutes. M—— hates lateness—he thinks it is rudeness—and I know this will get the day off to a bad start.

He is waiting for me in the sculpture garden of the Museum of Modern Art. He does not look pleased to see me, but it is not his way to look pleased. He says he hates his first sight of people he loves: they always expect too much from his face and it makes him feel a failure.

I apologize nervously, excessively, for being late. He steers us silently toward the cafeteria. I am wearing the baby in a front pack sling, when I take her out and give her to M——— to hold, she screams. He asks me what she likes to eat. "Me," I say, but he is not amused. "Get her some yogurt," I say, feeling foolish.

"And you?" he asks.

"Oh, anything," I say.

"You always say that," he says, frowning, "and you always have something specific in mind. You've lost an earring."

He looks at the baby. "Your mother is always losing earrings in the most extraordinary places, at the most extraordinary times." She looks him squarely in the eye and screams. He moves off with a shudder.

Finally, the yogurt pleases the baby, and her good temper is restored. I ask M——— about his visit, and he is noncommittal, uninformative. I begin to fear that he has crossed the ocean to see me. He wants to talk about the past, our past; he keeps bringing up details in a way that makes me know he thinks about me often. He keeps taking my hand, squeezing it in studied, meaningful patterns of pressure, but I keep having to pull my hand away to take things from the baby, or to hold her still. Besides, I don't want to hold his hand. Not in that way. I begin to feel unsettled, and start chattering, diverting much of my foolish talk to the baby, a habit in mothers I have always loathed.

"I've got us theater tickets for tonight," says M———. "And you must tell me where you would most like to have dinner."

I look at him with alarm. "I can't possibly go to the theater with you. I have to get home with the baby. You should have said something."

"I thought you'd know that's what would happen. It's what we always did."

"I never had a baby before. Or a marriage, not a real one. Surely you must know we can't go on a *date.*"

"Obviously I don't know anything about you any more. Come on, let's look at the pictures."

I try to put my arms through the sling, but it is a complicated arrangement if one is trying to hold the baby at the same time, and I know she will not go with M——. He stands behind me, helping me to put my arms through the straps. His hand brushes my breast, but instead of moving his hand away, he cups my breast with it.

I am covered over in panic. For the first time in my life, I am shocked by a man's touch. I understand for the first time the outraged virgin, for I am offended by the *impropriety* of such a gesture, indicating, as it does, a radical misunderstanding of my identity. He cannot have free access to my body, not just because it is mine, but because it stands for something in the world, for some idea. My body has become symbolic. I laugh at the idea as soon as it occurs to me, and M—— looks hurt, but I continue to laugh at the notion of myself as icon. My actual virginity I gave up with impatience and dispatch; an encumbrance I was eager to be rid of. Now, fifteen years later, I stand blushing.

We try to look at pictures, but it is no good, the baby cries incessantly. Besides, we really do not want to be together any more. He puts me in a taxi and tries to embrace me, but the baby is strapped to me and all he can manage is a chaste and distant kiss on the cheek. It is the first time I have disappointed him; and I feel the failure all the way home. The baby falls asleep the minute she gets on the bus; she was crying from exhaustion. I do not know what I was thinking of, making this expedition. Or I know precisely what I had been thinking of, and cannot now believe I was so foolish.

IV

It is evening. My husband and I are going to dinner at our favorite restaurant. The girl who is taking care of the baby is a girl I love. Seventeen, she is the daughter of a friend, a woman I love and admire, a woman of accomplishment whose children are accomplished and who love her. E—— is beautiful, a beauty which would be a bit inhuman if she understood its power, and were it not tempered by her sweetness and her modesty. I know her well; she lived with us in the summer. I was relieved to be unable to assume a maternal role with her; I believed, and still believe, that she sees me as a slatternly older sister, good at heart but scarcely in control. She plays the flute; she gets my jokes; she speaks perfect French; she does the dishes without being asked. The baby adores her. We can leave telling her nothing but the phone number of the restaurant. She knows everything she needs to know.

It is not a good dinner. I want to tell my husband about M—— but cannot. It is not his business; spouses should never be able to image their fears of their beloved's being desired by another. And I may want to see M—— again. I am distracted, and my husband knows me well enough to know it. We are both disappointed for we do not have much time alone. We do not linger over after-dinner drinks, but come home early to find E—— in the dark, crying. My husband leaves her to me; he has always said that a woman, however young, does not want to be seen in tears by a man who is not her lover. In the car, I ask her what is wrong.

"It's R——," she says, her first boyfriend, with whom I know she has broken up. "It's awful to see him every day, and not be able to talk to him."

"Mm," I say, looking at the dark road.

"It's just so awful. He used to be the person in the world I most wanted to see, most wanted to talk to, and now I rush out of classes so I don't have to pass him in the halls."

"It's hard."

"Was it like that for you? First loving someone, then running away from the sight of them?"

"Yes, it happened to me a lot." I conjure in my mind the faces of ten men once loved.

"Do you think people can ever be friends when they fall out of love with each other?"

"I suppose so. I've never been able to do it. Some people can."

She looks at me with anguish in the dark, cold car. "It's such a terrible waste. I can't bear it, I don't think. Do you think it's all worth it?"

"I don't think there's an alternative," I say.

"What a relief it must be that it's all over for you."

So this is how she sees me: finished, tame, bereft of possibilities. I kiss her good-night, feeling like that German woman with thick legs. Lightly, E—— runs through the beam of the headlights over the grass to her house. I wait to see that she is in the door.

Her urgent face is in my mind as I drive home, and M——'s face and the face of ten loved men. I realize that I am old to E——, or middle-aged, and that is worse. The touch of M——'s hand on my breast gave me no pleasure. That has never happened to me before.

I have never thought of myself as old; rather I fear that I am so young-seeming that I lack authority in the outside world. I feel the burdens of both youth and age. I am no longer dangerous, by reason of excitement, possibility—but I cannot yet compel by fear. I feel as if the light had been drained from my hair and skin. I walk into the house, low to the ground, dun-colored, like a moorhen.

My husband is in bed when I return. I look in at the baby. Under her yellow blanket her body falls and rises with her breath. I wash my face and get into my nightgown. It is purple cotton, striped; it could belong to a nun. I think of the nightwear of women in films whose bodies glow with danger: Garbo, Dietrich, Crawford. Faye Dunaway, who has a baby and is not much older than I. I see my husband is not yet asleep. He takes me in his arms. I ask, "Do you ever think of me as dangerous?"

He laughs. "Let me try to guess what you've been reading. *Anna Karenina? Madame Bovary? Vanity Fair?*"

"I'm serious. I'll bet you never think of me as dangerous."

He holds me closer. "If I thought of you as dangerous, I'd have to think of myself as unsafe."

I pull him toward me. I can feel his heart beating against my breast. Safe, of course he must be safe with me. He and the baby. Were they unsafe, I could not live a moment without terror for myself. I know that I must live my life now knowing it is not my own. I can keep them from so little; it must be the shape of my life to keep them at least from the danger I could bring them.

In a few hours, the baby will awaken, needing to be fed again. My husband takes my nightgown off.

THE DANCING PARTY

know why you're in this mood," says the angry wife, "I just wish you'd admit it."

They drive in darkness on the sandy road; she has no confidence that he will find the house, which they have only seen in daylight. And she half wishes he would get a wheel stuck in the sand. She would be pleased to see him foolish.

"I'm in a bad mood for one reason," says the husband. "Because you said to me: Shape up. No one should say that to someone: Shape up."

"I could tell by your face how you were planning to be. That way that makes the other people at a party want to cut their throats."

"Must I sparkle to be allowed among my kind?"

"And I know why you're like that. Don't think I don't. It's because you watched the children while I swam. For once."

"Yes, it's true, the day was shaped by your desires. But I'm not resentful. Not at all. You must believe me."

"But I don't believe you."

"Then where do we go?"

"We go, now, to the party. But I beg you: Please don't go in with your face like that. It's such a wonderful idea, a dancing party."

The house is built atop the largest dune. In daylight you can see the ocean clearly from the screened-in porch. The married couple climb the dune, not looking at each other, walking far apart. When they come to the door, they see the hostess dancing with her brother.

How I love my brother, thinks the hostess. There are no men in the world like him.

The hostess's brother has just been divorced. His sister's house is where he comes, the house right on the ocean, the house she was given when her husband left her for someone else. Her brother comes here for consolation, for she has called it "my consolation prize." And it *has* been a consolation, and still is, though she is now, at forty-five, successful. She can leave her store to her assistants, take a month off in the summer, and come here. She earns more money than her ex-husband, who feels, by this alone, betrayed. She comes, each morning, to the screened-in porch and catches in the distance the blue glimpse of sea, the barest hint, out in the distance, longed for, but in reach. She'd brought her daughters here for the long, exhausting summers of the single mother. Watched their feuds, exclusions, the shore life of children on long holiday, so brimming and so cruel. But they are grown now, and remarkably, they both have jobs, working in the city. One is here, now, for the weekend only. Sunday night, tomorrow, like the other grownups, she will leave. The daughter will be in her car, stuck in the line of traffic, that reptilian creature that will take her in its coils. Exhausted, she will arrive in her apartment in Long Island City. She will wait till morning to return her rented car.

I will not be like my mother, thinks the daughter of the hostess. I will not live as she lives. How beautiful she is, and how I love her. But I will not live like that.

She lifts an angry shoulder at the poor young man, her partner, who does not know why. She is saying: I will not serve you or your kind. I will not be susceptible.

She sees her mother, dancing, not with her brother any longer, but with another man. She sees her mother's shoulder curving toward him. Sees her mother's head bent back. Susceptible. Will this be one more error of susceptibility? Oh, no, my mother, beautiful and still so young, do not. Shore up and guard yourself. As I have. Do not fall once more into those arms that seem strong but will leave you. Do not fall.

The daughter leaves the young man now to dance with the best friend of her mother. This woman has no·husband and a child of two. The mother with no husband and a child of two dreams of her lover as she dances with the daughter of the hostess. She thinks: I have known this girl since she was five. How can it be? I have a child of two; my best friend has a daughter who lifts her angry shoulder and will drive away on Sunday to the working world. Do not be angry at your mother, the mother with no husband wants to say. She is young, she is beautiful, she needs a man in her bed. The mother with no husband thinks of her own lover, who is someone else's husband, and the father of the two-year-old child. Someday, she thinks, it is just possible that we will live together, raise together, this boy of ours, now only mine. She longs for her lover; she spends, she thinks in anger, too much life on longing. But she chose that. Now she thinks about his hair, his ribcage, the feel of his bones when she runs her fingers up his back, the shape of his ear when she can see him in the distance. She thinks: He is torn, always. When the child was conceived she said, being nearly forty: I will have it. There is nothing you need do. He said: I will stand with you. He came on the first day of their son's life and visits weekly—uncle? friend?—and puts, each month, three hundred dollars in a small account and in a trust fund for college. Says: I cannot leave my wife. The mother with no husband longs sometimes to be with her lover in a public place, dancing, simply, like the married couple, without fear among the others of their kind.

The scientist has come without her lover. He has said: Oh, go alone. You know I hate to dance. She phoned her friend, a man in love with other men. Come dancing with me. Yes, of course, he says. He is glad to be with her; he too is a scientist. They work together; they study the habits of night birds. They are great friends. The lover of the scientist is brilliant, difficult. In ten years she has left him twice. She thinks now she will never leave him.

The daughter of the hostess puts on music that the angry wife, the mother with no husband and the scientist don't like. So they sit down. Three friends, they sit together on the bench that rests against the wall. They look out the large window; they can see the moon and a newly lit square white patch of sea. They like each other; they are fortyish; they are successful. For a month each summer they live here by the ocean, a mile apart. The angry wife is a bassoonist of renown. The mother with no husband writes studies of women in the ancient world. These women, all of them, have said to each other: What a pleasure we are, good at what we do. And people know it. The angry wife has said: You know you are successful when you realize how many people hope that you will fail.

And how are you? they ask each other. Tired say the two, the angry wife, the mother with no husband, who have young children. I would like to have a child, the scientist says. Of course you must, say the two who are mothers. Now they think with pleasure of the soft flesh of their children, of their faces when they sleep. Oh, have a child, they tell the scientist. Nothing is better in the world.

Yes, have a child, the hostess says. Look at my daughter. See how wonderful. The daughter of the hostess has forgotten, for a time, her anger and is laughing with the young man. Asks him: Are you going back on Sunday? Would you like a ride? The hostess thinks: Good, good. My daughter will not drive alone. And maybe he will love her.

I am afraid of being tired, says the scientist to her three friends.

You will be tired if you have a child, they say to her. There is no getting round it. You will be tired all the time.

And what about my work?

You will do far less work. We must tell you the truth.

I am afraid, then, says the scientist.

The widow sits beside them. And they say to her, for she is old now: What do you think our friend should do?

The widow says: Two things in the world you never regret: a swim in the ocean, the birth of a child.

She says things like this; it is why they come to her, these four women near the age of forty. She has Russian blood; it makes her feel free to be aphoristic. She can say: To cross a field is not to live a life. To drink tea is not to hew wood. Often she is wrong. They know that, and it doesn't matter. She sits before them, shining, like a bowl of water colored, just for pleasure, blue. They would sit at her feet forever; they would listen to her all night long. She says: I think that I have made mistakes.

But they do not believe her.

She says: In my day we served men. We did not divorce. I do not think then we knew how to be good to our children and love men at the same time. We had wonderful affairs. Affairs are fine, but you must never fall in love. You must be in love only with your husband.

But only one of them has a husband. He is sitting, drinking, talking to another man. His wife would like to say: Look at the moon, don't turn your back to it. But she is tired of her voice tonight, the voice that speaks to him so cruelly, more cruelly than he deserves. She would like to say: Let's dance now. But she doesn't want to dance with him. Will I get over being angry, she wonders, before the party ends? She hopes she will and fears that she will not.

The widow greets her friend across the room. They have both understood the history of clothes. And so they watched, in the late 1960's, the sensitive and decorative march of vivid-colored trousers and light, large-sleeved printed shirts, of dresses made of Indian material, of flat, bright, cotton shoes. So, in their seventies, they greet each other wearing purple and magenta. As they kiss, the gauzy full sleeves of their blouses touch. Tonight to be absurd, the widow's friend has worn a feather boa. Her husband, her fifth husband, stands beside her, gallant and solicitous for her and for her friend.

The widow says to her old friend, pointing to the four women sitting on the bench: I think they've got it right. Their lovely work.

The friend says: But look, they are so tired, and so angry.

The widow says: But we are tired at that age, and angry. They will have something to show.

Who knows, the widow's friend says, turning to her husband. Dance with me, she says, I think this one's a waltz.

He kisses her, for she has made him laugh. They dance, they are the only ones now dancing with the hostess's daughter and her friends. The music has gone angular and mean, it seems to the four women on the bench. The hostess's daughter thinks: Perhaps, then, I should marry a rich man. I am not ambitious, but I like nice things.

The mother without a husband thinks about her lover. Of his mouth, his forearms, his way of standing with his knees always a little bent, the black hairs on the backs of his small hands.

The hostess thinks: Perhaps I will ask this new man to stay.

The scientist thinks: I will live forever with a man who hates to dance.

The daughter of the hostess thinks: I love my mother, but I will not live like her.

The widow thinks: How wonderful their lives are. I must tell them so that they will know.

Her friend thinks: If this man dies I will be once more alone.

The angry wife wishes she were not angry.

Suddenly a funny song comes on. It has a name that makes them laugh, "Girls Just Want To Have Fun." The daughter of the hostess claps her hands and says: No men. The women, all of them: the hostess and her daughter, the scientist, the mother with no husband, the angry wife, the widow and her friend, stand in a circle, kick their legs in unison and laugh. And they can see outside the circle all the men, ironical or bored looking, the kindly ones amused. They all look shiftless there, and unreliable, like vagabonds. The two old women cannot bear it, that the men should be unhappy as the women dance. The widow's friend is first to break the circle. She takes her husband's hand and leads him to the center of the room. The widow dances with the handsomest young man. The daughter of the hostess walks away. But the four women near to forty sit down on the bench. The angry wife can see her husband's back. His back is turned against her; he is looking at the moon.

VIOLATION

I suppose that in a forty-five-year life, I should feel grateful to have experienced only two instances of sexual violation. Neither of them left me physically damaged and I cannot in truth say they have destroyed my joy of men. I have been happily married for fifteen years before which I had several blissful and some ordinary disappointing times with lovers. In addition, I am the mother of two sons, my passion for whom causes me to draw inward, away, when I hear the indiscriminate castigation of all males, so common and so understandable within the circles I frequent. I rarely think of my two experiences, and I'm grateful for that, for I don't like what they suggest to me about a world which I must, after all, go on inhabiting. And I don't like it when I start to feel in danger in my house, the Federalist house we've been so careful in restoring, in the town not far from Hartford where we've lived now for ten years, and when I wonder if, perhaps, safety is a feeling open to men alone. It is then, especially that I am glad to be the mother only of sons.

I am thinking of all that now as I stand at the wooden counter cutting celery, carrots, water chestnuts, so un-vegetative in their texture, radishes that willingly compose themselves in slices decorative as shells. Courageously, we've kept the kitchen faithful to its period: We have not replaced the small windows by large sheets of glass that would allow a brightness our ancestors would have shunned. Leaves make a border at the windows; farther out—beech, locust—they become a net that breaks up the white sky. I arrange the vegetables, green, orange white, white circled by a ring of red on the dark wood of the chopping board, as if I had to make decisions like a painter, purely on the basis of looks. As I handle the slices of vegetable, cool and admirably dry, I think about myself as a young woman, traveling abroad or "overseas" as my parents then called it, truly away from home for the first time.

At twenty-two, I must have thought myself poetical. This is the only thing I can surmise when I look at the itinerary of that trip—my parents' present to me after college graduation—that I took with my college room-mate and best friend. Lydia had majored in economics like me, although like me she had adopted it as a practical measure, rejecting a first love (for her it had been Art History, for me English). But we both prided ourselves on being tough-minded and realistic; we knew the value of a comfortable life, and we didn't want to feel we had to be dependent on a lucky marriage to achieve it. We'd both got jobs, through our fathers' connections, at large Manhattan banks; we'd take them up in the fall, and the knowledge of this gave us a sense of safety. We could be daring and adventurous all summer, have experiences, talk to people (men) we never would have talked to at home, reap the rewards of our secret devotion to the art and poetry we hadn't quite the confidence to give our lives to. We considered ourselves in the great line of student pilgrims admiring ourselves for our self-denial, traveling as we did with backpacks and hostel cards and a few volumes of poetry. Not for a moment did we understand the luxury of a journey made on money we had never had to earn, and that the line we followed was that of young people on the grand tour: a look at the best pictures, the best buildings, some introduction to Continental manners, the collision of which with our young natures would rub off the rough edges but leave our idealism smooth. We would return then to the place that had been held for us in the real life that had been going on without us, not forgetting us, but not requiring us yet.

Our plane landed in Amsterdam. We saw the Rembrandts and Vermeers, and the Van Goghs my friend thought, by comparison, jejune, and then we took an all-night train to Florence. We stayed in a cheap *pensione* with marble floors and huge mirrors and painted ceilings above the iron cots that were our beds. And in Piazzole Michaelangelo, I met Giovanni, who sold Electrolux vacuum cleaners. Poor Italian, he was over-mastered by the consonants of his employer's name and pronounced his product E-LAY-TRO-LOO. Luckily, he worked all day so my friend and I could see the *Ufizzi*, the *Palazzo Pitti*, the *Duomo*, the *Museo San Marco*, and I need leave her alone only at night when Giovanni drove me around Florence at breakneck speed and snuck me into his *pensione* until midnight, then miraculously got me back into mine. (Now I see he must have bribed the concierge.) He agreed to drive us to Ravenna, where I could do homage to Dante and my friend to the mosaics, but even after he'd done this nice thing for the both of us and paid for both our lunches, my friend was put out with me. She felt that I'd abandoned her for a man. She hadn't met anybody possible, the friends that Giovanni had introduced her to were coarse, she said, and she was afraid to go out alone at night, she was always being followed by soldiers. It wasn't her idea of a vacation, she said, sitting in her room reading Kenneth Clark. Punitively, she suggested that when we got to England, where we both could speak the language, we should split up and travel alone. It would open us up to experiences, she said. Clearly she felt she hadn't had hers yet, and I'd had more than my share.

I left Giovanni tearfully, vowing to write. He bought us chocolates and bottles of *acqua minerale* for the train. Then we were off, heartlessly, to our next adventure. We were both sick crossing the channel; it made us tenderer to each other as we parted at Dover and hugged each other earnestly, awkward in our backpacks. She would go to Scotland, I to Ireland; in two weeks we would meet in London, stay there for a week, then travel home.

I decided to cross the Irish Sea from Wales, the home of poets. I would spend the day in Swansea and cross over at Fishguard to Rosslare. From

Dylan Thomas' home, I would proceed on a pilgrimage to Yeats'. I felt ennobled but a bit lonely. It might be a long time, I knew, before I found someone to talk to.

Swansea was one of the least prepossessing cities I had ever seen: it might, despite the hints left by the poets, have been some place in Indiana or worse, Ohio, where I was from. I decided to look for a pub where Thomas must have got his inspiration. I found one that looked appropriate, ordered bread and sausages and beer and read my Yeats.

So I was not entirely surprised to hear an Irish voice ask if it could join me, and was pleased to look up and see a red-haired sailor standing with a pint of beer. I was abroad, after all, for experience, to do things I wouldn't do at home. I would never have spoken to a sailor in Cleveland, but then he wouldn't have been Irish. I thought he'd noticed me because he saw that I was reading Yeats.

"Yer American, then," he said.

"Yes."

"Great place, America. What yer doin' in this part of the world?"

"I'm traveling," I said.

"On yer own?"

"Yes."

"Brave, aren't ye?"

"No, not especially," I said. "I just don't see that much to be afraid of. And an awful lot that's fun and exciting. I'd hate to think I'd let fear hold me back."

"It's a great attitude. Great. Ye have people over here in Swansea?"

"No."

"What brings ye here?"

"Dylan Thomas, the poet. You've heard of him?"

"I have, of course. You're a great poetry lover, aren't ye? I seen ye with the Yeats. I'm from the Yeats country myself."

"That's where I'm going," I said, excitedly. "To Sligo."

"Yer takin' the ferry?"

"Nine o'clock."

"What a shame. I won't have much time to show ye Swansea. But we could have a drink or two."

"Okay," I said, anxious for talk. "You must have traveled a lot of places."

"Oh, all over," he said. "It's a great life, the sailor's."

He brought us drinks and I tried to encourage him to talk about himself, his home, his travels. I don't remember what he said, only that I was disappointed that he wasn't describing his life more colorfully, so I was glad when he suggested going for a walk to show me what he could of the town.

There really wasn't much to see in Swansea; he took me to the Catholic Church, the post office, the city hall. Then he suggested another pub. I said I had to be going, I didn't want to be late for the boat. He told me not to worry, he knew a shortcut; we could go there now.

I don't know when I realized I was in danger, but at some point I knew the path we were on was leading nowhere near other people. When he understood that I was not deceived, he felt no more need to hesitate. He must have known I would not resist, he didn't have to threaten. He merely spoke authoritatively, as if he wanted to get on with things.

"Sit down," he said. "And take that thing off your back."

I unbuckled my backpack and sat among the stalky weeds.

"Now take yer things off on the bottom."

I did what he said, closing my eyes. I didn't want to look at him. I could hear the clank of his belt as it hit the ground.

"What's this," he said. "One of yer American tricks?"

I had forgotten I was wearing a Tampax. Roughly, he pulled it out. I was more embarrassed by the imagination of it lying on the grass, so visible, than I was by my literal exposure.

"Yer not a virgin?" he said worriedly.

I told him I was not.

"All right then," he said, "then you know what's what."

In a few seconds, everything was finished, and he was on his feet. He turned his back to me to dress.

"I want ye to know one thing," he said. "I've just been checked out by the ship's doctor. Ye won't get no diseases from me, that's for sure. If ye come down with something, it's not my fault."

I thanked him.

"Yer all right?" he said.

"Yes," I told him.

He looked at his watch.

"Ye missed yer ferry."

"It's all right," I said, trying to sound polite. "There's another one in the morning." I was afraid that if I showed any trace of fear, any sense that what had happened was out of the ordinary, he might kill me to shut my mouth.

"I'll walk ye to the town."

I thanked him again.

"I'm awful sorry about yer missing the boat. It's too bad ye'll have to spend the night in this godforsaken town." He said this with genuine unhappiness, as though he had just described what was the genuine offense.

We walked on silently, looking at hotels blinking their red signs FULL.

"I'll be fine now," I said, hoping now we were in public, I could safely get him to leave.

"As long as yer all right."

"I'm fine, thank you."

"Would you give me yer name and address in the States? I could drop you a line. I'm off to South America next."

I wrote a false name and address on a page in my notebook, ripped it out and handed it to him.

He kissed me on the cheek. "Now don't go on like all these American ladies about how terrible we are to ye. Just remember, treat a man right, he'll treat you right."

"Okay," I said.

"Adios," he said, and waved.

I stepped into the foyer of the hotel we were standing in front of and stood there a while. Then I looked out onto the street to be sure he was gone. There was no sign of him, so I asked the hotel clerk for a room. I wanted one with a private bath, and he told me the only room available like that was the highest priced in the house. I gladly paid the money. I couldn't bear the idea of sharing a bathtub. It wasn't for myself I minded; I cared for the other people. I knew myself to be defiled, and I didn't want the other innocent, now sleeping guests, exposed to my contamination.

I traveled through Ireland for ten days, speaking to no one. It wasn't what I had expected, a country made up of bards and harpists and passionate fine-limbed women tossing their dark red hair. Unlike the other countries of Europe, there was nothing one really *had* to look at, and the beauty of the landscape seemed to wound, over and over, my abraded feelings; it made me feel even more alone. The greasy banisters of the urban hotels I stayed in sickened me; the glowing pictures of the Sacred Heart in the rooms of the private houses that, in the country, took in guests, disturbed my sleep. I felt that I was being stared at and found out.

And that, of course, was the last thing I wanted, to be found out. I've never said anything about the incident to anyone, not that there's much reason to keep it from people. Except, I guess, my shame at having been ravished, my dread of the implication, however slight, that I had "asked for what had happened," that my unwisdom was simply a masked desire for a coupling anonymous and blank. And so I have been silent about that time without good cause; how, then, could I ever speak of the second incident, which could, if I exposed it, unravel the fabric of my family's life?

My Uncle William was my father's only brother. He was two years older, handsomer, more flamboyant, more impatient, and it was said that though he lacked my father's steadiness, my father hadn't got his charm. Their mother had died when they were children, and their father drowned before their eyes when my father was seventeen and William nineteen. They agreed between them, teenage orphans, that my father should go off to college—he would study engineering at Purdue—and my uncle would stay home and run the family business, a successful clothing store my grandfather had built up and expanded as the town's prosperity increased and its tastes became more daring. When my father left for school it was a thriving business and it was assumed that with William's way with people, women especially (he planned to build his line of women's clothing; his first move was to enlarge the millinery department) it could only flourish. But in two years, everything was lost and my father had to leave college. The truly extraordinary aspect of the affair, to my mind, is that it was always my father who was apologetic about the situation. He felt it had been unfair, a terrible position to put Uncle William in, making him slave alone in the hometown he had never liked, while my father had been able to go away. William was really smarter, my father always said. (It wasn't true; even my mother, a great fan of Uncle William's and a stark critic of my father, corrected him, always, at this point in the story.) My father and my uncle agreed that it would be better for my uncle to go away; he'd put in his time and it was my father's turn; there was no reason for Uncle William to stick around and endure the petty insults and suspicions of uncomprehending minds.

In five years, my father had paid all the debts, a feat that so impressed the president of the local bank that he offered him a job. His rise in the bank was immediate, and it led to his move to Cleveland and his continued steady climb and marriage to my mother, the daughter of a bank president. I've never understood my father's success; he seems to trust everyone; wrongdoing not only shocks but seems genuinely to surprise him; yet he's made a career lending people money. I can only imagine that inside those cool buildings he always worked in, he assumed a new identity; the kind eyes grew steely, the tentative, apologetic yet protective posture hardened into something wary and astute. How else can I explain the fact that somebody so lovable made so much money?

In the years that my father was building his career, my uncle was traveling. We got letters from around the country; there was a reference in one, after the fact, to a failed marriage that lasted only sixteen months. And occasionally, irregularly, perhaps once every five years, there would be a visit, sudden, shimmering, like a rocket illumining our ordinary home and lives, making my father feel he had made all the right decisions, he was safe, yet not removed from glamour. For here it was, just at his table, in the presence of the brother whom he loved.

I, too, felt illumined by the visits. In middle age, William was dapper, anecdotal and offhand. He could imitate perfectly Italian tailors, widows of Texas oilmen, Mexican Indians who crossed the border every spring. In high school, my friends were enchanted by him; he was courtly and praising and gave them a sense of what they were going away to college for. But by the time we had all been away a couple of years, his stories seemed forced and repetitious, his autodidact's store of information suspect, his compliments something to be, at best, endured. For my father, however, my Uncle William never lost his luster. He hovered around his older brother, strangely maternal, as if my uncle were a rare, invalid *jeune fille*, possessed of delicate and special talents which a coarse world would not appreciate. And while my father hovered, my mother leaned toward my uncle flirtatious and expectant and alight.

Once, when I was living in New York, his visit and my visit to Ohio coincided. I was put on the living-room couch to sleep since my uncle had inhabited my room for two weeks and I would be home for only three days. At twenty-five, any visit home is a laceration, a gesture meanly wrought from a hard heart and an ungiving spirit. No one in town did I find worth talking to, my parents were darlings, but they would never understand my complicated and exciting life. Uncle William, in this context, was a relief; I had, of course, to condescend to him, but then he condescended to my parents, and he liked to take me out for drinks and hear me talk about my life.

One night, I had gone to dinner at a high school friend's. She had recently married, and I had all the single woman's contempt for her Danish Modern furniture, her silver pattern, her china with its modest print of roses. But it was one of those evenings that is so boring it's impossible to leave; one is always afraid that in rising from the chair, one is casting too pure a light on the whole fiasco. I drove into my parents' driveway at one-thirty, feeling ill-used and restless, longing for my own bed

in my own apartment and the sound of Lexington Avenue traffic. In five
minutes, I was crankily settling onto the made-up couch, and I must have
fallen instantly to sleep. I have always been a good sleeper. `

It was nearly four when I realized there was someone near me, kneeling
on the floor. Only gradually, I understood that it was my Uncle William,
stroking my arm and breathing whiskey in my face.

"I couldn't sleep," he said. "I was thinking about you."

I lay perfectly still; I didn't know what else to do. I couldn't wake my
parents, I could see behind my eyes years of my father's proud solicitude
for the man now running his hand toward my breast, scene after scene of
my mother's lively and absorbed attentions to him. As I lay there, I kept
remembering the feeling of being a child sitting on the steps watching my
parents and their guests below me as they talked and held their drinks and
nibbled food I didn't recognize as coming from my mother's kitchen or
her hand. A child transgressing, I was frozen into my position: any move
would mean exposure and so punishment. At the same time that the
danger of my situation stiffened me into immobility, I was paralyzed by
the incomprehensibility of the behavior that went on downstairs. Could
these be people I had known, laughing in these dangerous, sharp, un-
provoked ways, leaning so close into one another, singing snatches of songs,
then breaking off to compliment each other on their looks, their clothes,
their business or community success. My childish sense of isolation from
the acts of these familiars now grown strangers made me conscious of the
nerves that traveled down my body's trunk, distinct, electric, and my eyes,
wide as if they were set out on stalks, now lidless and impossibly alert.
Twenty years later as I lay, desperately strategizing, watching my uncle I
knew the memory was odd, but it stayed with me as I simulated flippancy,
the only tactic I could imagine that would lead to my escape. My uncle
had always called me his best audience when I'd forced laughter at one
of his jokes; he'd say I was the only one in the family with a sense of humor.

"Well, unlike you, Uncle William, I *could* sleep, I *was* sleeping," I said,
trying to sound like one of those thirties comedy heroines, clever in a jam.
"And that's what I want to do again."

"Ssh," he said, running his hand along my legs. "Don't be provincial. Have some courage, girl, some imagination. Besides I'm sure I'm not the first to have the privilege. I just want to see what all the New York guys are getting."

He continued to touch me, obsessive now and furtive, like an animal in a dark box.

"I'm not going to hurt you," he said. "I could make you happy. Happier than those young guys."

"What would make me really happy is to get some sleep," I said, in a tone I prayed did not reveal all my stiff desperation.

But, miraculously, he rose from his knees. "You really are a little prude at heart, aren't you? Just like everybody else in this stinking town."

And suddenly, he was gone. In the false blue light of four o'clock, I felt the animal's sheer gratitude for escape. I kept telling myself that nothing, after all, had happened, that I wasn't injured, it was rather funny really, I'd see that in time.

My great fear was that I would betray, by some lapse of warmth or interest in the morning, my uncle's drunken act. I longed for my parents' protection, yet I saw that it was I who must protect them. It had happened, that thing between parents and children: the balance had shifted; I was stronger. I was filled with a clean, painful love for them, which strikes me now each time I see them. They are gallant; they are innocent, and I must keep them so.

And I must do it once again today. They are coming to lunch with my Uncle William. I will be alone with them: my husband is working; my children are at school. In twenty years, I've only seen him twice, both times at my parents' house. I was able to keep up the tone: jocular, tough-minded, that would make him say, "You're my best audience," and make my father say, "They're cut from the same cloth, those two." It was one of those repayments the grown middle-class child must make, the overdue bill for the orthodontists, the dance lessons, the wardrobe for college, college itself. No one likes repayment; it is never a pure act, but for me it was a possible one. Today, though, it seems different. Today they are coming to my house, they will sit at my table. And as I stand at the kitchen window where I have been happy, where I have nurtured children and a husband's love and thought that I was safe, I rage as I look at the food I'd planned to serve them. The vegetables which minutes ago pleased me look contaminated to me now. Without my consent it seems, the side of my hand has moved toward them like a knife and shoved them off the cutting board. They land, all their distinction gone, in a heap in the sink. I know that I should get them out of there; I know I will; for I would never waste them, but for now it pleases me to see them ugly and abandoned and in danger, as if their fate were genuinely imperiled and unsure.

What is it that I want from Uncle William? I want some hesitation at the door, as if he isn't sure if he is welcome. I want him to take me aside and tell me he knows that he has done me harm. I want him to sit, if he must sit, at my table, silent and abashed. I don't demand that he be hounded; I don't even want him to confess. I simply want him to know, as I want the Irish sailor to know, that a wrong has been done me. I want to believe that they remember it with at the least regret. I know that things cannot be taken back, the forced embraces, the caresses brutal underneath the mask of courtship, but what I do want taken back are the words, spoken by those two men, that suggest that what they did was all right, no different from what other men had done, that it is all the same, the touch of men and women; nothing of desire or consent has weight, body parts touch body parts; that's all there is. I want them to know that because of them I cannot ever feel about the world the way I might have felt had they never come near me.

But the Irishman is gone and Uncle William, here before me, has grown old and weak. I can see him from the window, I can see the three of them. Him and my parents. They lean on one another, playful, tender; they have been together a lifetime. In old age, my parents have taken to traveling; I can hear them asking my uncle's advice about Mexico, where they will go this winter, where he once lived five years. They are wearing the youth-endowing clothing of the comfortably retired: windbreakers, sneakers, soft, light-colored sweaters, washable dun-colored pants. They have deliberately kept their health, my parents, so that they will not be a burden to me; for some other reason my uncle has kept his. Groaning, making exaggerated gestures, they complain about the steepness of my steps. But it is real, my father's muscular uncertainty as he grabs for the rail. They stand at my front door.

What happened happened twenty years ago. I've had a good life. I am a young and happy woman. And now I see the three of them, the old ones, frail, expectant, yearning toward me. So there is nothing for it; I must give them what they want. I open my arms to the embrace they offer. Heartily, I clap my uncle on the back.

"Howdy, stranger," I say in a cowboy voice. "Welcome to these parts."

MRS. CASSIDY'S LAST YEAR

*M*r. Cassidy knew he couldn't go to Communion. He had sinned against charity. He had wanted his wife dead.

The intention had been his, and the desire. She would not go back to bed. She had lifted the table that held her breakfast (it was unfair, it was unfair to all of them, that the old woman should be so strong and so immobile). She had lifted the table above her head and sent it crashing to the floor in front of him.

"Rose," he had said, bending, wondering how he would get scrambled egg, coffee, cranberry juice (which she had said she liked, the color of it) out of the garden pattern on the carpet. That was the sort of thing she knew but would not tell him now. She would laugh, wicked and bland-faced as an egg, when he did the wrong thing. But never say what was right, although she knew it, and her tongue was not dead for curses, for reports of crimes.

"Shithawk," she would shout at him from her bedroom. "Bastard son of a whore." Or more mildly, "Pimp," or "Fathead fart."

Old words, curses heard from soldiers on the boat or somebody's street children. Never spoken by her until now. Punishing him, though he had kept his promise.

He was trying to pick up the scrambled eggs with a paper napkin. The napkin broke, then shredded when he tried to squeeze the egg into what was left of it. He was on his knees on the carpet, scraping egg, white shreds of paper, purple fuzz from the trees in the carpet.

"Shitscraper," she laughed at him on his knees.

And then he wished in his heart most purely for the woman to be dead.

=======

The doorbell rang. His son and his son's wife. Shame that they should see him so, kneeling, bearing curses, cursing in his heart.

"Pa," said Toni, kneeling next to him. "You see what we mean."

"She's too much for you," said Mr. Cassidy's son Tom. Self-made man, thought Mr. Cassidy. Good time Charlie. Every joke a punchline like a whip.

No one would say his wife was too much for him.

"Swear," she had said, lying next to him in bed when they were each no more than thirty. Her eyes were wild then. What had made her think of it? No sickness near them, and fearful age some continent like Africa, with no one they knew well. What had put the thought to her, and the wildness, so that her nails bit into his palm, as if she knew small pain would preserve his memory.

"Swear you will let me die in my own bed. Swear you won't let them take me away."

He swore, her nails making dents in his palms, a dull shallow pain, not sharp, blue-green or purplish.

He had sworn.

On his knees now beside his daughter-in-law, his son.

"She is not too much for me. She is my wife."

"Leave him then, Toni," said Tom. "Let him do it himself if it's so goddamn easy. Serve him right. Let him learn the hard way. He couldn't do it if he didn't have us, the slobs around the corner."

Years of hatred now come out, punishing for not being loved best, of the family's children not most prized. Nothing is forgiven, thought the old man, rising to his feet, his hand on his daughter-in-law's squarish shoulder.

=====

He knelt before the altar of God. The young priest, bright-haired, faced them, arms open, a good little son.

No sons priests. He thought how he was old enough now to have a priest a grandson. This boy before him, vested and ordained, could have been one of the ones who followed behind holding tools. When there was time. He thought of Tom looking down at his father who knelt trying to pick up food. Tom for whom there had been no time. Families were this: the bulk, the knot of memory, wounds remembered not only because they had set on the soft, the pliable wax of childhood, motherhood, fatherhood, closeness to death. Wounds most deeply set and best remembered because families are days, the sameness of days and words, hammer blows, smothering, breath grabbed, memory on the soft skull, in the lungs, not once only but again and again the same. The words and the starvation.

Tom would not forget, would not forgive him. Children thought themselves the only wounded.

Should we let ourselves in for it, year after year, he asked in prayer, believing God did not hear him.

Tom would not forgive him for being the man he was. A man who paid debts, kept promises. Mr. Cassidy knelt up straighter, proud of himself before God.

Because of the way he had to be. He knelt back again, not proud. As much sense to be proud of the color of his hair. As much choice.

It was his wife who was the proud one. As if she thought it could have been some other way. The house, the children. He knew, being who they were they must have a house like that, children like that. Being who they were to the world. Having their faces.

As if she thought with some wrong turning these things might have been wasted. Herself a slattern, him drunk, them living in a tin shack, children dead or missing.

One was dead. John, the favorite, lost somewhere in a plane. The war dead. There was his name on the plaque near the altar. With the other town boys. And she had never forgiven him. For what he did not know. For helping bring that child into the world? Better, she said, to have borne none than the pain of losing this one, the most beautiful, the bravest. She turned from him then, letting some shelf drop, like a merchant at the hour of closing. And Tom had not forgotten the grief at his brother's death, knowing he could not have closed his mother's heart like that.

Mr. Cassidy saw they were all so unhappy, hated each other so because they thought things could be different. As he had thought of his wife. He had imagined she could be different if she wanted to. Which had angered him. Which was not, was almost never, the truth about things.

Things were as they were going to be, he thought, watching the boy-faced priest giving out Communion. Who were the others not receiving? Teenagers, pimpled, believing themselves in sin. He wanted to tell them they were not. He was sure they were not. Mothers with babies. Not going to Communion because they took the pill, it must be. He thought they should not stay away, although he thought they should not do what they had been told not to. He knew that the others in their seats were there for the heat of their bodies. While he sat back for the coldness of his heart, a heart that had wished his wife dead. He had wished the one dead he had promised he would love forever.

The boy priest blessed the congregation. Including Mr. Cassidy himself.

"Pa," said Tom, walking beside his father, opening the car door for him. "You see what we mean about her?"

"It was my fault. I forgot."

"Forgot what?" said Tom, emptying his car ashtray onto the church parking lot. Not my son, thought Mr. Cassidy, turning his head.

"How she is," said Mr. Cassidy. "I lost my temper."

"Pa, you're not God," said Tom. His hands were on the steering wheel, angry. His mother's.

"Okay," said Toni. "But look, Pa, you've been a saint to her. But she's not the woman she was. Not the woman we knew."

"She's the woman I married."

"Not any more," said Toni, wife of her husband.

If not, then who? People were the same. They kept their bodies. They did not become someone else. Rose was the woman he had married, a green girl, high-colored, with beautifully cut nostrils, hair that fell down always, hair she pinned up swiftly, with anger. She had been a housemaid and he a chauffeur. He had taken her to the ocean. They wore straw hats. They were not different people now. She was the girl he had seen first, the woman he had married, the mother of his children, the woman he had promised: Don't let them take me. Let me die in my own bed.

"Supposing it was yourself and Tom, then, Toni," said Mr. Cassidy, remembering himself a gentleman. "What would you want him to do? Would you want him to break his promise?"

"I hope I'd never make him promise anything like that," said Toni.

"But if you did?"

"I don't believe in those kinds of promises."

"My father thinks he's God. You have to understand. There's no two ways about anything."

For what was his son now refusing to forgive him? He was silent now, sitting in the back of the car. He looked at the top of his daughter-in-law's head, blond now, like some kind of circus candy. She had never been blond. Why did they do it? Try to be what they were not born to. Rose did not.

"What I wish you'd get through your head, Pa, is that it's me and Toni carrying the load. I suppose you forget where all the suppers come from?"

"I don't forget."

"Why don't you think of Toni for once?"

"I think of her, Tom, and you too. I know what you do. I'm very grateful. Mom is grateful, too, or she would be."

But first I think of my wife to whom I made vows. And whom I promised.

"The doctor thinks you're nuts, you know that, don't you?" said Tom. "Rafferty thinks you're nuts to try and keep her. He thinks we're nuts to go along with you. He says he washes his hands of the whole bunch of us."

The doctor washes his hands, thought Mr. Cassidy, seeing Leo Rafferty, hale as a dog, at his office sink.

The important thing was not to forget she was the woman he had married.

================

So he could leave the house, so he could leave her alone, he strapped her into the bed. Her curses were worst when he released her. She had grown a beard this last year, like a goat.

Like a man?

No.

He remembered her as she was when she was first his wife. A white nightgown, then as now. So she was the same. He'd been told it smelled different a virgin's first time. And never that way again. Some blood. Not much. As if she hadn't minded.

He sat her in the chair in front of the television. They had Mass now on television for sick people, people like her. She pushed the button on the little box that could change channels from across the room. One of their grandsons was a TV repairman. He had done it for them when she got sick. She pushed the button to a station that showed cartoons. Mice in capes, cats outraged. Some stories now with colored children. He boiled an egg for her lunch.

She sat chewing, looking at the television. What was that look in her eyes now? Why did he want to call it wickedness? Because it was blank and hateful. Because there was no light. Eyes should have light. There should be something behind them. That was dangerous, nothing behind her eyes but hate. Sullen like a bull kept from a cow. Sex mad. Why did that look make him think of sex? Sometimes he was afraid she wanted it.

He did not know what he would do.

She slept. He slept in the chair across from her.

———

The clock went off for her medicine. He got up from the chair, gauging the weather. Sometimes the sky was green this time of year. It was warm when it should not be. He didn't like that. The mixup made him shaky. It made him say to himself, "Now I am old."

He brought her the medicine. Three pills, red and grey, red and yellow, dark pink. Two just to keep her quiet. Sometimes she sucked them and spat them out when they melted and she got the bad taste. She thought they were candy. It was their fault for making them those colors. But it was something else he had to think about. He had to make sure she swallowed them right away.

Today she was not going to swallow. He could see that by the way her eyes looked at the television. The way she set her mouth so he could see what she had done with the pills, kept them in a pocket in her cheek, as if for storage.

"Rose," he said, stepping between her and the television, breaking her gaze. "You've got to swallow the pills. They cost money."

She tried to look over his shoulder. On the screen an ostrich, dressed in colored stockings, danced down the road. He could see she was not listening to him. And he tried to remember what the young priest had said when he came to bring Communion, what his daughter June had said. Be patient with her. Humor her. She can't help what she does. She's not the woman she once was.

She is the same.

"Hey, my Rose, won't you just swallow the pills for me. Like my girl."

She pushed him out of the way. So she could go on watching the television. He knelt down next to her.

"Come on, girleen. It's the pills make you better."

She gazed over the top of his head. He stood up, remembering what was done to animals.

He stroked her throat as he had stroked the throats of dogs and horses, a boy on a farm. He stroked the old woman's loose, papery throat, and said, "Swallow, then, just swallow."

She looked over his shoulder at the television. She kept the pills in a corner of her mouth.

It was making him angry. He put one finger above her lip under her nose and one below her chin, so that she would not be able to open her mouth. She breathed through her nose like a patient animal. She went on looking at the television. She did not swallow.

"You swallow them, Rose, this instant," he said, clamping her mouth shut. "They cost money. The doctor says you must. You're throwing good money down the drain."

Now she was watching a lion and a polar bear dancing. There were pianos in their cages.

He knew he must move away or his anger would make him do something. He had promised he would not be angry. He would remember who she was.

He went into the kitchen with a new idea. He would give her something sweet that would make her want to swallow. There was ice cream in the refrigerator. Strawberry that she liked. He removed each strawberry and placed it in the sink so she would not chew and then get the taste of the medicine. And then spit it out, leaving him, leaving them both no better than when they began.

He brought the dish of ice cream to her in the living room. She was sitting staring at the television with her mouth open. Perhaps she had opened her mouth to laugh? At what? At what was this grown woman laughing? A zebra was playing a xylophone while his zebra wife hung striped pajamas on a line.

In opening her mouth, she had let the pills fall together onto her lap. He saw the three of them, wet, stuck together, at the center of her lap. He thought he would take the pills and simply hide them in the ice cream. He bent to fish them from the valley of her lap.

And then she screamed at him. And then she stood up.

He was astonished at her power. She had not stood by herself for seven months. She put one arm in front of her breasts and raised the other against him, knocking him heavily to the floor.

"No," she shouted, her voice younger, stronger, the voice of a well young man. "Don't think you can have it now. That's what you're after. That's what you're always after. You want to get into it. I'm not one of your whores. You always thought it was such a great prize. I wish you'd have it cut off. I'd like to cut it off."

And she walked out of the house. He could see her wandering up and down the street in the darkness.

He dragged himself over to the chair and propped himself against it so he could watch her through the window. But he knew he could not move any farther. His leg was light and foolish underneath him, and burning with pain. He could not move any more, not even to the telephone that was half a yard away from him. He could see her body, visible through her nightgown, as she walked the street in front of the house.

He wondered if he should call out or be silent. He did not know how far she would walk. He could imagine her walking until the land stopped, and then into the water. He could not stop her. He would not raise his voice.

There was that pain in his leg that absorbed him strangely, as if it were the pain of someone else. He knew the leg was broken. "I have broken my leg," he kept saying to himself, trying to connect the words and the burning.

But then he remembered what it meant. He would not be able to walk. He would not be able to take care of her.

"Rose," he shouted, trying to move toward the window.

And then, knowing he could not move and she could not hear him, "Help."

He could see the green numbers on the clock, alive as cat's eyes. He could see his wife walking in the middle of the street. At least she was not walking far. But no one was coming to help her.

He would have to call for help. And he knew what it meant: they would take her away somewhere. No one would take care of her in the house if he did not. And he could not move.

No one could hear him shouting. No one but he could see his wife, wandering up and down the street in her nightgown.

They would take her away. He could see it; he could hear the noises. Policemen in blue, car radios reporting other disasters, young boys writing his words down in notebooks. And doctors, white coats, white shoes, wheeling her out. Her strapped. She would curse him. She would curse him rightly for having broken his promise. And the young men would wheel her out. Almost everyone was younger than he now. And he could hear how she would be as they wheeled her past him, rightly cursing.

Now he could see her weaving in the middle of the street. He heard a car slam on its brakes to avoid her. He thought someone would have to stop then. But he heard the car go on down to the corner.

No one could hear him shouting in the living room. The windows were shut; it was late October. There was a high bulk of grey cloud, showing islands of fierce, acidic blue. He would have to do something to get someone's attention before the sky became utterly dark and the drivers could not see her wandering before their cars. He could see her wandering; he could see the set of her angry back. She was wearing only her night-gown. He would have to get someone to bring her in before she died of cold.

The only objects he could reach were the figurines that covered the low table beside him. He picked one up: a bust of Robert Kennedy. He threw it through the window. The breaking glass made a violent, disgraceful noise. It was the sound of disaster he wanted. It must bring help.

He lay still for ten minutes, waiting, looking at the clock. He could see her walking, cursing. She could not hear him. He was afraid no one could hear him. He picked up another figurine, a bicentennial eagle and threw it through the window next to the one he had just broken. Then he picked up another and threw it through the window next to that. He went on: six windows. He went on until he had broken every window in the front of the house.

He had ruined his house. The one surprising thing of his long lifetime. The broken glass winked like green jewels, hard sea creatures, on the purple carpet. He looked at what he had destroyed. He would never have done it; it was something he would never have done. But he would not have believed he was a man who could not keep his promise.

In the dark he lay and prayed that someone would come and get her. That was the only thing now to pray for; the one thing he had asked God to keep back. A car stopped in front of the house. He heard his son's voice speaking to his mother. He could see the two of them; Tom had his arm around her. She was walking into the house now as if she had always meant to.

Mr. Cassidy lay back for the last moment of darkness. Soon the room would be full.

His son turned on the light.

A WRITING LESSON

*F*airy tales, we have been told, have within them the content of all fiction. As an exercise, write the same story as a fairy tale, and then as the kind of fiction we are more used to.

If you are writing a fairy tale, you can begin by saying that they had built a house in the center of the woods. And they sat in the center of it, as if they were children, huddled, cringing against bears. He had to go outside, for food or fire; she never went out. He was clever, and hidden, and got by the bears when he was outside. The walls of the house were thick, and they were safe, sitting in the center.

If your story is not a fairy tale, begin by saying that the husband and the wife lived a life that was somewhat isolated. In the first paragraph, be sure that you introduce the other major character: the girl. Say, before you go any further, that the girl is strong and young and the man is a good man. Say at this point that the wife is frail and beautiful. The reader will know from the beginning that you mean the wife to win in the end, if you are writing the fiction we are familiar with. In a fairy tale, the prize usually goes to the young, the strong, the courageous and the good. But perhaps even in fairy tales there is no possibility that the frail and the beautiful will not, in the end, win. And so you can apply your description of the characters to either of your stories.

You will, by this time, have prepared the reader for the end of the story and indicated the direction you would have his sympathies take. This both is and is not the technique of the teller of tales. The main feature of the technique is that the teller gets to the point.

Quickly, then, whichever mode you are writing in, let the reader know that the girl is someone else's wife, and should not be called a girl if the fiction you are writing is realistic. She is called a girl simply to distinguish her (and it is important that she be distinguished) from the man's wife with whom, as things would happen, she has more in common than she can know or would admit. But you must let the reader see these similarities only gradually; it is part of the craft of concealment.

When you are writing the fairy tale, go on to say that the wife sat all day combing her beautiful hair. The man and the girl worked together, cutting up wood, tying it in bundles. Sometimes their fingers would touch and she would tell him with her eyes, "How I love you. It is unbearable to me." The man will understand, although the girl will not speak because she has seen the wife, pale and fragile, combing her beautiful hair.

This is the way to describe the situation if you intend to write a fairy tale. If you are writing realistic fiction, your approach will be different. It is possible to say that the wife did have beautiful hair and that the man and the girl worked together, but it must be a perfectly ordinary job; it will have nothing to do with bundling wood (wood should not even be mentioned); they can share an office, a secretary. And sometimes she *will* try to tell him something with her eyes. But if you are not writing a fairy tale, you must remember that the language of the eyes is silent, and often unheard or misunderstood. As a humorous touch, you can say that the girl once tried to tell him with her eyes, and he asked if she were ill. And so the girl will remain silent, for she has seen the wife with her husband, frail and tentative, sitting beside him at dinner, touching him often. And the sight will have moved her; such fragility, in any mode of fiction, must move any but the coldest hearts. But because outside of fairy tales, if you are not writing a fairy tale, the feelings of the characters are not always clear, you must make the point that the girl hated the woman, for the girl was a hewer of wood. That is to say, she believed that love was earned and could be lost, and the wife was loved for her beautiful hair. How the girl would have loved that: to be loved for her frailty, her hair, not to have to work at love like a cabinetmaker (you can see that we are using the image of wood without actually mentioning wood), but to be loved for what she was born with, what she had nothing to do with, what she could neither improve very much nor change very much. How she would have loved to be loved for what she could not do.

A problem now arises: How do you describe endurance, silence, in the language of the fairy tale? And how do you say that in the midst of her silence there was talk, a paradise of talk, a wilderness of talk, about everything else? And how do you describe his fine bright eye: a bird's? a horse's? For you, the craftsman, this will be a difficult problem. Perhaps you will have to leave all these things out of the fairy tale and put in their place definite, visible action.

In the fairy tale, something definite must happen: It is in the nature of the narrative. In the fairy tale, she will weep. The girl will weep in the woods and someone, someone old or magical, will hear. Something will happen, something outside her, so that her intention of silence will remain pure, and yet he will know. Something dramatic will happen, so that she can remain silent, but he will come to her, to her deathbed, to her bed of leaves, knowing.

Even in the course of the fiction we are familiar with, there is one central event around which the story centers, around which it fans, like a peacock's tail. You should be searching your narrative for a central event, a significant event. In the fiction we are familiar with, it is possible that the central event will be an event in the mind: a decision. For example, it would be perfectly consistent with the rules of fiction and with the character of the girl as you have created her, if you have her decide not to act but to keep her love a secret. You can refer back to the scene of the husband and the wife at dinner. You can depict the girl watching the wife afraid to eat anything until her husband has eaten something first, then giving him half her dinner. You may describe the fear that that engendered in the girl: you may discuss the fear that may exist in the heart of a strong person in the presence of vulnerability. You may mention, here, the girl's sense of superiority: she would, she knew, never wait to see what anyone was eating before she began to eat. And you may include here her sense that, being stronger than the wife, she was more able to bear loss.

The central event of a fairy tale often involves loss. The theme of the quest is also prevalent. In the fairy tale, for example, the girl can go to the man for help because she has lost something magical: a comb made of pearls, a ring in the shape of a lion's head. And they will search in the woods until it is dark, and then they will lie down with the animals.

In a story that is not a fairy tale, the difficulties in getting them into the woods alone may be distracting. He is married; she is married, so you can see the implications for your narrative. In addition, the image of a couple in the woods may be comic or prurient. And besides, the girl has decided that nothing of that nature will happen. You must convey that her decision involved some sorrow, but you must not say that the girl is weeping: it is not consistent with her character. You may make the wife weep; you could create a moving scene in which you describe the wife, combing her beautiful hair, weeping. Only you have decided that the girl will remain silent. So there is no reason for the wife to weep. But you may depict the wife weeping anyway: it will be beautiful and consistent with her character.

And the man? The man loved them both, each according to what he believed she needed, each according to his needs. The girl he loved in a paradise of talk, a wilderness of talk, and his wife he took to him, flesh to flesh. If we were to end the fairy tale, this would be a happy ending: each having what she needed, which was what he thought she needed: each happy. But, in realistic fiction, this apportionment will not satisfy the character of the girl as you have created her.

Perhaps even in the fairy tale, apportionment will not be enough for the girl, and she will turn into a kind of witch, stirring her love in a dark pot, over and over, with things from old nightmares: heads of animals, curious mangled limbs, herbs that are acrid, dangerous. Even this could lead to an event or an ending: the girl could bewitch the wife and take the husband. But you want the girl to be the hero of the story, and now the girl has become a witch, so you can see the problem for your narrative.

But the problem is not insuperable because the form of the fairy tale, unlike the realistic form, allows for the possibilities of transformation. So you can depict the girl transformed from a girl to a witch, and then you could transform her back to a girl, sadder, more silent, perfectly beautiful in the woods, having learned in her witchhood the language of animals. You can have her send the man and the wife off, having cured them of their enchantment, and leave her in the woods, full of secrets, full of lore. This will compel the reader with the attractions of the supernatural.

It is possible in realistic fiction as well to create the witch as hero, but you must place her in another moral context, and you cannot call her a witch. The use of multiple contexts is an option of the writer of the fiction we are now used to, but you must be sure that your values are clear to the reader. You must create a context in which you extol the values of silence and endurance. You must make the reader interested in the girl's interesting and understandable hatred; you must make him sympathize with her fear and her sense of superiority. You will praise the girl for swallowing her power like a spell she wants to forget, for loving, in spite of herself, the beautiful wife, frailly combing her beautiful hair by the window. And this is the image that will stay in the reader's mind. Of course you can see the problem for your narrative.

You must be sure that the reader can only interpret the story as you would have it interpreted. If you have written a fairy tale, it may be possible for the reader to find everyone a hero: the girl, the man, the wife. All may live on, each inhabiting his particular beauty. But if you are not writing a fairy tale, the center of your fiction is the avoidance of action, the will, steadfastly clung to out of love and hatred, not to change, but to be silent. This may be interpreted as cowardice or bravery, depending upon the context you have created. If it is cowardice, the wife will be the hero of the story, because the reader will have seen her do nothing cowardly. And if it is bravery, the reader will still remember the wife, sitting at her window, fraily combing her beautiful hair.

Once you have decided upon the path of your narrative and have understood its implications, go back to the beginning of the story. Describe the house.

FOR THE BEST IN PAPERBACKS, LOOK FOR THE

In every corner of the world, on every subject under the sun, Penguin represents quality and variety – the very best in publishing today.

For complete information about books available from Penguin – including Pelicans, Puffins, Peregrines and Penguin Classics – and how to order them, write to us at the appropriate address below. Please note that for copyright reasons the selection of books varies from country to country.

In the United Kingdom: Please write to *Dept E.P., Penguin Books Ltd, Harmondsworth, Middlesex, UB7 0DA*

In the United States: Please write to *Dept BA, Penguin, 299 Murray Hill Parkway, East Rutherford, New Jersey 07073*

In Canada: Please write to *Penguin Books Canada Ltd, 2801 John Street, Markham, Ontario L3R 1B4*

In Australia: Please write to the *Marketing Department, Penguin Books Australia Ltd, P.O. Box 257, Ringwood, Victoria 3134*

In New Zealand: Please write to the *Marketing Department, Penguin Books (NZ) Ltd, Private Bag, Takapuna, Auckland 9*

In India: Please write to *Penguin Overseas Ltd, 706 Eros Apartments, 56 Nehru Place, New Delhi, 110019*

In Holland: Please write to *Penguin Books Nederland B.V., Postbus 195, NL–1380AD Weesp, Netherlands*

In Germany: Please write to *Penguin Books Ltd, Friedrichstrasse 10–12, D–6000 Frankfurt Main 1, Federal Republic of Germany*

In Spain: Please write to *Longman Penguin España, Calle San Nicolas 15, E–28013 Madrid, Spain*

In France: Please write to *Penguin Books Ltd, 39 Rue de Montmorency, F-75003, Paris, France*

In Japan: Please write to *Longman Penguin Japan Co Ltd, Yamaguchi Building, 2–12–9 Kanda Jimbocho, Chiyoda-Ku, Tokyo 101, Japan*

FOR THE BEST IN PAPERBACKS, LOOK FOR THE 🐧

A CHOICE OF PENGUIN FICTION

Money Martin Amis

Savage, audacious and demonically witty – a story of urban excess. 'Terribly, terminally funny: laughter in the dark, if ever I heard it' – *Guardian*

Lolita Vladimir Nabokov

Shot through with Nabokov's mercurial wit, quicksilver prose and intoxicating sensuality, *Lolita* is one of the world's greatest love stories. 'A great book' – Dorothy Parker

Dinner at the Homesick Restaurant Anne Tyler

Through every family run memories that bind them together – in spite of everything. 'She is a witch. Witty, civilized, curious, with her radar ears and her quill pen dipped on one page in acid and on the next in orange liqueur . . . a wonderful writer' – John Leonard in *The New York Times*

Glitz Elmore Leonard

Underneath the Boardwalk, a lot of insects creep. But the creepiest of all was Teddy. 'After finishing *Glitz*, I went out to the bookstore and bought everything else of Elmore Leonard's I could find' – Stephen King

Trust Mary Flanagan

Charles was a worthy man – a trustworthy man – a thing rare and old-fashioned in Eleanor's experience. 'A vivid, passionate roller-coaster of a book, which is also expertly crafted and beautifully written' – *Punch* 'A rare and sensitive début novel . . . there is something much more powerful than a moral in this novel – there is acute observation. It stands up to scrutiny. It rings true' – *Fiction Magazine*

The Levels Peter Benson

Winner of the Guardian Fiction Prize

Set in the secret landscape of the Somerset Levels, this remarkable first novel is the story of a young boy whose first encounter with love both bruises and enlarges his vision of the world. 'It discovers things about life that we recognise with a gasp' – *The Times*